In the Beginning

And the Truth Will Set You Free

SJ ALTY

authorHOUSE

AuthorHouse™ UK
1663 Liberty Drive
Bloomington, IN 47403 USA
www.authorhouse.co.uk
Phone: 0800.197.4150

© 2019 SJ Alty. All rights reserved.

No part of this book may be reproduced, stored in a retrieval system, or transmitted by any means without the written permission of the author.

Published by AuthorHouse 04/22/2019

ISBN: 978-1-7283-8748-2 (sc)
ISBN: 978-1-7283-8749-9 (e)

Print information available on the last page.

Any people depicted in stock imagery provided by Getty Images are models, and such images are being used for illustrative purposes only.
Certain stock imagery © Getty Images.

This book is printed on acid-free paper.

Because of the dynamic nature of the Internet, any web addresses or links contained in this book may have changed since publication and may no longer be valid. The views expressed in this work are solely those of the author and do not necessarily reflect the views of the publisher, and the publisher hereby disclaims any responsibility for them.

PROLOGUE

In the beginning; The Truth will set you free.

Yes, not original but if it starts the writings of the Bible its good enough for me, I have always had what I call a knowing, others call it psychic, clairvoyance etc. This is nothing new there are many instances of knowing ability in all Human beings throughout history, in biblical terms they used to call them Profits.

In fact, the writing you are about to hopefully enjoy, have been given to me by this very Medium, I think referred to as automatic writing, written simply so there can be no misinterpretation of the story, and the message contained within.

I am aware, This Book will invoke emotional responses in all who have read the bible and follow the associated Religions, this book is not written for any Religion or Cult on Earth.

All Without exception, because God and Jesus have nothing to do with them, suffice to say all Religions are about control especially over Women, and to conquer the minds of the populous, Religion is a man-made concept. God however exists and is freedom, and everlasting Life.

There are already many versions on religious belief, the world is bursting with them, supposing that there is an alternative to being brainwashed from birth into a judgemental religious' zealot's culture.

This stands regardless of where you just happened to be born in this world, Brain washing, or culture starts from birth from our Parents, from School, education from the work you do, culminating in the church or religion you are a member of, Imagine no religion, only God.

I hope to show the reader what I have been told by my psychic walk with the other side, especially what they shared with me.

Did you ever hear the story of Chinese whispers, one that sticks out in my mind is "send reinforcements were going to advance "after the whisper passed down the line, finally reaching the person who could take this command and respond, the whisper said "send three and four pence were going to a dance".

Add to this concept that the bible was written 300 years after the year of our Lord AD, then it isn't wrong to assume that this is exactly how the Word of God and Religion has developed, I mean all religions, and just to provoke your mind and thinking further.

Have you ever asked yourself? Why? do all Male dominated cultures with Religion, fear Women so much? Keeping them as slaves, abused or controlled.

Why? after 300 +years after the death of Jesus did the Cesar Constantine decide to endorse one God concept, leading to the great Religious movement which shaped all our destiny from Rome 375 years after the murdering of Jesus the God, declaring Christianity to be the true faith, commissioning the Bible to be written by Monks, who used to be priests worshiping the many Gods of Rome, eventually leading to the building of the great St Pauls Cathedrial, dedicated to the worship of the Roman Catholic Church.

So, all Modern Religions only came into conception about 2019+AD years ago, not even a blink in the eye of evolution. Have you ever asked Why? in some contexts especially the Bible do we say Jesus as God on earth and then the Son of God, how can he be both?

Throughout our history there have been many questions unanswered, and varied clues, the DaVinci code, painting the Last supper, Further to this, ask yourself Why? was the murder of thousands of Women as witches, sanctioned by the Roman Catholic Church, why? did Hitler want to breed a master race through DNA of Arian blond blue eyed people? was he aware of something we were not permitted to know?

Why does God still love us, despite all the abhorrent wars, Jeehads, and horrors committed in his name.

And what makes us so different from the rest of the vast array of Animals. Why have we been able to develop incredible technology within the past 100 years, instant communications, Cars travel commerce, trade, Music that moves the soul, health cures remember penicillin, transplants, great innovations in Health the conquests of all major killer's smallpox, black death Tuberculosis.

The www.wonderfull inventions, why have these exceptional Human inventors been able to achieve all this, and its only right at the beginning, have you ever asked why?

I am just an ordinary Woman and Mother, I can't even begin to describe myself as a literary guru I am not even an accomplished writer.

However I was given this task to write this story, why You, You may Ask, who are you to be able or conceited or deluded enough to assume you are doing Gods or Spiritual work, why not others much more educated or spiritually inclined and able than you?

I don't know? I have become upset and angry with spirit and the Angels, and asked many times why Me? Why not give this task to a powerful well-known Medium, who would have the knowledge and funds to promote and use many ghost writers (no pun intended) to get this task done so much quicker and easier?

like the monks who transcribed the first Bible,350 + years after the Murder of Jesus the God, could it be that it was simply the fact that ordinary people remembered and passed on to future children, The memory, of how wonderful the world was when he walked amongst us, especially within the so called holy lands.

A time when crops flourished, illness was cured by the touch of his, or her hand, no one starved people laughed, and loved more despite being ruled by Rome.

I am still waiting for the answer, the beautiful Beings on the other side treat me with kind patients, then remind me of all the times God himself tried to instruct the powerful and must have felt as frustrated with them, when they still refused to believe in Him.

Even after witnessing the miracles, and how the powerful in our society abuse Power to own wealth, control the public, and gain even more power by keeping the Women beneath them.

Please try to enjoy my story and then do your own research our ansestorage history is fascinating littered with clues to the truth if you dare to look.

I was amazed at some of the historical facts I was given by automatic writing and checked through the writings of history and found them to be a fact.

After reading I dare you to do just that, then ask yourself openly and honestly the questions above its very evocative when you can use your God given Free will and choice, to come to your own conclusions.

Furthermore, despite all the progress made by Human Beings, nothing has changed, even if God himself stood in front of them many would still refuse to believe, even today would crucify him. I hear you say, OH NO I would believe, no my Friend you would believe whatever today's media and television told you to believe.

Like the terrible vitriolic Things said about Donald Trump to discredit him, calling him a racist a bigot woman hater, even women paid to come forward with any accusation that may harm him, and his family, remarks printed that he would never be President.

Trial by gossip media, yet that incredible man held fast, proving all that bore false witness against him lyers.

"And behold a pale rider will come from the west, out of the house of eagles bringing fire, righteousness, and truth" (revolations bible) maybe against all odds and with God's blessing, becoming the president of the USA.

The Pharisees and Socrates of the bible are still, the ones who own the media, TV and religions of today, these are the wealthy, the ultimate world leaders that control the world, the ones that stand to lose the most, if the Truth was told.

They must have quivered with horror when Mr Trump triumphed against the odds, despite all the hurdles, still being thrown in front of him.

Ask yourself, what right, do these so-called leaders, on capitol hill have to refuse the Leader of one of the greatest countries on earth, support and help, rather than leave him on his own to defend his country from the Enemy within. Praise God and pass the hat.

By writing this book, I have come to believe that Religion is used only to control the growing and general populations, a rather lucrative business venture, run by Men who crave land, wealth and power over Women, as far removed from the message of Love, God has tried to give us.

Our Father which art in heaven gave us free will, for good or bad, He gave us a loving home after this physical life, he told us that I am not in big wealthy buildings, I am in my flesh and blood in YOU.

I hope you find this out for yourself. I hope that the truth will quietly set you free, and above all remember. God the Father and Mother of modern Man really does love you unconditionally. Now is time to know the truth.

CHAPTER 1

In the Beginning

On a blazing-hot day, a small group walked into Jerusalem, in the district of Judea. They came out of the dust from the sandstorm-ravaged desert, walking from the direction of Egypt.

Jerusalem was a thriving city—the capital of trade from the East and a rich stronghold for wealthy merchants and rich spoils for the Roman masters. As they walked on the road to the city, crowds gathered and followed them. These people looked very different from the indigenous population.

At this point in human evolution, people were much smaller in stature. The average height of men stood at about five feet five, hence the great plumes worn on the helmets of the Roman centurions to give a fearsome height.

Women were less than five feet. The group received curious attention. The small camel train numbered seven.

They were led by a large man, approximately six feet tall. He was very striking to look at—bright skin; blond, sun-kissed hair; and blue-green eyes that were so vibrant they seemed to change brightness and colour in the light of the day.

When he cast his gaze on any individual, they felt stunned and shocked at his incredible ability to know them. A simple look, and most felt absolutely naked and unworthy. At the same time, one was filled with awe and love. He instilled great presence and charisma unequalled by anyone. He was God—a supernatural being living in and getting to know and understand the natural world. He presented as a simple male human. His name, for the purpose of explanation, was Jesus.

At his side was an equally striking woman possessing much of the same virtues. She had a blaze of burnished copper hair and the same compelling eyes.

The five others presented themselves as students—disciples following their master, hanging on his every word. Jude looked about a frail sixteen-year-old. Jesus referred to him as Beloved of Brothers. He was an expert on botany and knew every plant, tree, and bush. His task was to name and record his findings.

James looked about eighteen years old. He was a sturdy and steadfast warrior. He saw his purpose as protector and second beloved brother. Luke was a very studious youth, about seventeen years old. His purpose was to record all accounts of the wonders of the life and times of Jesus and Mary Magdalene.

Mark, twenty-two, the oldest of the companions, was a scribe who wrote the words and teachings of God for the benefit of future generations. Miriam, sixteen and unmarried, preferred to spend her time in devotion to Jesus and Mary. They referred to her as Beloved Little Sister.

They were a very strange sight, and people started to follow them. Every mile or so they would rest, and this strange fellow would address them, asking where they lived, if they were happy, and what were the politics of the day. He spoke to them in a way that made them question themselves. Instead of answering their questions, they started to form judgements in their own minds and make their own conclusions.

The crowds studied them, noticing that they were particularly well dressed in the white and purple of the Roman elite. Were they high-born Romans? Their skin was light and golden. Why were they walking? He must be a great scholar. He spoke and understood many dialects as if he was a native speaker.

They marvelled at the stunning beauty of his closest companion. He introduced himself simply as Jesus, and the woman, Mary Magdalene, as his beloved wife. Someone joked that he must have paid a lot of camels for this one. The crowd laughed, and the group laughed with them. Mary blushed and acted coy, hiding her face behind a veil. Jesus found this particularly funny, throwing his head back and laughing loudly. The group walked on in good spirits.

As he walked, he started to sing, and the companions and growing crowd joined him. The crowd simply didn't want to leave. They felt so compelled that they followed them along the dusty road into Jerusalem, walking into history and the terrible lie.

As they passed through the causeway into Jerusalem, they noticed a terrifying sight. Bodies, some newly crucified and some left for some time, lined the side of the road—a frightening reminder of who was in charge.

Roman domination loomed ominously above them. Jesus looked up at the ravaged bodies hanging on crosses, their pain and torment on display for all to witness. His eyes welled with tears of compassion and sorrow for their suffering. He became quiet and withdrawn, shaking his head at the abhorrent scene and contemplating the sorrow he knew would come for the beautiful few who travelled with him.

The merry band became mellow, and they walked in silence as they approached the gates of Jerusalem.

Two Roman guards stopped the band of weary travellers and demanded to know their identities.

Jesus replied, "Why, don't you know me, Tiber Drusus?"

The centurion noticed their dress and concluded that these people were obviously high-born Romans. Being very aware of his social position, he always tried to gain as much favour as he could with the wealthy high-born Romans and merchants. He decided that he must know him, as he addressed him with his given name.

"Oh, of course, sir. Sorry about that; I didn't recognise you. Be careful on these roads; they are full of thieves and vagabonds." The crowd roared with laughter. To them, the biggest criminals of the day were the Romans.

Usually the centurion wouldn't have spared the whip or sword on anyone daring to mock him, but for some reason that he couldn't fathom, he was in quite a good mood and returned the humour. Jesus asked if he knew of a fine inn for the evening.

Tiber Drusus took it as his mission to deliver them to a safe refuge, dispelling the crowd to go about their business and escorting them through the narrow smelly streets.

As dusk fell, they walked, marvelling at the change of colours in the sky. Red-violet hues turned from blue to amber to darkness, and fabulous bright stars appeared. A large moon loomed over the land. Jesus looked at the spectacle with wide eyes as if he was seeing this marvellous site for the first time. He smiled and turned to Mary Magdalene, holding her gaze with such knowing love between them and kissing her gently.

Jesus asked Tiber Drusus if the governor was in residence and if he would deliver a tablet to him. "Of course," Tiberius readily agreed. He didn't understand why, but he trusted this man with every sense of his being.

As he was directly responsible for the governor's safety in the region, this would be an easy task. Tiber Drusus never missed a chance to network with the elite. After all, one never knew when favours could be returned, and as he had his usual audience with Pontius Pilate first thing in the morning, it would pose no trouble to him.

The lodgings were quite beautiful. From the narrow street, it appeared as just a strong, large dusty door. The pleasant home was only visible when they walked through the doorway. They were greeted by a lovely courtyard with a central well, well-lit with palm-oil lamps. The smells of blooming jasmine plants and herbs filled the air. Two large fig palms and climbing grapes spread over a cushioned sitting area and low eating table. One could simply reach out and take the succulent grapes right from the vine. The four walls surrounding the yard were a story high, with steps leading up to the rooms of the inn. The pleasant surroundings were suitable for their stay.

The innkeeper welcomed them, calling to his wife to bring refreshments. Jesus thanked Tiber Drusus for his help and gave him a tablet to give to the governor.

Tiber Drusus left, and the small group ate and laughed together.

Mary Magdalene asked if she and her female companion could bathe, as the heat and dust of the road made her feel unclean. The innkeeper was a little taken aback, as this was a rare request. Clean water was a very prized possession. Nevertheless, he shouted orders to his servants to make the ladies a bathing area, away from sight, between the palms.

Mary smiled at Miriam, her dearest friend and companion. Miriam was devoted to Mary and loved to do anything she could to make Mary and Jesus comfortable. One would think she was a devoted servant. She fussed over her like a mother. Her labours were given out of pure love. She positively enjoyed every task. She was far from a servant. She never felt exploited and always felt beloved.

Miriam was a brilliant and skilled woman. She could make a wonderful meal out of the most meagre ingredients. She could cure a fever by picking a few herbs and arrange any material into the most beautiful gown. This woman was incredibly skilled.

Mary was just as accomplished; however, she was also a natural inventor. She never saw a problem. She only talked of solutions to challenges through her ingenuity or whatever natural resource she could use. She was a truly happy and emancipated woman. Her love, Jesus, was her equal, not her master. He consulted with her above all others. His love and passion for her was devout, without question. He admired her. Every minute with her was so precious that they needed few words. A gaze or a touch of her hand was enough to sustain him.

He showered her with the greatest public show of his love, as if no one else could see, often leaning over and kissing her, brushing the hair from her beautiful cheek. No human being was ever loved as much. She never showed anger. She never talked behind anyone's back. She never berated anyone or hurt another's feelings. She never cursed or used profanity. She was simply the perfect woman, with a wicked since of humour and wit. She filled Jesus with joy, love, and longing, completely complimenting him.

When they were alone together, they made the most satisfyingly fabulous love.

They wondered at the beauty of each other's bodies, he spoke of her fine graces, the sensuous curves of her incredible body, She was the omega the perfect Woman, She amazed him, loved him without any condition, for her it was more than enough just to be beside him, sometimes the love of him was too much and she would weep at the very thought of not being at his side.

Mary was also blessed with a psychic knowing, no one could ever lie to her, She simply knew the truth, She felt others illness, others emotional pain, on occasions she would be able to tell others about their lives and guide them without judging them, She seemed to advise without any regard for customs ownership or Religion, She silently knew and wept in private for the future. She knew to savour every moment of this life with her beloved as if it was her last.

Eve the inn keepers wife asked if she could join them, She had been so long without friendship and desperately wanted these lovely women's company, Mary looked at Eve and said of course you must and let us fix up your lovely hair, and help you wash your pain away, Eve gasped and instinctively put her hands over her mouth, how do you know?

Miriam said, ask what She doesn't know.

The three women Laughed, hugged each other, then Miriam threw a whole pitcher of water over them.

Whilst the women washed, splashed and laughed, the Men relaxed talking, drinking the wine which tasted full bodied and sweeter than was usual, The Inn Keeper, Adam joined them sitting on the cushions Jesus asked him.

Adam why do you feel so angry. Adam replied what do you mean? Forgive me I noticed that you shout curse and hit your Wife and Servants, why do you feel so angry.

Adam was dumfounded why I? well I? I have to show them whose boss or else nothing will be done; they are such a lazy lot I have to show them.

Jesus said Why? Adam, looking right into his eyes, I don't really know that's the way of it, the way it's always been. My Father and his Father all worked hard and had to fight hard to provide for the Family, sometimes a Man must rule by the whip or back of the hand to prove his Manhood, I will be obeyed and served in my own house.

Jesus said Do you think that to show them love instead of berating them, asking instead of ordering loving instead of forcing, If it is her free will, your wife will then Love you, the companions Jude, James, Luke and Mark fell into an uncomfortable silence.

Adam felt the look from Jesus and fell into thought, if any Man would have questioned how he ran his household business he would throw him out in the street, but not this man when he looked in his compelling eyes he felt something move in his chest his heart ached to be loved.

He had watched with amazement at how with great reverence Jesus treated his wife he saw the look of love in her eyes for her husband, and he wished with all his breaking heart that his Wife would look at him and love him like that, he had dismissed the thought immediately as he watched his wife spill the wine and shouted at her at her stupidity giving her a good smack across the head for good measure.

Poor Eve she had been sold into marriage at only thirteen a business Marriage, arranged for the benefit of her Father, being pulled from the arms of her dear mother left with this awful brute who was ten years her senior an old Man who stank, and She hated him, Eve would have been a very pretty Woman if the awfulness of her existence hadn't taken its toll, bearing four children without much assistance or kindness had made her hate the thought of any manly intentions especially her Selfish angry abusive husband.

She loved her Children and cared for them well, she was resigned to living only for Her Children, an awful loveless life waiting with silent indignation for the end, the only hope she had was wishing her husband would drop dead before he raped her again, oh yes, she silently hated.

Jesus looked into Adam's eyes, Adam gasped as he saw his own behaviour being played back to him like watching a horrible movie, he suddenly pulled from Jesus's gaze and fell in wracking sobs, every pain he had ever inflicted every horrible indignant act he had ever committed on his wife every awful thing he had said all the tears emotional horror he gave out, he felt everything.

After a while the sobs subsided and Adam composed himself as best, he could, Jesus held out his arms and Adam fell into them saying forgive me. How can I ever put the things I have done right, Jesus replied with love Adam, with love?

Love Eve as you love yourself, love your Children as you love yourself, love your servants as you love yourself, Win their love, earn their love, over time they will serve you gladly with full hearts because they love you, not because they fear you, above all love God, and you will be happy forever.

Tomorrow as the sun comes up you will be a loving and good man, tonight ready yourself for this great change for a start, you stink go and bathe as the women have, shave your beard, lift your eyes to the Sun and do to others as you would have done to yourself. Know that God loves you.

Adam walked away sadly deep in thought.

The ladies joined the Men laughing and skipping towards them Eve was still with them, although now she looked completely transformed, She always wore a black barker no one ever saw her, and before them was a most handsome woman, the girls had coiffed her hair and a hint of henna on her cheeks and lips.

She was wearing a simple white shift, she looked beautiful as did the others She beamed at the compliments given to her. they continued to enjoy each other's company, just before they retired to bed Eva looked very anxious, she knew she would have to go to bed, but dreaded the thought.

She anticipated her Husband's great displeasure at her being washed and dressed in garments that other Men may admire, He would be furious, and she knew he would beat her without mercy.

She wondered where Adam was and it crossed her mind that he must have gone to bed already She was glad for that, Mary looked into her eyes, and said you have nothing to fear tonight dear one, Eva smiled back then went to bed, and was relieved to find that her husband wasn't there. She slept long and peacefully and dreamed of paradise.

James asked, Lord Jesus what will happen tomorrow what does the day hold for us what are we going to do, Jesus looking deeply into James eyes replied Do you love me James, with all my heart lord, then Wait and Trust.

Later that night, Mary held Jesus in her arms and watched him sleep.

And so, ended the first day. and with it the first supernatural miracle.

CHAPTER 2

The New Day

In the beginning of a new day, A bright sun lit the sky, the earth was warming up, a beautiful day, there was much activity in the courtyard servants were preparing breakfast for the guests and Children, Eva was busy directing everyone and Adam was nowhere to be seen She was beginning to get worried and curious as to where he was, He did not come to bed all night.

The Children all four, ate a hearty breakfast, John the oldest a small version of his Father had reached the age of eight years, Benjamin six years, Samuel four, and little Sasha at two, she was a sickly child delicate, as pretty as her Mother but very small for her age, she had an obvious disability in that her right foot seemed to turn inward at two years, She had failed to take her first step Eve worried that she would fail to thrive as the others, the thought gave her much torment, She felt that She would simply die herself if she lost her beloved baby.

Eve pushed these thoughts away as she caught the Children giggling at their Mother who appeared in front of them without the traditional barker, she turned and danced in front of them laughing with them.

She still looked lovely and the Children were telling her this just as their guests arose and joined them, at the same time their Father appeared clean shaven washed with combed hair, with a clean tunic.

They gasped and became immediately silent, eyes wide with bread hanging out of their mouths, as if they had never seen their Parents before,

They cringed waiting for the blows, their eyes looking terrified towards their Mother because they knew She would be first to feel their Fathers wrath.

Silence, no one moved for an age, Sasha gave a little frightened wimper, and then their Father looked at them all very sternly and then started to laugh He stared at Eva, my dear how lovely you look, Eva was to stunned to speak come on now everyone, breakfast for our guests.

Everyone ate millet a kind of porridge and bread with honey fresh figs and cool water with sweet wine delicious breakfast. The Men appeared preoccupied studying an ancient map.

Jesus sat with little Sasha on his lap, Mary and Miriam talked with the Boys, Mary turned to look lovingly at Jesus and stared shocked at little Sasha's legs, She and Jesus shared a knowing look, Marys eyes filled with tears, Jesus simply smiled back at his love and laid his hand on Sasha's little twisted foot, he stroked the little foot and then kissed her forehead, Sasha looked up into His eyes and smiled, She placed her little arms around His neck and snuggled into His chest totally content. As if She had known and loved him all her life.

Whilst everyone was eating, talking and enjoying the company, Adam took Eva's arm and led her into a room he wanted to talk with her privately.

Eva I am so sorry for everything I have done can you, will you forgive me, I swear on my life that I have changed, Eva was so overcome she burst into tears replying with shaking voice I I don't know, will you give me time it's all been such a shock, She looked down to the floor never before would She dare speak to him in such a manor, He simply said of course, of course, I will prove I am a changed Man

But Eva could you, well, do you think, you may learn to love me, Eva looked up and between her tears She looked into his Face as if She saw him for the first time, She thought actually without the beard and his hair combed, He wasn't that bad, She smiled and quietly said we will see.

Adam had hope, even after his terrible treatment of Her, there was a chance She could love him it was up to him, He would be the happiest Man in the world if he could just once see the same look of love he had witnessed Mary giving to Jesus.

However he quietly hoped that she would not go outside without her Berker, what would the neighbours and the Jewish community say, He began to worry, he needn't have, because as she was getting ready to take the children to the synagogue he observed her putting on her Berker, Eve felt that it would be just two much of change to cope with outside of her home. Adam breathed a sigh of relief.

Eve busied herself telling the Children as Mothers do to get ready for morning prayers and the days lessons, She whisked Sasha into her Arms as She always did placing her on her hip for the short walk to the Synagogue, Eve felt something, she couldn't fathom what, but something in her daughter was well simply different, She looked at her little Girl as if for the first time, lifting her up and observing her intently, Eve let out a scream that stopped the whole household in its tracks, She whirled round to Jesus, and threw herself down at his feet between uncontrollable sobs all everyone could hear was thank you thank you my lord thank you.

Adam stood in complete stunned shock at his Wife's outburst, If not, finding himself a little annoyed at her lack of reserve, in front of the guests, he moved to bring her to her feet, as he did so Eve held Sasha out to him still crying tears of absolute joy, Adam nearly fainted he took hold of his little girl and scrutinised every part of her legs observing them to be absolutely beautiful and normal, fell down to the ground himself praising Jehovah for the miracle.

Mary lifted little Sasha from her Father's arms as She feared the Child may be harmed by her Parents joy and ecstatic praises.

Jesus stood in front of them both, and said to Mary, place Sasha on her own two feet She can walk very well, Mary gently placed Sasha standing in front of her, Jesus held out his arms to the Child and she ran into them.

Jesus said suffer little Children to come unto me, for theirs is the kingdom of heaven.

A great cheer followed by all the household guest and Family shared in the joy, the youngest was cured. Adam looked up with tear stained face into the loving eyes of Jesus and asked WHO ARE YOU.

Jesus said I am the light, the new, the beginning, the love, in the world, the Father of the future, the living God.

I bless you Adam and he whoever believes in me and follows me will never know death or grief will reside with me in my heavenly kingdom for all time, do you believe in me Adam.

Yes, Lord Jesus, I do.

then you must honour me by trying to live with these values in your life, and I will always be with you.

Honour your father and mother, honour your family, your wife, honour yourself, show compassion especially love those that are bigots and live with the great burden of hate, cherish every other human being as if they were your own family.

Spread this word tell everyone you meet every day you have seen the living gods their names are Mary and Jesus.

At this moment, a loud commotion could be heard from the street, someone shouting orders and the familiar noise of marching feet clad with clanging armour, a small garrison of legionnaires marched through the street gateway, standing to attention inside the courtyard, their leader approached Jesus.

Hello, greetings Tiber Drusus, do you bring us news of my good friend Pontius Pilot our lustrous governor.

I bring greetings and this Armed garrison to escort you and your entourage to the Governors Palace you are invited to stay with him as his esteemed Guest, you and your good Lady will be escorted by carriage.

Jesus thanked him for his kindness taking Mary by the hand and guiding her to the awaiting Sudan, Mary and Miriam will ride, I would like to walk with you Tiber Drusus.

Tiber Drusus thought that this was most irregular but offered only token resistance, He secretly felt pleased that this very important Guest of the Governor wanted to walk and talk with him.

Jesus passed pleasantries with Tiber Drusus as they walked and asked, Tiber I see you have the civic crown as your decoration this is one of the highest honours any centurion could earn you must be a fierce and loyal servant of the Emperor Tiberius Julius Cesar Augustice, Yes indeed Sir, I hope to earn my military diploma after my term serving the governor.

I have served and fought under Cesar Tiberius on many campaigns I believe myself to be his most trusted servant, Jesus said, That is so commendable, but have you not grown weary of always fighting, well no sir that is my life, however when I receive my military diploma I will be proclaimed a free Citizen of Rome, and with that a certain purse, lands, and freedom of Rome.

I intend to marry you know, settle down and raise my own army of children he laughed, Jesus placed a hand on his arm and said Sevilla Maximillia would be honoured to have you right now, her Father is placing much pressure on her and arranging suitors to marry her as we speak, He will use her beauty, goodness and chastity to procure more lands and wealth, unless you declare your love and intentions soon you will lose her, and commit her to a loveless miserable life.

Tiber Drusus looked crestfallen He felt tears of despair and Anger sting his eyes, he turned to Jesus, so you know her Father, of sorts Jesus replied.

My Lord I cannot declare my love until I gain My Military diploma, until then I am but a servant of Rome without place or substance how can I ever hope without hope to ask for her, it will probably be another five years in which time, She will be lost to me.

Jesus looked thoughtful may I make a suggestion, write to her Father asking for her hand, also write to Sevilla Maximillia at the same time declaring your great love for her, That you will be returning to Rome presently, ask them to put aside any arrangements for suitors until that time.

I ask you Tiber Drusus, to trust me, Yes my Lord I do trust you, but Sir, Yes Tiber, I can't write, with that they both burst out laughing, no matter my friend, I must introduce you to my dear companion Luke, a scribe and great scholar he will help you write, by the time you receive a reply you will be able to read it yourself.

Tiber Drusus felt his heart become lighter as if the very words this strange Man gave him hope and joy something in his very soul believed, every word, and he knew then that he would follow this Man and love him far more than the emperor or Governor forever.

Jesus asked Tiber Drusus what of Pontus Pilate was he a good and just Prefect, Tiber gave an account the Roman Emperor Tiberius appointed Pontius Pilate Prefect of the Roman provinces of Judaea, Samaria and Idumæa.

Cesar Tiberius Augustin granted Pilate the power of a supreme judge, which meant that he had the sole authority to order a criminal's execution.

His duties as a Prefect Governor included such mundane tasks as tax collection and managing construction projects. perhaps his most crucial responsibility was that of maintaining law and order, Pontius Pilate attempted to do so by any means necessary. What he couldn't negotiate he accomplished through brute force, with his Centurion Garrison as was the custom of Roman rule.

Tiber Drusus intimated that, Pontus Pilate collaborated with Jewish authorities 'and many People would describe him as cruel and unfair, furthermore weakly succumbing to the Jewish Sanhedrin council.

Tiber felt that Pontius Pilate was a very good negotiator, using his skills to bring more peace and prosperity for the general population, and coffers of Rome. He was a particular favourite of Tiberius Cesar, Tiber Drusus realised that he had spoken too freely to Jesus about his Governor and fell silent.

Jesus asked and what of his Wife and household, Tiber replied Pontius has a wife and large household of in-law's slaves and numerous Family Members, who reside with him, of which he was sure he would meet presently.

At that moment they reached the palatial domain of Pontius Pilate Prefect Governor of Judaea.

The party was escorted towards the most beautiful large palatal room plaster paintings depicting the emperor Tiberius in battle victory, various busts, statues depicting late Emperors and Roman Gods in regal splendour, soft white and purple viols hung and swayed in the breeze of open windows, Gold reliefs etchings of the most splendid Art work, cushions and large seating areas, and tall roman pillars held up the dome roof, one could hear the servants whisper as clear as day right at the other side, as this building was cleverly constructed as a chamber where the governor could cleverly hear any words of treason, or unrest before he entered.

Everyone who waited in that room came under scrutiny, always left a while to contemplate the meeting to come and talk amongst themselves believing their words not to be heard by the Prefect.

Servants came into the room bringing large palm fans which was a welcome relief from the heat of the day, trays of sweet meets and flagons of wine large bowls placed on the tables full of fresh fruit they waited patiently for the host.

Mark rose from his seat and made to pour some wine into a flagon, Jesus simply gestured with his hand, and he sat back down, Jesus said our Governor and host will give us leave to eat and drink when he joins us, I will take nothing without his permission and neither will you.

After consulting with Tiber Drusus out of site of the guests, Pontus Pilot asked Tiber Drusus directly if he felt these guests had been sent by the Cesar himself, Tiberius then possibly Augustine, As Rome was governed by duel Rule of joint Cesar's.

Pontus observed them for a while listening intently to their conversations which only consisted of uninteresting small talk and pleasantries.

Pontus Pilot walked into the room with his entourage of advisors his secretary scribe, and his wife Solicitous, after introducing everyone Jesus returned the compliment and Pontus gestured for them to sit down and enjoy his hospitality, Servants busied themselves pouring wine and offering lunch, Pontus sat directly opposite Jesus observing him, tell me Jesus, your name suggests Jewish princely background, yet Tiber Drusus tells me you must derive from Rome as you know quite a few of the roman gentry, has my dear Tiberius or Augustus Cesar seen fit to send you as a spy to report on my efficiency as Governor.

The group held their breath, Jesus looked into the eyes of Pontus Pilot, neither can be farther than the truth, however yes I am from the highest Royal household, I own no allegiance with the Jews or any other band of men on this world, my kingdom is far away.

I am not here to spy on you, only to help you in all ways and manor in your life that I can, I am your humble servant Sir, I wish only your happiness and well-being you will find no conspiracy in myself or companions.

Then why are you here, Jesus replied I believe you prefer straight talking so I will get right to the point I have come to visit with you so that I may make your greatest wish come true, and Sir what is my greatest wish, To Father a Legitimate son, Pontus Pilot became ill at ease, and how do you know this, who informed you and how do you propose to help me with this delicate dilemma, when all the so called physicians', medicine men, and appeasing the gods have not worked.

By curing you and your Wife of the reason why She has not yet conceived. Oh I see you are a physician sent by my true Friend and Cesar Tiberius, He is the only one that I ever confided in, indeed he even sent one of his own slave girls so that I could use her as surrogate, My Wife however would hear nothing of it, Jesus sat back and locked his gaze on Pontus Pilot, he said nothing.

Well this puts a totally different light on the matter of course you must stay, you are welcome in this house when would you want to examine my wife.

Pontus seamed totally at ease, for some reason that he couldn't fathom he totally trusted this Man and if he could give him the one thing in the world he wanted more than anything, a legitimate Son when his wife was obviously barren, yes that would make him a very happy Man. Jesus said we will talk later, When with your permission I will talk with your Wife.

Yes of course I leave you to be taken to your rooms and rest, this evening we will have a feast in your honour, and you will meet the rest of the Family.

The Women, had taken their leave of the Men, Solitous wished to Show Mary and Miriam the gardens and had met the Children of the household along with Solitouses Mother and Sister

Whose two Children they were entertaining, Mary looked intently at Solitous, and was moved by the loving looks she gave to her nephews, have you any Children Solitous, sadly No the Gods have not yet blessed us, is this something you wish, with all my heart Mary, well we will have to do something about that won't we, What? What are you mocking me Madam, said Solitous indignant Oh know, know, please don't take offence I meant non, I would never mock you?

Solitous fell into wracking sobs and her Mother ran to comfort her, Mary said to the group of Women, would you leave us I wish to talk to Solitous, Dear Mother she will be much happier afterwards.

I promise, signalling to Miriam to take them inside, Miriam immediately sprang into action steering the women and Children away whilst Mary comforted Solitous, it's all right dear Solitous, dabbing her eyes, cry away until you feel you cannot cry anymore, tears are designed to wash away frustration they help a Woman to face adversity, and then with great bravery solve all the problems of Men.

IN THE BEGINNING

I am sorry to behave so haughtily, please do not tell my Husband he will be very angry that I had acted in such a silly manor towards his guests.

Mary replied, do not worry I will say nothing of the matter, but I can help you if you wish it, but how, well firstly by asking a few questions are you ready, Mary and Solitous walked and talked for some time.

Miriam observed them from a distance only when She saw them hug and laugh did, she approaches them knowing that Mary with her skill and love had reached an accord of friendship and love with this Woman who was obviously very troubled.

Miriam had discerned from Solitouses' Mother and Sister that they feared they would all lose the protection of Pontius pilot and be sent back to Rome in disgrace, if Solitous failed to give him a Son, or a Daughter, the atmosphere in the home was tense and although Pontius had always declared his love for her, they felt he would take on another childbearing Wife and Solitous would lose her status and be devastated.

Mary was right Solitous was much happier after their talk, Miriam advised them that it was time to join the others, Jesus and Pontius were also locked in deep talks and hardly felt the time, as the group joined again Jesus held out a hand towards Mary and kissed her, Pontius mirrored the gesture with Solitous.

Pontius gestured towards the waiting servants to show his guests their rooms, so that they may rest and prepare for the evening's entertainment.

Jesus and Mary were shown to the most sumptuous apartments a large bath like a small swimming pool had already been filled with fragrant water, they both slipped into it sighing with pleasure, and dismissing the servants fell into each other's arms, making love in the warm fragrant water was wonderful they savoured every moment.

afterwards they realised that garments had been laid out for them, clean and soft tunic for Jesus and a beautiful gown for Mary, as if by magic as they rose out of the bath the servants returned drying them with warm clothes, anointing their skin with oils, Mary giggled unashamedly, Jesus smiled at Her.

Both enjoyed such pampering and luxury, the servants worked without making a sound preferring to gesture, Fixing the gown perfectly, gestering Mary to sit down, whilst they coiffed her hair with gold braid, finishing by slipping her feet into soft slippers, the young Men attending Jesus worked with skill, shaving and combing styling them completely.

When they finished, they simply backed out of the room and disappeared into the shadows.

A loud Dinner gong startled them, and a house servant appeared and said My Lord Pilot wishes your attendance please follow me this way.

They Followed the servant into a dining room, Pontus Pilot and Solitous greeted them showing them to sit down at the low table, the custom was to lie down for comfort, the rest of the Family and Group joined them, the feast before them was sumptuous to say the least, roast Meats fresh vegetables and fruit, the display was breath-taking it was finished off by a fountain of wine which ran constantly, one only had to hold a goblet out to be filled with delicious sweet wine.

The company was very relaxed and pleasant, each guest enjoyed conversations with the family, and a delicious banquet, entertainment was provided by dancing Girls, a band of acrobats, the evening ended by singing everyone joined in, a very pleasant evening was enjoyed by everyone and was instrumental in forging firm friendships, especially between Jesus and Pontus Pilot.

The following morning there was more than a few bad heads, the group was positively subdued after enjoying a bit more wine than was wise, nevertheless Jesus and Pontus pilot were walking and talking in the garden. Pontus Pilot enquired when Jesus would begin his work healing his barren Wife.

Jesus stopped and looked at Pontus, there isn't anything wrong with your wife the problem is with you my Friend, WHAT! There is nothing wrong with me Pontus said indignantly, I beg to differ Jesus replied, remember the orgies you attended at Tiberius's invitation, Pontus stood with his mouth open, in his defence said, well yes, it's expected.

Jesus went on remember that particular beauty that took everyone's attention, She passed on an illness to you, havnt you wondered why the stinging sensation when passing water or that you haven't been able to make love to your wife, the unpleasant fever that indisposes you, from time to time, it has rendered you infertile, you cannot Father a Child, the constant discomfort and fever, is the result of this illness.

Yes, it's true I do feel this way, I will have that Woman flogged and thrown out.

No Pontus it isn't her fault, She was used and abused all her life by Men like you, She merely gave a gift back from the Man who gave it to her, Her Husband died in service of Tiberius That Woman is sole provider, for her two Children, in her despair She used the only asset she has, her body.

She is a very brave and loving soul whose sacrifice is the only way of providing for her Family, to sell her poor body, No Man has the right to judge her, less he be judged in turn.

Are you seeking to make me feel bad about Her plight, she is very well paid for her services, Jesus replied I merely want you to explore your own conscience, then except responsibility for your own actions, instead of blaming your Wife or Concubine except that this situation is your fault not there's

Until you do, I cannot heal you, I suggest my Friend that you think about our conversations, we will talk again later.

Jesus left Pontus in turmoil he was turning over in his mind reflecting, if anyone else had spoken to him in such a way he would be incensed offended infuriated, and would have him thrown in jail for his impudence, however Jesuses words hit home He knew He had just been told the whole ultimate truth, and now he had to face his imperfections he felt Sad melancholy wretched, then after contemplating, remorseful and then repentant.

Pontus set out to find Jesus, He found him in conversation with Solitous.

Pontus worried for a moment that Jesus had told Her about his indiscretions, He needn't have worried, Jesus would never betray his trust or confidence.

Solitous greeted her husband with a kiss, Darling she said Mary has made an infusion of herbs and plants She bids me to take the drink to help me conceive, I ask you permission to take the mixture, Yes of course my Dear, you go to Mary, leave me to talk with Jesus.

Pontus watched Solitous walk away then turned to Jesus, Sir how do I make up to her, how do I express my sorrow at my own behaviour, Pontus my dear Friend you already have.

Jesus held out his arms, and Pontus fell into them, embracing as Lifelong Friends, Strangely Pontus felt a jolt run through him and for a moment went quite faint.

He immediately regained his composure, Jesus said tell me Pontus how do you feel, Pontus looked thoughtful, better Sir, like a great weight has been lifted from me. Indeed, it has, go, make love to your wife, Jesus you know I physically cannot.

Yes, you can you are both cured.

WHAT!! how can that be? Who are you, what are you? Pontus Jesus replied, I am the living God I have the power and will, to mend or destroy all things if I so wish.

believe me you are cured you are fit and healthy so is your Dear Wife, I tell you now that together We will reach out to all human beings giving healing Love and Hope for their everlasting Life, bringing the essence of my life, into all the Human Beings on earth, I am not Natural I am Supernatural, I told you once that my kingdom is far away, That I am King and Lord of that Kingdom, do you believe in me Pontus.

Jesus looked deep into Pontius's eyes. Pontus Pilot felt in utter shock, yet he believed every word, he fell prostrate before Jesus.

My Lord I am your Servant; please give me your direction and I will follow you as your most dedicated disciple.

You will present yourself as my Friend Pontus, no more and no less, we will travel together over all this land, I will gather Men and Women who wish to make Heaven on earth, I will give talks and sermons to all the people so that they may use their free will to follow my word or not. This is what will happen Pontus.

My Lord then I fear for you, there are those who enjoy power, that will seek to oppose you not least Tiberius, if he fears you to be popular, He sees threat in everyone his mania is famous for putting many to Death, No one is safe, even I live in fear of his wrath, I have worked hard to earn his trust.

Fear not Pontus I will deal with it when the time comes, Now go to your wife.

Jesus went to find Mary and the first disciples, The Men were pouring over maps, planning a journey Through Nazareth to Galilee, how goes it James my dear Brother, oh well My Lord we have mapped our journey, and we are ready to travel at your instruction, we will use the camels to

IN THE BEGINNING

ride and donkeys to carry tents, we will not need tents Mark, and I would appreciate a good Horse on this journey.

Luke said but Lord much of our journey will take us through remote and desolate planes, we will need to put up tents to rest.

Mark and James stood up and agreed with Luke, Jude stated that there only concern was His and Marys comfort the journey will be hard going, Mark fell in supporting Luke and Jude, with his concerns for their safety.

Jesus fell back laughing, gasping for breath he said, do you not know me, you of all people, do you not know who you are addressing, The Men looked at each other than burst out laughing themselves.

Mary and Miriam came hurrying into the room, we heard you laughing are we having fun Miriam asked, clapping her hands in glee, this just set everyone off laughing again.

Do not worry my Dearest, I will explain the joke later, Jesus placed his arms around Mary and Miriam, kissed each on the forehead fondly.

I intend to travel tomorrow to see John the Baptist, He will be outside Jerusalem baptising in the river Jordon, I will travel with Mark, Luke James and Jude, My Darling Mary and Miriam I ask them to stay here.

It pains me so much to be away from you my Dearest Mary, the road is hard and the climate very hot, It will be hard going for us, I for you and delicate Miriam, That the conditions would prove too much for you both, so I ask you to stay we will return in two days. Mary looked crestfallen.

If that is your wish then I will do as you ask, but may I remind you of your promise to me that we will never part, that we will be at each other's side no matter what, and have you forgotten that I can ride walk and run as fast, and far. as any Man.

I need to be baptised as well, so does Miriam, I have heard a lot about John the Baptist, according to some of the servants, They say he has just returned from the wilderness with much to say, he is telling everyone he comes into contact with to repent before the coming of Christ, who will deliver us all from Evil.

I want to be there when he comes face to face with you, I want to experience the joy, when he recognises you.

Jesus replied If he recognises me, I also heard he is barking mad from spending weeks in the desert, Mary said if he is half the profit gossip says he is, he will recognise you, Alright if you feel you must come along We will all go together.

The following morning Jesus spoke to Pontus about his plan to seek out John the Baptist, Pontus gave instructions to have good horses ready for them, and immediately after breakfast they set off to find John.

The road was hard going for the horses and Mary noticed her mount seemed to be moving in pain so she dismounted to look at the hooves of her Horse, sure enough she found a stone stuck in the poor creatures hoof, She removed it, and called to the others that they should find shade and rest for the Horses, and to check each horse's hooves,

She felt that after rest and water they should walk for a while and spare the horses, Jesus and everyone agreed.

They rested for a while letting the animals graze at the meagre grass, Jesus noted that this was poor forage for the magnificent Animals and they deserved much better, He lifted his hands and made a gestor as if calming the earth, immediately new lush growth succulent grass appeared before each Horse they all turned towards Jesus dropping their heads in thanks and praise.

The group sat in the shade watching the Horses enjoy grazing, I don't know about you, but I am beginning to feel Hungry Mark said.

OH I nearly forgot said Miriam running towards her Horses saddle bags she pulled out a virtual feast, I am sorry everyone I only had time to put a few things together, spreading a cloth on the floor She produced Bread, sheep's cheese, grapes, and bowl of hunny, with two large flagons of sweet wine with a gourd of water.

Dearest Miriam Jesus praised her good thinking, Mary gave her a hug you are quite remarkable little sister, Miriam blushed but secretly loved the praise and positive comments.

Mark especially praised her saying that one day She would make someone blessed if she became their wife, Mary and Jesus exchanged a look of recognition as if they read each other's mind, everyone ate heartily.

Strangely the food seamed to keep replenishing itself, there was the same amount left as was consumed, Jesus said that they would need more later, so Miriam packed them away back into her saddlebag, and settled back for a little sleep, in the shade the sun was high and very hot.

After a while the quiet was replaced by chattering voices horse's hooves, and wagons, wooden wheels pulled by Oxen, moving along the perilous road.

James called out to a group of travellers Hello where are you going, OH Hello several voices at once called, We are going to see the great Profit and Preacher John He is Baptising People in the River, thank you replies James We will follow you if you have no objections.

Non, please come along with us, Jesus called to the Horses who had wondered a fair way, they came at a gallop, kicking up a great dust storm as they came near, Jesus spoke to the Horses.

calm now children walk with us, be careful of the stones underfoot, are you all feeling better, the horses nodded neighing approval, we will come to the river very soon and you will be able to have cool water to drink, please be kind to your riders they have your best interest at heart, and that is why we will be walking until the road gets better.

Marys mount nuzzled her hair making her laugh, OH stop it you silly boy, he playfully pushed her to start walking, She was laughing so much that she stumbled immediately, her Horse grabbed her clothing to stop her falling. This was witnessed by everyone on the road they started laughing in unison.

The horse stood still looking shocked at his own boldness, still holding Marys clothing in his mouth, all right thank you for helping me you can let me down now, the horse immediately let go. Mary walked with as much grace as she could muster, still laughing Mary held Jesuses hand, the Horses obediently followed behind.

As They walked along, they found themselves in the company of a group of women who were drumming, one playing the lyre the sounds of the women were mesmerising.

although they did not sing in words as such, it was more of an accompaniment to the drums, crowd of people on the road joined in humming the tunes, as did Jesus Mary and their group, it was a very merry band of travellers on the Demasks road.

Within a few miles the road split into a crossroads. The People hummers drummers and players took the road to the left, so did our band of travellers.

After a short walk the road came to a river, this is the river Jordon only a short walk now, and we will see him, someone called out.

They carried on a while, until they saw many people standing by the bank a somewhat dishevelled looking Man was shouting at the crowd, to repent of their Sins, before He that will come after Me arrives.

John had just finished his Sermon and waded into the water, a single file line of people Men and Women wearing their white slips are positioned to receive the baptism and blessing from John, each entered the water, each were received by the water as John held them momentarily under the water.

He asked each person, do you repent of your sins, the recipient saying Yes, then he dunked them saying you have bean cleansed by the word, and water of god go in peace.

Jesus instructed the others to go before him, Mark Miriam, James and Jude joined the line, Mary and Jesus behind them as they moved up the line of baptism, John kept stopping looking around him, saying to his helpers can you feel it can you see a light, they shook their heads.

John carried on, until he got to Jesus and Mary, John placed his hand on Marys head, he immediately withdrew his hand as if scorched, he looked into Marys eyes and then saw Jesus.

Oh, my lord is it you, He couldn't get anything else out of his mouth for the great tears in his eyes and sob in his throught.

Yes, John I come to be baptised, No, no lord Jesus, I am not worthy to baptise you, for you are without any sin to renounce.

I have told of your coming to many, this baptism is to prepare them for you, then baptise Mary and Me John and then I will baptise you in return.

John did as he was told, baptising Mary and Jesus, and when he had finished onlookers were amazed when Jesus baptised John, the strange thing was that the whole river appeared fresh and cleansed people who had already been baptised exclaimed how well they felt, all their blemishes had healed, strange indeed, when Jordon was considered a bit of a cesspit containing much of the waste from Jerusalem, the water felt fresh revised and clean.

This was not the only miracle witnessed that day, as soon as John finished baptising Jesus a beautiful white dove flew above his head.

Standing either side of Jesus, in fact, helping to dip him, and Mary backwards into the water stood two beautiful Angels, John stood trembling before them speechless.

It happened that they were the last to be baptised, which meant that no one would be disappointed because Poor John was in no fit state to baptise anyone else that day.

After making their way back to the dry land, everyone stood in a state of shock especially as the Angels dried them, and slipped over their heads fine tunics, and outer garments, fit for any king, they also dressed john in similar attire, smoothing his wild hair back from his face, and combing his unkempt beard.

John was far to shocked to object, it took quite a time before he came to his senses, Jesus led him into a large tent that suddenly appeared at the bank of the Jordon River, a feast was prepared waiting for them.

before them, the drum players, lyre, singers and everyone baptised that day was welcomed to celebrate with them, Jesus sat John down on comfortable cushion's as this feast was in his honour.

The celebrations went two nights, when Jesus was satisfied that John had eaten and drank his fill, He asked John to take a walk with him, along the banks of the Jordon river, they left the revelries and strolled along together.

My Lord said John why do you honour me so, when it should be me honouring you, My Dear John, how many injustices have you seen, how many times of great suffering have you come through, How cold and hungry you have bean and still your faith in me as your God has never wavered.

As a profit of God you have had to endure the temptations in the wilderness, yet your faith and love for me has never wavered, You have suffered greatly in this life and I am here to tell you that when this life is through, you will be escorted to your rightful place, in my kingdom you shall have your home.

John stopped and threw himself at Jesuses feet, my lord I am not worthy of all these blessings, I am not used to unconditional love, it is not that I am ungrateful just overwhelmed.

Jesus laughed as he lifted John to his feet, John please except my blessings with a happy heart because my friend before you go home, there is much work for you to do, you will come up against a terrible foe, you will have to remain steadfast not waver in your belief for one moment, can you do that in my name John.

Yes, Lord I will, after this time you will be taken home so have no fear, when you are at your darkest hour, I Will be with you, I want you to continue to act as my profit, very shortly a delegation will ask you to go with them they will arrest you in the name of King Harrod because he and his new wife are very angry you have condemned them as unworthy and immoral as not only is Herodias his brother's wife She is also his Niece and A Jewish princess.

there is great unrest between the Brothers who reside in kingdoms split into four regions by their Father, John replied yes lord I have criticized them, call me old fashioned, but I don't think stealing your brother's Wife is a good way to calm family relations ensuring stability in the regions, yes I have judged them to be immoral because they are.

Jesus replied, yes John your words to the People have decimated Harrods plan of becoming the king of the Jews over all the regions.

Herod believed that He would bring all the twelve tribes together under his Kingship he believed that marrying Herodias, would give him the position, and status to lay claim to the consortium, His ambition has been severely damaged by your criticism.

Many follow you John and as a result, his plans have been dashed, He is an unstable emissary at the best of times and only a token king ruled by Rome, although he is angry with you, he hopes to persuade you, that his plans would be best for the whole country, thereby ensuring your dedication.

He does not want to kill you, He wants you to do a prophecy for the King He wants you to tell your God or Maduk, as they prefer to call Me, to grant him a further year of prosperity, for him and his people, you must go with them, and cast this work for Him, you must only tell what your gifts tell you to give him.

Above all tell him the absolute truth about himself, his relationships, and how his future will be, if he denies the one true God. That is all for now John I think it time for you to sleep, you must be very tired.

They walked back into the tent where Johns place for him to rest was already prepared Jesus laid John down on the comfortable pillows and bade him goodnight.

In the first light of the morning Jesus Mary Miriam and the others left John sleeping peacefully, they joined the horses grazing nearby and set off on their next journey.

John was woken by a delegation of palace guards who came storming into the tent, demanding that John the Baptist come with them immediately, so thought John, it comes swiftly as my Lord said it is to be.

John was taken to a fortress near the small town of Mari, at the side of the Euphrates river, King Harrod went there himself and all his court, after John was held for six months, He thought that this time of solitude, and despair, being held as a prisoner may force john to be more sympathetic towards Harrod.

It didn't, John was known to shout up from the dungeons calling out that they should all repent, as the living God walked the very earth they stood on, and the apocalypse was near, this greatly upset Herodias, and caused many arguments, between them She thought, that Harrod showed weakness and fear in not allowing Johns swift death, therefore silence him for good.

She did not know that Harrod Antipas, witnessed the death of his Father after giving the command to kill all the Boy Children, after a profit soothsayer, and astrologer, told him that an important Child would be born around Bethlehem.

A Child that would make the People rise in defiance and answer his cruel regime by turning the People and Jewish Church against Him.

Harrod realised the Child that got away was indeed John the Baptist, John had talked at length with Harrod of the times to come, as he cast Harrods future, Harrod felt foreboding, and only saw enemies, coming to oust him out of his Kingdom.

He could not get the sight of his Father, clutching his chest as he collapsed, when his chief soldiers, informed him that the deed was done, and He did nothing to help save his father whom he hated.

Herodias had only contempt for everyone, especially Harrod for placing her in this awful place, and hated John, especially when his dungeon was placed by the latrine, the shaft would carry his voice right into Herodias private apartments, John constantly called everyone Vipers, and her the whore of Babylon, this would drive her to become so enraged,

She would beat and kick at the slaves and Harrod, as a result married life was not the harmonious bliss, She and Harrod envisaged.

It was even more infuriating for her as Harrod would spend hours talking to John, becoming morose and then more hours getting drunk and molesting the servants.

Herodias was a very jealous and unhappy Woman, which was even more hard to bear as She had noticed how Harrod was looking at Her Own Daughter Salome.

This family was even more dysfunctional than even She had realised, as Harrod was lechering after every younger woman, with a pulse. Including her beautiful Daughter.

She blamed John for all her suffering, which was rapidly becoming unbearable, Harrod was even more uneasy when She was sweet,

He knew there would be a price to pay for any sexual favours She gave him, she wasn't content with a priceless bauble, it seemed the only thing She craved, above everything was the death of John the Baptist, so that they could return to Babylon and start enjoying her status as Harrods Queen.

In the beginning of the twelfth month was Harrods birthday

A grand birthday party was arranged by Herodias as it was a Major celebration.

Herodias asked that John be gagged and bound, she didn't want his guests to see or hear him, and She did not want her Husband to be emberaced by his rantings.

Harrod reluctantly agreed as many guests had arrived and the celebrations were in full swing Harrod was enjoying himself being very drunk, he asked Salome to dance for him.

She looked towards her Mother for approval after gaining a nod of her head approached Harrod she leaned forward and asked what you will give me for my dance, Harrod laughed, why if your dance is sufficiently pleasing, He will give her anything She desired.

Anything yes Anything, the music started, and Salome gyrated, the dance was premiscuace to say the least, which greatly delighted the male guests,

Harrod was sweating with lustful desire, He proclaimed that She should be allowed anything, Salome looked towards her mother and said, I want the head of John the Baptist on a silver platter.

Harrod was furious and at an impasse, could not appear in front of his guests as not giving Salome what She asked, he had given his word and everyone had witnessed it, on the other hand he thought she would simply asked for make up or gold bangle, Not the head of someone, Herodias was smiling at her Daughter, Harrod realised who had put Salome up to this.

Harrod felt that He had no choice and ordered the execution to be carried out, and the head delivered to Salome on a silver platter.

CHAPTER 3

After leaving John, Jesus said that they should ride towards galilee He Laughed as he stated that he wanted to fish for Men, twelve Men, who would eventually after instruction from Jesus become the twelve apostils their task would be to look after the Apostle Women.

Furthermore, they would take the word of God, through the Son of God, to all nations, they were surprised by someone shouting after them and waving frantically.

The group stopped and waited until the person and his Companion caught them up.

Oh, thank goodness, I have caught up with you I have some news of John the Baptist, He has been taken by King Harrods Men.

Thank you, my Friend Jesus said please tell me your name, Philip Sir, May I introduce, John my Friend we followed John the Baptist and now I don't know what to do.

Following is a synoptic of the known disciples according to the Bible, however there were Many disciples, Jesus and Mary called them their beloved hundreds, many were Women, these were especially blessed because they never denied or abandoned Jesus and Mary.

Even when confronted by the most violent Roman Soldiers, these women held fast in their adoration, while the Men ran away terrified.

Philip: He was a close friend of Andrew and Peter, and a native of Bethsaida) "Philip was given instruction as a disciple to protect he who was to come, and to encourage and protect the important Three disciples His Mother Sarah, and Sisters Deborah and Demelza ".

IN THE BEGINNING

Well Philip Jesus replied, you are more than welcome to join us, we go to preach in Galilee.

Philip replied, that is very near my home town, I would like to accompany you, can I ask you, is its true what John said that you are the one that John preached about, could I become your disciple. Jesus smiled at Philip and said welcome Philip.

They carried on a few miles, Jesus saw that Mary and Miriam looked tired, Jesus said let's rest for a while and eat some lunch, Miriam packs the most wholesome food, you must join us Philip.

Miriam's saddle bag was again filled with food more than enough for everyone they sat and chatted whilst the horses grazed

Jesus asked Philip if he knew of a family of fishermen who worked on the sea of galilee, Philip said why yes, there is Peter and Andrew who is a very good friend, I live in Bethsaida I know practically all the fishermen, I would be honoured if you let me introduce them to you, and you and your companions must stay at my home this evening.

Following is an account of the Disciples, taken from the Bible, however there were many Disciples the most devout being Women.

Peter– became one of the most prominent of the supposed 12 disciples. He was a natural spokesperson His main purpose was to protect He who was to come and provide safety to two Disciples His wife Sarah and her Mother Mary. He was a Fisherman by occupation on the sea of Galilee, He lived in Capernaum.

John: (John was originally the disciple of John the Baptist. (He was the younger brother of James and the son of Zebedee. He lived in Capernaum in Galilee, but most probably a native of Bethsaida. He was a fisherman on the Sea of Galilee along with his brother and father. He was one of the three disciples, closest to Jesus the Son, the others being Peter and James.

James: (Greek *Iakobos*– the English word for Jacob meaning Israel or he who supplants his Brother). James was the son of Zebedee (Mark 4:21), the older brother of John (Mat 17:1), by occupation a fisherman along with his brother and father in partnership with Peter and Andrew. (Luke 5:10). He was the first disciple (apostle) to be martyred. (Acts 12:2)

Andrew: (Greek –*Andreas*, meaning 'Manly', man), was the brother of Simon Peter, the son of Jonas, lived in Capernaum like his brother, was a fisherman by occupation. He brought Peter, his brother, to Jesus. (John 1:25-42)

Bartholomew: (Greek –*bartholomaios* meaning Son of Talmai). He is mentioned in all the four lists of the apostles in the New Testament. There is no other reference to him in the New Testament. Nothing much is known about him. However, He played an important role in the story of Jesus and Mary

Thomas: (Greek –*Thomas* from Aramaic –*te'oma* meaning 'twin') He is also called 'Didymus' or 'the Twin' (John 11:16, 20:24, 21:2). When Jesus appeared to the apostles after His resurrection, Thomas was not present with them. Later, when the disciples told him about Jesus' appearance, he would not believe them, until Jesus showed Himself a week later. (John 20:24-29). His occupation is unknown, from which comes the saying (doubting Thomas)

Matthew: (Greek –*maththaios*– meaning 'gift of Yahweh') is also called 'Levi' (Mark 2:14, Luke 5:27). Jesus called him to be one of his disciples, when he was at the tax office (Mat 9:9, Mark 2:14). He is ascribed to be the author of the Gospel according to Matthew. However as the New testament was written by Monks 250 years after his death this is most unlikely; He did look after the coffers donated to the Christian cause

James: He was one of the apostles of Christ. With Jesus and Mary from the beginning

Thaddaeus: or Jude He is mentioned in two of the four lists of Jesus' disciples. (Mat 10:3, Mark 3:18). In the other two lists he is variously called as Jude of James, Jude Thaddaeus, Judas Thaddaeus or Lebbaeus. Nothing else is known about him apart from the mention of his names in the two lists.

Simon the Zealot: He is another disciple of Jesus. He was a member of a party later called as the 'Zealots' (Matthew 10:4, Mark 3:18)

Judas Iscariot: He is the disciple who it is said betrayed Jesus. His last name 'Iscariot' is from the Hebrew word '*Ish Kerioth* 'meaning 'a man from Kerioth', a place in the south of Judah (Joshua 15:25). He was a scribe and treasurer of the group. However, there was another Man called judas Hiscariot, he was the Son of a temple elder, Simon Hiscariot, it is this person who betrayed Jesus not Judas Iscariot.

Matthias: the eleven disciples selected Matthias as the twelfth disciple. After the Murder of Jesus.

Although the Bible only mentions the Men who were picked for their devotion to God, there was Many more Women who were just as important if not more important than the Men. unfortunately, they were completely omitted from the History and truth of the living Gods, they worked with Mary and Jesus and were instructed by them personally, this did cause jealousy from the Men.

Who proclaimed that Jesus and Mary had no right to attend to these women as the movement the Men wanted, would not support the Woman as church leaders, Jesus became angry with them and told them that if they valued his and Marys love, they would act as Men, not petulant little boys if they had a problem with the teachings of God.

then it would be wiser for them to go back to their fishing boats, as idiots, when they could show as much unconditional Love as the women, only then will they be as worthy to utter the word of God with as much understanding as the Women. He stated that it will be the women that would stand fast at the moment of his need, not the Men, it is for them that he will give the greatest gift of all to the Human race.

two women above all Joanna and Salome, would become heads of the first Christian movement, The Men were taxed by Jesus to be their protectors above everything.

Jesus Mary and the rapidly growing companions arrived at Philips house, they were greeted warmly by Philips Mother Sara and Sisters, Deborah and Demelza.

They were thrilled that Philip had come home, Sara did not approve of her Son following John the Baptist, She felt he should be helping to support his family, especially after the sudden loss of His Father, last year who fell to the ground and did not get up again.

Sara was still in full mourning She missed her Husband desperately although Her husband Philip the Elder, left her suddenly, He had ensured before his death that there would be enough money coming in to the family so they would not be destitute, He owned Cattle, Sheep, a fishing boat, which was rented to Andrew and his Brother Simon Peter, Jesus asked Philip to introduce him to Andrew and Peter in the morning.

Philip said that they would have to get up before day break as they would be fishing early in the morning so the fish would be fresh to be sold on the Market at Galilee.

Philip and John were very worried about John the Baptist and asked Jesus if he would help him, Jesus replied that John the Baptist has an important role to play, and the Pharisees and Socrates could have him freed if they wished, by partitioning Harrod, as for himself and Mary.

They had already helped John except his fate, and that he would probably be martyred, His story and life would not be forgotten with time, He would always be referred to as cousin and Family to God and his work revered by generation to come. A true Profit of God.

Jesus stated, His position in my Kingdom is secure.

Jesus took Sara's hand and looked deep into her eyes beautiful Mother I see and feel your pain and sorrow, fear not, your husband is merely sleeping, He will rise again and if you both wish it, you will be reunited because of your love for each other, in my Kingdom.

Mary and I understand the bonds you share with your Husband and Children, If Mary was to be taken from me, I would find the pain unbearable, as would I, Mary added if my beloved Lord of all Men wasn't by my side.

Mary went on talking to Sara, your grief has made you ignore your own body, have you not had a painful lump in your breast for some time, why yes Sara replied.

I thought it would repair itself I have tried poultices, but they haven't worked, and I have felt so very tired lately, Her Children expressed shock at knowing their Mother was gravely ill, she didn't tell them because She didn't want them to worry.

Jesus turned towards all the group and said, This Woman has shown unconditional Love for her Children She has always put her needs second to theirs, take this as an important lesson, if you can love as Sara does for every Man Woman and Child you come into contact with, Love them, as if they were your own Family regardless of race, creed, or culture then, as my Disciples you will see and know my kingdom.

Mary embraced Sara and said go to your bed and sleep well, In the morning this affliction will be gone and you will feel like a new Woman, Deborah and Demelza came forward wrapping their arms around their Mother crying what would we do without you, please make her well again.

Jesus replied it is already done, take your dear Mother put her to bed then sleep yourselves in the morning you will witness a miracle.

Philip stood staring at Jesus and Mary as if he had never seen them before, he fell to his knees and sobbed, it is true John the Baptist was right, you are the Jehovah, one true god.

Are you capable of working all miracles? tell me it's so, Jesus bent down to Philip and lifted him to his feet, Philip cried I am not worthy Lord, Jesus replied, yes Philip John the Baptist was right, I and Mary am God,

We have come to this earth with an important mission, but first we must know if Human beings are capable and worthy of the greatest gift I could bestow on them, I still haven't made my mind up yet, as to the human races fitness to receive such a great honour.

Time will tell Philip, for now please show Mary and myself where we are to sleep tonight. Philip immediately obliged.

The others lied on straw beds they were strangely comfortable, Miriam went with the girls, Jesus and Mary into a private bedroom.

It was 4.30 in the morning Philip was tip toeing through the house so as not to wake anyone except Jesus, as he promised to introduce him to the local fishermen first thing, Jesus was already up and waiting for Philip and they set off together towards the sea of galilee.

They walked together; Jesus watched as the day dawned the beautiful morning carousel of the birds as the first light of the sun greeted a new day.

Jesus marvelled at the golds reds and blue of the dawn Philip said that he hadn't noticed before just how beautiful the dawning of a new day was, it was as if he had been blind to the world, and now he could see mother earth, in all her splendid glory, He found himself smiling feeling at peace and Happy for the first time since His dear Father had Passed away so suddenly.

It's as if a great weight has been lifted from me, he said to Jesus, Lord, is this the rapture John told us would happen at your coming, because just by walking at your side I feel so liberated.

Yes, I am in awe of you, I am not afraid of this world anymore, my heart feels full and Happy.

Yes, Philip that is exactly what I want for you and this world, for everyone born into it to feel as you do at this moment, however there is opposition, A dark presence which moves in the shadows, Will work hard to instil fear, and terror in the hearts and minds of Men, so gaining dominium over this world.

I have come into this realm to give something to the whole Human race, Myself as a Human being, and my Son, Who will bring the seed of God to the world, and the greatest gift of all is the Woman, Mary Madelaine great, and wonderful Mother of Man, she is the chalice, the beginning and end, the secret of life everlasting.

They walked and talked until they reached the shore of Galilee, Philip noticed that all the boats were already out on the great lake, looks like we missed them Lord. should we wait for them to return or come back tomorrow.

No Philip, would you please gather some wood, I wish to make a fire and cook some fish, Whilst Philip went gathering wood as Jesus asked, Jesus looked out over the see shadowing his eyes from the strong sun, he could just make out a fishing boat coming towards him.

As they got nearer Jesus waved and shouted have you a good catch, Andrew replied No Sir sorry we haven't caught anything in our nets today.

Jesus shouted back to the fishermen throw your nets on the other side, Peter grumbled to himself and the others, saying Oh yeah another bloody know it all, every ones an expert fisherman, but the fishermen, who have 20 years' experience, Andrew you're not seriously considering doing what he said.

Andrew was deep in thought, what would it cost us to try, This Man maybe no fisherman and then maybe he is the greatest fisherman that ever was, we don't know unless we take a leap of faith Simon says, we will be no worse off by trying, Andrew let's throw the nets on the other side of the boat as the Man says.

The crew gathered the nets, putting them onto the water on the opposite side, almost immediately the Fishermen felt the tug of a good catch.

they heaved together to bring the brimming wriggling catch into the boat, the catch was so large it started to tear the nets, another vessel was nearby James and John with their Father Zebedee.

Andrew shouted over for them to join them in bringing the catch in, both boats were filled to sinking point the Men were exuberant, laughing and whooping at their change of fortune, they worked swiftly to secure the catch into baskets ready for the sale.

When finished Andrew waved and shouted to the Man on the shore, thank you it seems you were right, our catch is secure, we can go to market early, thank you.

Jesus shouted back Andrew come ashore and bring some good fish and Simon Peter with you, you have time now to take breakfast with Me, Andrew was very curious at who this Person was, turning to Simon Peter, says well what about it? we wouldn't have this catch if it wasn't for him, let's go and break bread with this strange Fellow, he may be able to give us some more fishing tips.

They slid into the water after picking out some prime Fish for breakfast and swam the short distance to shore leaving their crew to make ready for the Market at Galilee.

Jesus stood on the shore waiting for the Men, Philip busied himself tending the fire ready for the fresh Fish he was looking forward to a good breakfast.

They sat around the fire drying themselves, waiting for the fish to cook, Simon Peter addressed Jesus, who are you, how did you know to cast the nets on the other side, are you the Rabbi everyone is talking about?

Jesus replied I am the light of the world, the living Father of Man, stay with me Simon Peter and I will make you Fishers of Men, Simon Peter and Andrew kneel before Jesus, and Simon said I am not worthy of such a call to follow, I have done wicked things, I am a married Man.

Andrew was knelt in front of Jesus crying great sobs and tears he was so overcome with emotion, that he could not speak.

Follow me Simon Peter Follow me Andrew come with me to tell all people from all nations the good news, the living Gods Mary and Jesus are here to learn about the human beings, and if they prove themselves worthy, to give a wonderful gift to this world, life everlasting.

Jesus held out his arms to them Andrew fell into the lord and Jesus kissed his eyes and said, you have no need to fear me Andrew and now your eyes can see properly again, I have chosen you to be my Student, to travel with me and bear witness to the teachings and miracles, Simon Peter are you with me, I lord, as he reached out to grasp Jesuses forearm.

There are two more Men that we must ask to follow James and John, I have already met John He is a good friend of Philip, but I must talk with James and his Father Zebedee.

First, we must have our good breakfast Philip said, its ready, they sat enjoying the Fish which was sumptuous, after breakfast they set off towards Philips house to re-join Mary and the others.

They walked towards the harbour the Boats had already arrived, the Men were busy unloading fish, and selling to the large crowd gathered around the boats.

John looked up and saw Jesus, He shook James arm for him to pay attention, the two Men stepped out of the boat to greet Jesus and the others, Zebedee their Father watched the men approach his Sons.

Zebedee had a twisted back which gave him great pain, he stooped to one side and walking was hard for him, nevertheless He jumped to his feet and approached Jesus, waving a fist he became enraged Saying, how dare you come here with your preaching, John has told me about you, and that he will be going with you as your Desciple, well I say hands off James.

I will have no one to help with my business, I do not approve of you taking my Sons away, what sort of person are you to take my Sons from me, their Mother will turn in her grave.

Jesus waited until Zebedee finished his rantings, Then He said Zebedee do you want me to cure your pain, Zebedee replied I know there is nothing to be done for Me, so what the hell can you do child stealer.

Jesus laughs out loud, your great pain in your Body and Heart is making you angry Zebedee, He replied enraged, What the bloody hell are you talking about, you don't know me, I can tell you now in front of my stupid Sons, You are a charlatan, just like that John the Baptist, My Son John, left us to become his disciple, I was so full of joy at his return home, and now you will be taking him and his Brother.

I felt like I had lost everything when their Mother Died these Sons of mine were the only reason I carried on, and now they are leaving me to, how can I keep fishing without them, how can I hold it altogether without my Sons.

Zebedee fell into a crumpled heap at Jesuses feet sobbing his heart out, Why have you come to destroy me, I know who you are, John and James ran forward to hold their Father and try to comfort Him, Jesus held out his arm to them in a gestor not to come forward to touch their Father.

Jesus knelt facing Zebedee and said, come out of him, Zebedee immediately started convulsing screaming obscenities, rolling around on the floor, Jesus said louder, come out of Him, and with a bloodcurdling scream the unclean spirit left the body of Zebedee.

Everyone who witnessed this were so astonished especially John, and James, who at Jesuses command ran forward to help their Father, who appeared to be awakening out of a long and deep sleep.

The crowd of People started to talk amongst themselves about what this all meant, is this merely a Teacher or what Teacher could command an unclean spirit to leave, when no one knew there was such a spirit in Zebedee. in the first place.

Everyone who knew him just assumed he was a particular bad tempered Man, who suffered pain, and temper tantrums especially when Drunk, a state Zebedee enjoyed on a regular basis, John and Joseph knew this state two well as they had suffered countless beatings from their Father as Children, and blamed his drinking and beatings on the death of their Mother.

John left His Father and Brother on the day their Mother was buried, preferring to search for spiritual enlightenment, He thought that he had found it, by becoming a disciple of John the Baptist, James longed to join his Brother, but felt strong loyalties tied to their father and Fishing business.

Jesus spoke to Zebedee, come to me Friend, the crowd, gathered gasped when they saw Zebedee walk towards Jesus, He was no longer bent to one side of his body, the hump on his back had gone, He walked as straight as any man, He was no longer in pain, who are you he asked Jesus.

He replied I am the living God come to walk with Men and Women, To understand them, To teach love instead of hate, To give these Human beings a very special gift, if they are deemed worthy, Zebedee cried, are we worthy of it Lord, Jesus replied, I cannot answer that question at this time Zebedee.

No matter, I have been blessed this day I walk straight and free, thank you Lord, I must go to the synagogue to give thanks and tell them, the living God of our Ancestors, is here in Galilee we are blessed by his presence, and you must take both my sons as your Desciples, teach them well lord, they go with my blessing.

Jesus said I will go to your Synagogue another day to preach the word of God, but I warn you Zebedee they will not want to hear what you have to say. It would be better for you if you tell no one.

Jesus walked to Philips house, He did not converse with the others, they followed him in silence, Jesus seemed to be in deep thought as he walked as if he was struggling with something in his own mind, he longed to be reunited with Mary he had much to discuss with her, and he needed her advice.

before long they arrived at Philips, before he opened the door he heard singing coming from inside the house and stopped to listen, He smiled at the sweet voices singing in perfect harmony, another of Marys blessings, She sang as beautifully as the birds and She was leading the other Woman in singing my lord is my shepherd.

The singing seamed to revived him, turning to the other Men gathered behind Him he said, let it be known by you Men, that the Woman are nearer to God, they are the right side of any Man, if a Woman loves you, you are greatly blessed, always treat your women with great respect and reverence.

For they are not only your equal they surpass you, their Love is pure unconditional, whilst yours carries conditions of which you think you are entitled as your right, I tell you now it is not your right, to take her against her will, or to abuse her in any way, observe how a woman greets her Man, when She and He. are enthralled with a great love equal to one another.

Jesus turned and opened the door, Immediately the Women ran to greet the Men, Mary throwing herself into Jesuses waiting arms He kissed her tenderly, I have missed you Darling She said, no more than I have missed you my dearest he replied.

Philip introduced John, James. Simon, and Andrew to his Mother, Mary, and the others, the women had prepared food, and after washing and sitting down together to share the meal, they talked of the day's events.

At first everyone appeared shy to start the conversation, then Philips Sisters said well go on tell us of your day, Andrew started by telling about the catch, then John came in with how Jesus helped his Father, as the conversations began to take excited momentum, with everyone joining in to tell of what they witnessed, Jesus watched each person as they told of the miracles they experienced, He remained silent observing each person's point of view.

When the excitement around the table was at its highest, a loud banging on the front door. Stopped all conversations immediately.

Philip was apprehensive of opening the door as the loud banging suggested that whoever was on the other side of the door meant business, everyone followed Philip with their eyes as he walked to open the door in antrepidation, Philip slowly opened the door then took a step backwards in shock.

facing him was a Roman Centurion in full battle dress Oh Shit he thought, we are for it now. Good day said Tibur Drusus, I wonder if you know the whereabouts of a Man called Jesus and his Wife Mary, they usually command a large crowd around them so relatively easy to spot, Philip was struck dumb, he simply didn't know what to say, Thank God, he breathed a sigh of relief when Jesus came from behind him and greeted the Centurion as if he was a long-lost Brother.

Tibur Drusus turned to his Men and commanded them to step down and rest outside, he then walked into the home with Jesus taking his fine plumbed helmet off in respect.

Mary immediately jumped to her feet and gave him a hug, great to see you Tibur, what brings you here, I came to find you Tibur replied, Pontus Pilot himself bade me to come and find you as he heard that John the Baptist had been arrested by King Harrods Militiamen, He knew you went to meet him at the baptism place.

He and His good Lady were worried about you all, they have heard nothing since you left, and feared that you had been caught up by the militia and arrested along with the Baptist fellow.

They gave me the mission to find you, I am to escort you safely back to Jerusalem.

Mary replied it is great to see you Tibur and thank you for caring so much about our welfare that Pontus and Solicitous have sent you to take us home to them.

Before we come back to Jerusalem, we will be taking detours along the way to preach and heal People, this will take more time and with all respect to you dear Tibur would be better conducted without a Roman Garrison as escort.

Please send our love and blessings back to our dearest friends and tell them we will have many stories of our encounters to tell them when we return. We have many new and old friends that are looking after us, so please tell them not to worry we will be back with them soon.

Thank you, my Darling that was so well put, Jesus said, would you like something to eat before you leave us Tibur, well yes but my Men haven't eaten today so I must look to them, we will take food out to them also.

Poor Sara was concerned the stew and bread they made had all but gone, there were no more vegetables and the fish needed scalping and dressing. Mary smiled at Sara she leaned over and whispered don't worry the pot is full and the bread is freshly baking.

Sara looked stunned as She went to stir the vegetable stew bubbling on the fire, Miriam opened the oven door and pulled out many loaves fresh bread and stew it is then Tibur said smiling.

Deborah and Demelza busied themselves getting bowls and Luke helped carrying out the large pot of stew to feed Tibur's troups, The Girls were very excited they hadn't seen so many young and Handsome young Men in their lives and both Girls were at the age where handsome young Men mattered, they fairly swooned at the compliments the young men gave them, they giggled and acted coyly, but secretly they were thrilled at all the attention.

as they moved along serving the dish and breaking the bread, Demelza stopped a few moments longer looking into the eyes of a very good-looking young man with the loveliest blue eyes.

in that moment which seemed to last a lifetime between them something strange happened they fell madly in love with each other, each felt they knew each other intimately.

before they could speak, everyone started shouting to move along and hurry up as they were starving, so Demelza moved quickly on, however She could not take her eyes of the young Man and He could not break her gaze for a moment.

Later that evening Demelza told her Sister what happened between her and the young Man Who She didn't even knows his name, yet She knew She would only love him forever.

After the house went quiet and She was sure everyone was asleep, She carefully climbed out of her bedroom window, She simply had to talk to the young Man, very carefully and quietly she crept through the sleeping bodies as She looked for her love, He was already awake just as disturbed by their encounter as She was.

He was Shocked seeing her creeping along bearfoot, something in his heart told him She was looking for him, so just as silently He moved towards Her, when they met He took hold of her hand lifted her up in strong arms and silently moved away from his sleeping comrads, He lifted her gently as if she was a precious flower.

they moved enough away so the others could not hear their conversation. He sat her down on a grassy bank, and sat himself facing Her, did you feel it too he asked Her, Yes and that's why I had to see you just once before you leave tomorrow.

He nodded I am glad you did, although I will do nothing to defile you, it is enough to talk and hold hands, I have never felt such a burning desire and love with anyone, Yes Demelza said I felt it just like you, what does it mean.

Well do you believe in love at first site, I really don't know I have never experienced love before and when I am Married well the bridegroom is usually chosen by Family Members, so love doesn't come into it. Mother says if God is willing, I will come to love my husband in time.

If truth be told I have never felt as whole as I did when you looked upon me, with those beautiful eyes. I could have wantonly kissed you to Death.

Am I so bad and wrong for thinking such things, not when I feel the same, I have never felt so moved by anyone as I am by you, but we can never be married, I am a Roman Legionary life is dedicated to my Emperor, I will probably die in battle. I cannot provide for you, Demelza replied I haven't asked you to, and She placed her hands on his face and kissed him gently then more passionately, their mutual passions got the better of both they fell together in a rapture that neither could resist.

Afterwards they lay in each other's arms so completely loved up that they fell asleep. They awoke suddenly with shouts of She's over here, with the devil that took her, before they were in their right senses hands grabbed them both and they were dragged towards the House, someone had delivered a blow to the young Man so he was knocked senseless unable to offer any resistance.

The Poor youngsters were thrown unceremoniously into the main room of the house where Sara Deborah, Philip and all the other guests, were praying, crying, wailing and carrying on in such a way that Jesus and Mary thought there must have been a murder.

They joined the scene as Tibur Drusus held the young legionnaire by the throat and amidst screams of NOOO from Demelza was about to cut him, Jesus shouted STOP, and everyone stopped, Mary ran past Jesus to administer healing to the young Man and calm poor Demelza.

Tibur what has happened here, why do you treat this young Man so badly, Philip stepped forward this Bastard pointing to the young soldier has defiled my sister, my property, He has rendered her virtually unmarriageable. And probably given her a bastard, she was innocent of such things until tonight and now she is forever changed I cannot look at Her. Sara was pleading with Her Son not to go to the synagogue as they would have her stoned for being with a Roman.

Jesus listened to the hysteria and ramblings of all the people in the room all the while looking and observing the young couple still on the floor, Demelza had her arms around the young Soldier She was crying and saying how sorry she was to bring him to this, although bound at the wrists, his face was turned to her trying to comfort her, knowing that he was about to be put to death.

He was smiling at her. His countenance was of someone who looked with absolute adoration and love.

Mary moved towards Jesuses side they held hands and considered each other's eyes, Jesus shouted OK THAT'S ENOUGH. If you are not a family member please leave quietly now, except you Tibur. Most of the throng consisting of searchers, neighbours, soldiers, shuffled out of the house Jesus promptly shut the heavy wooden door behind them.

Has anyone bothered to ask about the young people here, asked them why they crept away together? Philip shouted He abducted her, if you think that then why are you not more caring and sympathetic towards your Sister, let's ask Her, Jesus held out his hand towards Demelza and she took it and stood up in front of Jesus, meanwhile Mary took a knife from the kitchen walked behind the young man and cut his bonds, helping him to his feet.

Demelza told all of them how they both felt when first setting eyes on each other, Jesus turned towards the young Soldier and asked him how he felt at the same time, and if he had abducted the Girl against her will, to stand up for Demelza honour he was about to say yes he did, when Demelza screamed no he didn't I went to find him.

In that case Jesus said this young woman forced herself on the young Man, NO NO She did not, the young man cried he was determined to take all the blame so as not to tarnish the Girls standing with her Family and scar her future, or worst still the Holy men at the synagogue stoning her to death, He knew they loved a good stoning,

He turned to her and said I wish with all my heart that I could have been a part of your life, I wish with all my heart that I could love you forever and be married to you to, have a family with you would be worth laying down my life for, So please let them put me to death as guilty, this is the only thing I can do for you my only Love.

Demelza considered his eyes and said, I want to be put to death with you, because if I cannot live my life happily with you, I don't want to live without you. The young couple held each other, no one dared separate them.

The mood in the room had changed instead of hysteria a quiet peace came over everyone, as the young couple spoke of their connection to love experienced in a moment of recognition, the people were silently weeping for them, even Philip was moved by their commitment, however He stated How can they be in love, they have only just met. Jesus replied do you love me and Mary Philip, of course you know I do, we have only just met so how can you love me, because you are Jesus and Mary, God, yes but how do you know, well it's a feeling a knowing and all the miracles I have witnessed. Jesus replied yes you have just witnessed another miracle with your Sister and the Man She has chosen.

Jesus turned to the young couple and said if it was possible would you both want to spend eternity together, each replied yes Lord.

I know you have no Family Young Man would you want to take Demelza Family as your own, yes but that's impossible I am a legionnaire I will never be allowed to Marry a Jewish Woman.

I did not ask you that, Jesus exclaimed if there was no objection to you two being together would you renounce your old life in favour of becoming a Family Man, taking on a new identity as Husband of Demelza, Brother of Philip and Deborah, Son of Sara, would you devote yourself to your Family, working only for their good, bringing into this world the blessing of Children and promise to still love Demelza with all your heart into old age.

Yes of course it would be everything I have ever dreamed of and wanted.

Demelza would you swear before your God that you would honour this Man everyday of your life giving your body and love only to him. Yes, it would be a dream come true.

Do you both promise to marry for love. YES, YES, Then I now pronounce you Man and Wife. Let no man undo this tying together, I wish your Health Wealth and Happiness for the rest of your days.

Everyone stood with their mouths open contemplating what just happened, how could they object there was nothing to say but congratulations.

Tibur Drusus was the first to question the right of this marriage, saying hang on a Minuit, He is signed up as a legionnaire only Tiberius himself can grant him freedom. Yes, replied Jesus that is true, but what if you caught this legionnaire defiling a Jewish woman, and to keep the peace within the region you had no choice but to put him to death by your sword, you were going to do just that when we entered the room, think of your own predicament with Miss Maximus.

Tibur relented looking at the young soldier, He said is this what you want, the young Man replied Yes Sir I don't really have the stomach to be a good legionnaire. Alright then we had better get our story straight before another Soldier suspects the truth, I will take your uniform out to the Men and tell them you have been executed.

I will leave at first light for Jerusalem taking your messages with me.

Thank you, Tibur we can always count on you Mary, said, yes, I must be mad or becoming a right softy replied Tibur, by the way young Man what is your name, BIGGUS Dickyust sir.

for a moment no one said a word, then Jesus let out a big gawf then, everyone burst out laughing, every time someone mentioned Biggus Dickyust they started again.

Jesus and Mary were in hysterics, Mary suggested they find another name, Jesus suggested Ben, that was rejected when some bright spark shouted yeah Ben down and do it again, so they fell about laughing again, Jesus was trying to compose himself, but it was no good every time He tried to stop, someone would make another quip and they started again, this went on for quite a while until everyone became exhausted With sides aching they decided to go to Bed.

(note from writer, this joke was used in life of Brian, I said this to my orator his reply was yes, who do you think gave it to the writers it in the first place, incidentally they love life of Brian on the other side.)

Biggus took no insult, He laughed along with everyone poor Demelza didn't know what they were laughing at, until Biggus explained She still didn't think it was funny.

She said but I like your name, which made everyone start laughing again, Jesus asked for calm he wanted to bless the young couple, and could see that poor Demelza was looking bemused, Dearest Child he said taking hold of her hand, to laugh together is one of the greatest joys, if you can laugh at life and yourself and trust God with your future, you and Biggus will have a long and very happy union.

Blessed I am sure with many Children, who will fill you with happiness and sometimes tears of sadness and joy, when life becomes a burden, when you cannot share humour in everything you say and do, then life becomes sad, remember my dear, live love and laugh, leave everything else to God.

The House became silent, Biggus and Demelza laid together with arms around each other, Their lives spared and looking forward to a future together, Philip gave some clothes to Biggus.

Tibur took his legionnaires uniform out to the Men waiting outside telling them of the young soldier's fate, the legionnaires were not happy with Tibur's explanation, some openly objected to the young Soldiers demise.

Tibur was resolute saying to the Men this fate will fall on you all, if it undermines the peace and smooth running of the area. He immediately ordered the men to ready themselves and they left for Jerusalem immediately.

Everyone breathed a big sigh of relief when they realised the soldiers had left. The following morning Philip called a Family meeting they all sat down and waited for Philip to start,

Philip stood up to address all of the Family and Jesus and Mary, He stated a lot had happened in such a short time and he questioned that the union of his Sister and Biggus was legal, and if so what could Biggus bring to this Family having no money or land or any standing whatsoever,

He also stated that he was upset because a local landowner a rich man had expressed interest of marriage to Demelza, this would have brought a large amount of money into the household and felt that Demelza was being selfish in choosing for herself this Man that we know nothing about, for all we know he could slit our throats whilst sleeping, Jesus did not ask me if this union was right for all the family, Jesus and Mary said nothing they waited until Philip had finished.

Poor Demelza was crest fallen at her Brothers words, with tears welling in her eyes she addressed her Brother, Philip I never realised you of all people owned me, like I was born your Slave.

I always thought that I was a free Woman she cried, Philip replied angrily of course I own you, as the head of this Family, It is my duty to place you in a good marriage so that you and the rest of us leave a better life, yes I object to this union I was not consulted, as for you pointing to Biggus what can you bring to this family, nothing am I right.

Sir, Biggus replied I am sorry you were not consulted the events happened so quickly I could barely think, I am sorry you feel as you do, if we had stopped to consult with you would you have given us your blessing.

No, I would not, then what great and good fortune for us that Jesus intervened, because this day I would have been put to death, we would have had no future together, and your Sister would be sold into an unhappy life.

Philip was lost for words and Sara spoke, I have observed this young Man and Demelza together and it pleases my heart that they obviously love each other so much, who are we to say they cannot be together, Philip my dear Boy it is true that you are the head of this house, in Jewish law you alone have the right to bless your Sisters union.

I am your Mother so what I say in this family must count as I am the one who gave your life. I believe this young man will bring the greatest thing to this Family, LOVE, I for one, wish to welcome him as my Son, because if Demelza and Jesus and Mary favour him, then that's all the dowry this family needs.

She moved to the couple and kissed each one as a Mother does, Deborah ran to them I think hese lovely she placed her arms around his neck kissed his forehead and said welcome home Brother.

WELL, cried Philip I see you all stand against me, No No we don't cried Sara, we want you to see what is before you, so you can give your blessing to these two-young people and take this young Man as your Brother, you have much to teach him, and much to learn from him.

At this point Jesus spoke, Philip Why are you so angry, well I? I Don't know, I just am because of tradition I suppose I am the one to pick a Husband for my Sisters, I say what happens in my own household, Jesus replied Is it because you feel powerless where you once had power over your women folk.

Philip replied, this is the way our people have always lived, it is our culture set by god, marrying them goes against our culture and traditions they are from different faith race and culture;

how can they hope to survive in our community married to a Roman? Simple replied Jesus don't tell anyone.

Keep to yourself, that you have been blessed for this very brave and courageous young man to be part of your Family.

Be happy for your Sister, then you will feel your own joy within your heart.

If you say this is so then I am in no position to oppose them, but Jesus please explain, these values have always been in our Family we are Jewish and have worshipped you for centuries our way of life is on your word and church, so how can you say such things the synagogue leaders would be furious if they heard our conversations.

I will say this, listen closely, I am your Jehovian, am the one who released your ancestors from slavery, I will not be found in the synagogues nor in any religion on this earth, because they are there to suppress the free will, which I gave to you, they are power crazy, Religion is only a mask a front to control, by the taking of money and gifts from the masses they are made by Man not God to control the unknowing innocent,

No, my friend I do not dwell in those Grand houses, I am in the hearts blood and bone of the individual, I do not recognise any Religion, they are all cults without exception.

The sharing and giving of love is my only currency and purpose, observe if you will, a good Mothers love, this is a sacred love, She labours and toils in great pain to give life She doesn't blame her Child for that pain, as soon as She is delivered, her only thought is for the well-being of the Child, She holds that Child to her breast and gives and receives a powerful bond with her Son or Daughter and from then on She devotes all her life to that Child, If the child is hungry She will do anything to feed it going without food herself to provide the basic of needs Food, shelter and Love for another little human being.

Her love is nearer to Gods perfect love for you than you will ever understand, if you want to know if God loves you ask your Mother first, if She loves you, and if She says Yes, my darling Son more than my own life, you are blessed by God, your holy Mother and Father. For they love you also. Listen to your Mother Philip She is a very wise and blessed woman.

I wish to speak to those termed as my disciples, we will go outside into the Sun whilst I give you a fundamental lesson about CREATION, I especially want the Women to sit with us and hear the lessen.

The Men expressed concern at sitting with the Women as this was unacceptable in the synagogues, Jesus replied that they were not in the synagogue, as the women were the right side of Men they should sit right at the front.

Teaching about Creation

Jesus began, the first intelligent human let us call him Adam his name is immaterial, was begotten by Semjasa, the leader of the celestial sons who were the guardian angels of God, the great ruler of the travellers from afar Semjasa, the celestial son and guardian angel of God the great ruler of Zion or Heaven.

In short, the voyagers travelled here through vast expanses of the universe, took terrestrial women and begot Adam, the first father of the human population. They took up dominion on earth inhabiting the entire world, for our purpose we will examine the area known as Egypt.

IN THE BEGINNING

They Fast became the rulers and governors, they looked very different from any other race on earth having white skin and white or red hair, they also had large blue or Green eyes and were super intelligent.

They stood taller above any other race, commanded great technology which they introduced, teaching some of their Children, with this technology they were able to build enormous buildings, hence the great works of the pyramids which were originally used as great power houses, generating power from air, water, fire and Air a combination which gave out light, powering their crafts and machines, used for shaping and moving heavy objects of stone or carve great likenesses of the Rulers.

They were able to manipulate anything using vibration noise or music, all knowledge stemmed from them. It was easy for them to crush any uprising, they possessed staffs that rendered anyone paralysed if they refused the bidding of the celestial beings, they produced horns which when blown in a certain harmony rendered all completely in compliance to the Gods wishes, they became in time great ruler's dynasties of kings and queens that were beautiful in their continence, swift in judgement but fair to all their subjects, the Males looked attractive to the local women who bore them many sons and daughters.

Over much time a few thousand years their Children travelled to all corners of this earth and begot the human beings of today, however the Pure breeds living far longer than their Human Children became unhappy and unsatisfied with the unstable riot ridden offspring as they turned on the celestial being in uprisings, and the descendants being true to the long dead Celestial Sons of Egypt became obsessed with returning Home to God.

They became more interested in Death and returning home, to their original universe, preferring to shut themselves off from the world as such, this became an undoing because rather than taking Women and Men as Wives and Husbands from the general population saw themselves above that kind of thing, knowing the truth about where Human beings came from and why they are set a little apart from animals.

preferring now to keep the seed within their own families.subsiquently the seed became unbalanced within creation, the Children of these first Gods became deformed some having elongated heads and large hands or lived but a short time, they also became mentally unstable, causing great distress, they called to God to deliver them home.

The great dynasty crumbled and died with the last of its pure kind, only the writings on the great pyramids which became their burial tombs survived, which can still be seen and witnessed as marvels around the whole earth. However, the Kings and Queens were so attached to their golden comforts that their understanding of a part of the law of creation in that, whatever is created on this earth will be created in the other world.

They consequently filled their burial chambers with everything of value to them so that they could enjoy them in the afterlife, this was a misconception as it is only living beings that are recreated in My Kingdom from every blade of grass, Animals, plants everything that lives with a spirit is to be enjoyed in the afterlife, not inanimate objects.

Thus, it is the Human Beings birth right forever interested in finding their one true God and firing their Gods interest in them. The only way to do this is to be a Child of God.

Jesus preached powerfully, saying, "Behold, Creation stands above humanity, above God and above everything. It appears to be perfect by human comprehension, but this is not so. "Since Creation is spirit and thus lives, even it must forever perfect itself.

"But since it is one within itself, it can perfect itself by way of its own creations, through the generation of new spirit forms that dwell within humans, give them life, and evolve towards perfection through their learning on this beautiful planet Earth "The newly generated spirit is part of Creation itself; however, it is unknowing down to the smallest iota.

"When a new spirit is created, which is still unknowing in every way, it lives in a human body and begins to learn. "Persons may consider the unknowing spirit as stupid and say that the individual is confused. But it is not, because it is only unknowing and devoid of knowledge and wisdom.

Thus, may this new spirit live a life within a human being to gather knowledge.

Then, when this spirit enters the beyond, it is no longer as unknowing as it was at the time of its beginning. "And it returns into the world and lives again as a human being but is no longer quite as unknowing as it was at its beginning.

"Again, it learns and gathers further knowledge and new wisdom, and thereby increasingly escapes from ignorance. "So, after many renewed lives, the time comes when people say that this spirit is normal and not confused.

"But this is neither the end of the spirit nor its fulfilment, because, having become knowing, the spirit now seeks the greatest wisdom. "Thus, the human spirit perfects itself so extensively that it unfolds in a Creational manner and ultimately becomes one with Creation, as it was destined from the earliest beginning.

"Thus, Creation has brought forth a new spirit, allowing it to be perfected independently in the human body. The perfected spirit returns to Creation to become one with it, and in this manner, Creation perfects itself within itself, for in it is the knowledge and wisdom to do so.

"Truly, I say to you, the time will never come when Creation ceases to create new spirit forms and to broaden itself, "However, Creation also requires rest, a characteristic of all that lives, and when it slumbers it does not create.

Just as human life has day and night and is divided into work and rest, so Creation also has its times of work and rest. "It's period, however, is different from that of people, because its laws are the laws of the spirit, while human laws are the laws of material life.

The material life is limited, but the life of the spirit lasts forever and knows no end. I will go forward into creation and create a home of plenty where my Children will experience renewal, respite and above all love, I honour my Children by bringing them home to me, and their Holy Mother, at the end of their physical life.

Its secret is that which is immeasurable and is based on the number seven, which is counted in 'times.'

This is one of the secrets and laws the human mind will solve only when it reaches perfection. But let it be said that the laws of life are not hidden from the wise man, hence he can recognize and follow them.

Thus, the wise understand that the secret of Primeval-Creation lies in the number seven and in computations based thereon. Thus, they will gather and retain the knowledge that Creation has a time for work or rest that is also based upon the number seven. The number of God is *777*.

Creation rested in a state of slumber for seven million Great Times when nothing existed, not even the universe. Only Creation itself existed in slumber, and it brought forth no creature nor anything.

However, it did awaken from its slumber through the seven cycles of seven million Great Times and began to create creatures and everything.

Part of this Creation is primeval ooze, where lives the most putrid creatures spirits whose greatest pleasure and sport is to attack and overwhelm the uneducated simple Humans, their numbers are 666 always one behind the numbers of God because they are inferior to Creation and God, therefore when a spirit has lived by their number, that spirit is returned to the lowest point in creation.

After having rested for seven cycles of seven million Great Times, it is now creating living organisms and everything else, and it will do so for seven more cycles of seven Great Times, until it requires rest again and reposes anew in deep slumber for a further seven million Great Times. When it will rest again and lie down in slumber, nothing will exist except for Creation itself.

There will be neither creatures nor any other thing. Only Creation itself will exist during the seven cycles of the seven million Great Times, because it will rest and slumber until it awakens again and brings forth new creatures and everything else. Just as Creation is one within itself, however, so is all life, being and existence one within itself.

"It is by the law of Creation that all humans, plants, animals and all life are one in themselves and creation.

A person may believe that everything is two or three, but that is not so, because everything is one.in creation, Whatever people believe to be two or three is one, so they should make everything that is two or three into one. Since the spirit in a person is part of Creation, it is one with Creation;

I state that there is a unity and not, in any way or form, a duality or trinity. If it appears to people that there is a duality or trinity, then they are the victims of deception, for they do not think logically but according to human knowledge.

But if they think according to the knowledge of the spirit, they find the logic, which is also in the law. Of creation Only, human thinking can be incorrect, not the laws of Creation.

For this reason, it is said that everything emanates from a unity, and a duality seems apparent only because humans, in their limited thinking, cannot grasp the truth. Since everything is a unity and everything emanates from it, no duality or trinity whatsoever can exist because it would violate the laws of Creation.

Therefore, people should make the two or three into one and think and act according to the laws of Creation. Only in ignorance does a person fabricate a duality or trinity and give offense to the laws of Creation.

"When a person aligns everything into this unity, making everything into one, and then says to a mountain, 'Move away,' then it will move away. When everything is one in Creation, in its laws, in the creatures and in matter, it is without error.

Therefore, evil is one, because it is also good. Likewise, good is one because it is just as much evil. Since even when apart they are one and a unity, together they are also one and a unity, for this is the law of Creation.

Thus, the result is, that there are two parts in appearance, but they are both one in themselves and one when together. If, therefore, people say there exists also a trinity, then their consciousness has been addled by some cult, falsified teachings or confused thinking.

A unity always consists of two parts, which are one in themselves and are a duality only in appearance.

Since a person is a unity of two parts, the spirit is a unity of two parts, but both are one in themselves and one together.

The body cannot live without the spirit and conversely, because spirit and body are a unity despite their seeming duality. The spirit, however, lives according to the same law, because it also consists of two parts and is one in each part; thus, it is one.

The two parts of the spirit are wisdom and power.

Without wisdom of the spirit, its power cannot be utilized, nor can any wisdom emerge without spiritual power. Hence, two things are always required that are one within themselves, so there is a oneness within the unity but not a duality.

Thus, the creation law says that a human being is a unity, which consists of two equal parts that form a unity, both within themselves and together.

And the two equal parts in the human being, each of which constitutes a unity within itself, are the body and the spirit.

So, when the scribes teach that a person lives in a trinity, this teaching is erroneous and falsified, because it is not taught in accordance with the laws of Creation."

Now that I have your attention, let me get to the more serious parts of the spiritual teachings. Humans throughout the universe are destined to evolve spiritually over many reincarnations.

These are defined by seven levels of development.

Level 1 is concerned with simple survival. Primitive thought patterns and speech develop. Human beings develop a conscience, hence the development of lethal weapons, shape the world, constant wars, struggle to find other ways less costly of defusing conflict.

Level 2, Rational thought is cultivated. Societies are established. We have cultural activities and primitive science. Empires rise and vanish, through debate and Politics, Human beings develop a greater sense of compassion.

At Level 3, The first expressions of wisdom lead to intelligent use of knowledge. Men and Women start to think and act at a higher level, producing great insight and inventions.

Level 4 Technology is used to enhance the enjoyment of human life. We also see the beginnings of Earth human intelligence and spiritual advancement which covers a wide range within Level 1,2,3 and 4

Human beings can become stuck in this wheel of 2,3, and 4 until through knowledge and repetitive creation it frees itself and only then move on to level 5, However you are still far from spiritual advancement, Human beings seek spiritual enlightenment, however they are held back, because of the culture of that Human, and Religious beliefs, they are led to believe they can only achieve this by following the Holy Men or Wealthy Men in their communities,

Religion becomes tribal, Men seek to obtain power through force, using their Religion as an excuse to overcome other tribes by murder, gaining Land power over Women, and commerce.

There are, and will be, in the future calls to defend God through so called Holy wars, Men will say god is on our side, therefore we are righteous in the evil of war.

I say to you God is on no side in any conflict that takes a life, they are driven by evil minds and thoughts, as far away from God as they can be. God is only interested in the individual not in his or Hers religious beliefs.

There are those that say We study Holy books, we pray every day therefore we are the elite God has chosen us, I say to them you are delusional.

It will take hundreds or even thousands of years before the enlightened few are ready for level 5

At Level 5, humans are grasping the spiritual nature of reality and begin to utilize their spiritual power.

At Level 6, humans have learned to live in peace and harmony with the Laws and Directives of Creation.

Level 7 They can distort time and space for intergalactic space travel.

This is the level of Jesus. Or Jehovah, Yahuwah or Madoc the names given by Humans to one living God, who is both Male and Female,2 is 1 bringing righteousness and order out of the Chaos Therefore your God comes from advanced Creation

At Level 7 spiritual beings have become perfect, ending their journey by merging with the spirit of Creation. The Laws of Creation are the "Blueprint of Reality." They describe the way it is. Hence the number of God is 7

I will concentrate here on the spiritual aspects of the Laws of Creation; and so, I have arbitrarily extracted the most important aspects of Creation Creation's Love is Unconditional.

"Truly, I say to you, a love that is unlimited, constant and unfailing is unconditional and is a pure love, in whose fire all that is impure, and evil will burn. Such a love is Creation's love

"When one makes a mistake that serves the insight, knowledge, and progress of the spirit, there is "Through these laws and directives, which represent Creation, humankind in its irrationality will bring

And this is the way it is!

I have listed 7 action items under the FIRST DIRECTIVE:

1. PERFECT YOUR SPIRIT

Therefore, humans should try without ceasing to broaden and deepen their knowledge, love, truth, logic, true freedom, genuine peace, harmony and wisdom, so that the spirit may be perfected and lifted into its true home, becoming one with Creation."

"**2. ATTEND TO YOUR SPIRITUAL NEEDS FIRST**

First seek the realm of your spirit and its knowledge, and then seek to comfort your body with food, drink and clothing." Seek out your conscious mind

"What would it profit them if they should gain the entire world, yet still damage their consciousness?"

3. LEARN THROUGH LIFE'S EXPERIENCES

"Humans gain experience in the use of their powers and capabilities only by trying daily to unlock them."

"But if humans do not think and seek, they will not be able to attain wisdom and will remain fools."

Note that the living God can raise the dead and heal the terminally ill, but he is not able to cure the fools. If you remain a fool, nobody can help you.

The next item is:

4. CONQUER FEAR AND SEEK TRUE FREEDOM

Love cannot blossom in the presence of fear.

Personal power cannot blossom in the presence of fear.

Therefore, seek spiritual wisdom to banish ignorance and poverty of consciousness, so that fear may be replaced with love and confidence.

Free yourself from the enslaving power of Cults, false doctrines, evil passions, addictions, negative emotions, imagined needs and attachments.

"No greater darkness rules within humans than ignorance and lack of wisdom."

"Greatness of personal victory requires uprooting and destroying all influences that oppose the Creational force, …"

And now the last item:

5. GAIN SPIRITUAL POWER THROUGH ALIGNMENT.

Develop spiritual power by aligning with Creation. Create a will that is aligned with the will of Creation, so that you learn to control your destiny.

"Know this: Whatever a person may wish to accomplish, they must always first create the will to do so, because this is the law of nature. Thus, a person determines the course of his life, known as fate.

6&7 THE SECOND DIRECTIVE of CREATION is:
HONOR CREATION THEN GOD, ABOVE ALL.

"But the other directive, equal to the first, is this: You shall consider only Creation as omnipotent, for it alone is constant in all things and therein is timeless."

I say: "It is unwise and foolish for people to let others consider them greater or smaller than they really are. "In other words: Be neither arrogant nor meek but act according to your level of spiritual wisdom.

The Earth is destined to be ruled by wisdom, so that ignorance and poverty of consciousness will be banished, and so that love, peace and harmony can flourish.

This will not happen in our lifetime, but eventually, in times yet to come, wise spiritual people on Earth will gain the upper hand.

Jesus looked at the Disciples and asked any questions, each looked at Jesus with stunned silence, then Peter spoke My Lord you have given us so much to think about I am a bit overwhelmed what you say is contrary to my beliefs and Teachings of the phrases and Socrates at our Temple, are you saying that we should not trust the elders and betters in the Temple and synagogues.

Yes, Jesus replied that's right, and I have promised you that I will always tell you the truth if you are struggling to understand and need to go back over my teaching today, Jude my studious Brother has written everything down He will scribe at all your lessons, so you will have a written guide, which you may study between you at length, well my Friends.

I think you have much to mull over, talk amongst yourselves and feel free to ask any questions you wish of me, I tell you these things so that you understand the fundamental truth of Creation and God, how can you go about in this world preaching and healing your fellow men and Women and not know where you came from or why you came about.

That what dwells in your material body is spiritual therefore two the body and spirit are one also at one when re-joining creation, you must grasp this concept, when you move through the stages of enlightenment at your own pace and level of perception a great knowing will come about, you will need this knowing in the future to help you take the word to all people, and here ends your lesson for today.

The disciples rushed forward gaggling like geese to ask their own questions. Jesus held up his hand in a gesture to stop. Jesus said, "Let him who seeks continue seeking until he finds. When he finds, he will become troubled. When he becomes troubled, he will be astonished, and he will rule over All."

Jesus left them to go to Mary, as always, she greeted him with open arms and a lingering kiss, so my Darling tell me, "Whom are your disciples like?"

He said, "They are like children who have settled in a field which is not theirs. When the owner of the field comes, he will say, 'Let me have my field back.' At first the Children will argue with the Owners telling them of their sacrifice and arduous work to bring the field into producing a great crop.

eventually They will undress in the owner's presence standing naked and humble to let him have his field and then permit him rightful resolution, only then will the owner be able to give it back to them. Today they have learned a momentous lesson in the middle of the field, tomorrow the arguing and questioning will begin.

These Apostilles will eventually recognise the truth and right of all I have taught them, however I believe it is the Women who hold the most potential.

If they prove open and worthy, they will be in raptures standing naked before us ready and able to except the Devine, This will be a day full of joy as we give the field back to the worthy and rightouse, however I fear there are still many devils who would murder the Owners and take the field in this dimention, telling all and sunder, that they are the righteous ones.

justifying their evil behaviour taking the beautiful well grown field and destroying its fruitfulness for generations to come, This I feel disturbed by.

Therefore, I say, if the owner of a house knows that the thief is coming, he will begin his vigil before he comes and will not let him dig through into his house of his domain to carry away his goods. You, then, my dearest one. be on your guard against the world.

Arm yourselves with great strength and your unending knowledge, lest the robbers find a way to come to you, for the difficulty which you expect will surely materialize. Let there be among them a man or Woman of understanding. When the grain ripened, he came quickly with his sickle in his hand and reaped it. Whoever has ears to hear, let him hear."

Mary replied They have much to learn through their ears, she playfully tickled Jesuses ear, He started to laugh and held Mary in his arms, my dearest right side of me you always can lift my spirit even when teaching unruly Children.

The following morning Jesus called everyone around him, I will tell you of the plans for today and tomorrow, we will journey to Capernaum today as we journey People will want to talk to us and I will answer all their questions and Mary and myself will heal the sick.

My Dear Disciples will watch and observe, Philip you must leave Biggus as head of your household until you return, with Demelza He will look after your interests, Mother and Deborah I would like them to come with us at least for a short while.

With goodbyes' and embraces they left for Capernaum, along the road they met many people healed many and spoke good sense to the crowds that followed, In Capernaum Jesus and Disciples attended the synagogue held everyone enthralled at his preaching and teaching.

There was a Man who was possessed of an unclean spirit or Demon, He shouted loudly Ha what do you want here, to destroy us all with your blasphemy, I know who you are, Jesus shouted back sharply, Be quiet! come out of him and the Devil threw the man down and went out of him without hurting Him or anyone else, The whole communion were astonished after this the synagogue became packed with all the parishioners of the area and beyond daily, all hoping to see Jesus and be healed in body and spirit by him and Mary.

Jesus made the decision that they would set Capernaum as the Centre of his and Marys teachings, Mary talked and healed the women Mothers with Children, whilst Jesus and the disciples preached and debated answering questions at the synagogue.

Simon Peter lived in Capernaum, with his wife and Mother in law, and after the first evening at the synagogue Jesus Mary and growing followers went to stay at Simons Peters house, only to find that Simon Peters Mother in law Mary and Wife Sofie was very sick with fever, Simon asked Jesus and Mary if they could help them as he feared they were both near to death.

Jesus went to them and admonished the fever and it left them immediately, they got up from their sick beds and cooked a meal for them, Mary Capernaum, and Sofie became two more Disciples, Simon Peter was very grateful thanked them repeatedly for restoring happiness in his home, Jesus told him that in the future he would be responsible for their safety and delivery from Evil, the meal was a joyous occasion.

They stayed at Capernaum for several months preaching and healing, however the synagogue was writhe with its old ways of beliefs and superstitions the religious Leaders became to regard Jesus and Mary as something of a threat and feared that they would bring swift and cruel judgement from the Romans on them.

instead of discussing their fears with them they chose to order the people to ignore them, they did not threaten them or send them away they simply made it uncomfortable for them to stay.

they would walk away when they saw Mary or Jesus approaching them, they left the synagogue when Jesus was present, The Women stopped coming to see Mary, Jesus asked the Disciples what was being said behind their backs, but they also felt the same cold shoulder.

They still came, the steady stream of people wanting healing, but only at dusk or in the dark, where the Synagogue Elders could not see them, In the end Jesus became annoyed with Capernaum.

He addressed the Disciples to go back to their homes for now, he would send for them when he needed them again, He spoke to them saying that he needed to consult with his friend Pontus Pilot, they travelled back the next morning without goodbyes to Jerusalem.

With Mary Miriam and his original Brothers, yet he felt that this was a defeat and he did not understand Why? Mary Miriam and the Women Disciples ware particularly upset as they thought that She had made good friends with the Women, their rejection hurt Marys feelings so much that She wept.

Miriam was blazing with anger at how her beloved ones were treated, especially after all the love healing and help Mary and Jesus had given them, by the time the usual merry band reached Jerusalem, silence rejection and gloom came back with them.

As they neared Jerusalem shouts went around the city, they are back, People came running up the road to greet them, a small group of people suddenly became a large crowd, happy and greeting them with such open love, the small band of travellers started to feel elated and became caught up in the good mood of the People.

The crowd escorted them to the palace gates singing hosanna he is the greatest, Jesus and Mary smiled and touched the hands of the people as they passed them, eventually reaching the Palace whose gates opened immediately for them.

Tibur Drusus was first to welcome them, Pontus Pilot and Solitous were waiting for them at the great doors with heartfelt hugs and welcome food and drinks, after they had rested Pontus asked them to tell him about their adventures, and also adding that He was very happy that they had come back with his horses, after so long away, particularly as Solitous was nearing her time to give birth to their Child.

He felt so pleased that they would help her in her labours, Mary reached out and took Solitiouses hand, you have nothing to fear my dear friend, I will be with you, but you have at least eight weeks yet, What!oh my I am as big as a house now cried Solitous, I won't be able to walk if this Child grows any bigger, everyone laughed, Jesus said creation of a beautiful Child will take its own course, it will only come into this world when it is ready.

Pontus leaned forward and touched Solitouses belly, immediately he felt a kick, Wow did you see that My Son is strong and healthy, Indeed He is Jesus replied.

Jesus and Mary felt happy to be home again with Pontus and Solitous, they felt renewed by their Friends great happiness and love for each other.

However when on their own Mary expressed concern over Solitous her confinement was worrying her, Darling she said to Jesus I feel something is not the right way with Solitous, I fear that a hard labour would be too much to bear for her, She seems so frail, tired, and out of sorts, We must be near her when her time to deliver comes or I am afraid that we will lose Her, Then my dear near her we must be.

Jesus replied taking her into his Arms and Kissing her softly, I love you with all my heart, Solitous will be well delivered and bear no further ills as a result.

Thank you my Darling I love you to the moon and back, it feels so good to be back with People who love us as much as we love them.

CHAPTER 4

Pontus was sitting in the justice room judging the complaints of the day, the usual thefts, adulteries Divorces and acts of treason against Tiberius, which usually consisted of someone usually Jewish citizens complaining at the unfair Roman occupation.

There was a great commotion which bluntly interrupted proceedings, many people from the synagogue rushed into the room all shouting at once,

Pontus called for calm, and his sentinels drew their swords which immediately stopped the large crowd in their tracks, a Pharisee walked forward and greeted Pontus Pilot bowing low in respect of the Governor.

Lord Pontus Pilot forgive us this intrusion, but the word at the synagogue is that a living God our God Jehovah King of all the Jews has come to walk amongst us, it is rumoured that he healed a Child of being crippled.

The inn keeper Adam swore he was God come to walk amongst us, we believe he is your guest, his name is Jesus, we come to offer adoration to him and ask him to join us at the synagogue.

We only wish to ascertain whether this is true or not.

At that moment before Pontus had time to answer, Jesus walked into the room hand in hand with Mary, you asked after me Sir. The Pharisee turned towards Jesus.

Yes, we would like to invite you to the synagogue to answer some questions as to what your status is, Jesus looked steadfastly into the eyes of the Pharisee,

Sir you wish to prove that I am only a Man, and have no kingdom, and I am not God, He replied Sir, we would respectfully ask that you attend a meeting of the elders at the synagogue alone without the Woman.

Jesus was clearly Angry, how dare you demand of me, this Woman is the Right side of me, she is wiser than all of you Holy Men put together, twice as accomplished, take care how you speak about Mary Madeleine my beloved Wife and treasured companion

You do me, and her, an injustice by calling her a mere Woman used from your mouth in such a derogatory term.

All Woman are the best side of all Men, can a Man bear such pain as a Woman when she brings new life, your Children into this world and give such unconditional love as only She does, that Woman is nearer to God's love, then you Men will ever be.

You Men of this world are so arrogant, cruel and ungrateful you should be holding all your Women in great esteem for they are the right side of you all, yet you treat them as if they are unclean and keep them out of your synagogues, this practice I find abhorrent to my eyes it hurts my very being.

Why then do you assume that I want to walk into your synagogue when you treat the women with such distain, why do you want to invite me into this house of debauchery.

I tell you now, I do not reside in these great buildings of power and ill-gotten wealth.

The Pharisees were clearly taken back, Women were always regarded as being second to Men, they had never heard such talk, it went against everything they knew or felt comfortable with.

I am sorry Lord I meant no offence, I am respectfully asking you to come to the synagogue and be seen with your People, and I have brought my Son who has been struck down with illness, and if you are who you say and have already healed a sick child then you would be able to heal my Son he is near death, I beg you Lord help him.

With a command a stretcher was brought into the gathering, a small gravely ill boy was laid upon it. Jesus walked forward towards the Boy, he looked down at his pathetic little face, he was filled with compassion for the Child and said suffer little Children to come unto me for the innocents shall be healed and walk again in the sunshine.

This Child will be healed but remember I do this for the love of this Child not to prove something to you Men of religion, who will still in their arrogance, refuse to believe what their own eyes witness, rise Child look to your Father he needs you.

The Boy sat up and looked around for his Father, the onlookers gasped in astonishment, the Father was overjoyed holding his Son up so that everyone could see him healed and well again, The Father turned to Jesus and fell to his knees, Lord Jehovah you are truly the One, the crowd also knelt in praise and some in fear.

I will come to your synagogue when I am ready to. now you may take your leave. The crowd left however word of mouth travels very fast, in no time at all, Pontus was astonished to find that hundreds of sick and infirm people were camping outside the palace gates, waiting for a glimpse of Jesus and his companions, He asked Jesus if he felt it wise to declare himself so openly, Pontus did not trust the Pharisees, with worthy cause.

Jesus simply smiled at him Pontus you worry too much. I am taking a walk with Mary before dinner.

Jesus and Mary walked hand in hand towards the Gates keeping the People out, Tibor Drusus ran towards them my Lord for your own safety I implore you to turn back to the palace the crowd is growing unruly I cannot guarantee your safety.

Tabor Drusus don't pay any attention to us, we are merely taking a walk open the gates, Tibor Drusus reluctantly obeyed

Although keeping an eye on the throng and one hand on his sword, just in case he had to rescue the pair.

The crowd had grown to such an extent that they couldn't see where it ended, some members were singing hymns and praising God for deliverance from their disabilities.

Jesus began to speak to them, the great throng of people pushed forward to hear and Jesus gestured for them all to sit down and he and Mary would move amongst them as he spoke incredibly everyone could hear him, he spoke of the importance of Family honouring Father and especially Mothers, treat all Women with reverence and respect, Of the love of God for them, and that they should Love God in return for the great gifts that had been given them, He told them that God hears and Answers their prayers.

As they moved through the crowd they lovingly touched the people, each one was healed from whatever illness or demon possessed them, the touch from Jesus and Mary spread through the great throng of People like a great wave of energy, when everyone had been cleansed, Jesus bade them all to go home and on the way, tell everyone they see that the living God has come to stay for a while.

The crowd dutifully obeyed, dispersed with joy, full of the words of God and basking in his love went home to tell of their great deliverance. And so, the fourth miracle was complete

The word was well and truly out, People from all over the province came into the city, holy Men from as far as Syria Iraq Babylon, Greece, and Capernaum came_to the synagogue waiting for Jesus to come and speak to them.

Jesus knew of their arrival, Saturday was the holy day and He chose this day to visit the synagogue He was looking forward to witnessing himself with some amusement the pomp and ceremony.

As it was this specific religion of Moses above all other nominations, which had prompted his visit.

Jesus walked hand in hand with Mary, the other Disciples walked behind them with Miriam, as they walked beggars the blind and infirm reached out towards him, crying imploring Jesuses attention.

As they walked, Jesus and Mary touched the infirm, without stopping they walked on smiling hand in hand the incurable became visibly well, it seemed to the Disciples that all the unclean of the world had descended on Jerusalem.

Many thousands had come to witness the miracles for themselves, yet seeing the small band walk with ease without body guards, made them question, Is this honestly a God, when he walks and talks among us so normally, where are his legions, his army is he not to deliver us from Roman rule as was the teachings of the synagogue and the great book the Holy Men read to them on the Sabbath, Is it not true that he lives with the Governor enjoying all the spoils of occupation.

Nevertheless, despite some misgivings they followed them, murmuring among themselves.

IN THE BEGINNING

The Synagogue was significant in that it was the very one built by Solomon to house the Ark of the covenant, the ten commandments that God had given to Moses on their exile from Egypt, the Hebrews worshipped one God which they called Yahweh, incidentally the laws of their religion and the events of their history were gathered into a collection of books, now known to Christians as the Old Testament of the Bible, Or scrolls of laws directed at Men.

As they approached, sellers of all description descended on them, Lord buy my doves no better sacrifice on the alter guaranteed for any wish from Jehovah to be granted, No Lord buy my roosters, as good a sacrifice to god as any Lamb or goat and cheaper Don't listen to this dog buy my goat no better sacrifice and good eating afterwards, buy my barkers' shame on a woman that she should walk into Jehovah House uncoverered, buy my bracelets to adorn your lady blessed by the vestal virgins, buy my lamps and oil to light the way.

Jesus stopped on the steps and turned towards them his beautiful eyes had turned dark He was visually angry. a storm cloud gathered a role of thunder and the heavens lit up by lightening a flash flood was threatening, not unheard of at this time of year but unusual, the sky grew dark, but no rain fell.

How dare you offer blood sacrifices in my name, how dare you use the Sabbath to steel life, Murder lie, and grow rich on the misery of others, in my name, with that he turned the tables over, scaring the sellers and money changer were witless they ran terrified out of his way scattering their wares. How dare you offend me in this way.

Jesus stormed into the synagogue and was greeted by all the holy men seated around a large richly adorned room, it looked more like a court than a joyous greeting of their Living God.

The most senior Pharisees and Sadducees came forward, Jesus stood defiant before them.

Mary and Miriam were stopped from following. The Men followed Jesus into the great room

He told them the scriptures say my house should be called a place of worship, but you have turned it into a place where robbers hide. The Pharisees cried indignantly, what right do you have to say and do these things, who gave you this authority.

Jesus answered, I have just one question to ask you, if you answer I will tell you where I got the right to do these things, who gave john the right to baptize, Was it God or merely some Human Being?

They conferred with each other whispering in a close group, we can't say that God gave John the right, Jesus will ask us why we didn't believe John the Baptist on the other hand these People think that John is a great Profit, and we are afraid of what they might do to us, that's why we cannot say that it was a mere Human Being who gave John the right to baptize, so they said, we don't know.

Jesus said Then I won't tell you who gave me the right to do what I do.

The Pharisees and Sadducees cried if you are who you say give us a sign from Heaven.

Jesus told them, If the sky is red in the evening, you say the weather will be good, but if the sky is Red and gloomy in the morning, you say it's going to rain, you can tell what the weather will be like by looking up at the sky, But you don't understand what is happening right now in front of you, you want a sign because you are evil and won't believe, despite bearing witness to the many signs and miracles already given, the only sign you will be given is what happened to Jonah. Heed the sign it is already written in your scriptures or suffer a worst fate than any of your four fathers or Cesar's in Rome can deliver heed my warning and believe me there are worst punishments than Death.

Then Jesus left Them to deliberate.

As he joined Mary and the others beckoning them to come away, he was struck by a terrible sight Adam the Inn keeper his first Friend was trying to crawl towards him, he had been badly beaten Interrogated by the leaders, then thrown into the street, My Lord, Adam cried I was trying to warn you, Jesus caught him in his arms, My Lord I tried to tell them you had come the true God, They said I spread lies I did not betray you.

Adam you and yours are beloved of God I know you would never betray me, Jesus and Mary held Adam in their Arms, Mary gave a quiet sob on observing Adams injuries She knew he was close to death, she smiled at him through her tears, not today Adam your Wife and Children have need of you, Jesus gently ran his hands over poor Adams swollen bloody and bruised face, his eyes were all but completely closed, as Jesus past his hands over him it was as if Adam was completely new without the terrible swollen scars, his broken bones became strong again.

Some people waiting and watching a few feet away observed the miracle, fell to their knees praising God and Angels for bearing witness to the impossible.

Go home Adam be with Eve and the Children. I am not afraid Lord I will go back into the synagogue and show them that although they beat me within an inch of my life, my beloved God Jesus took pity on an old sinner and before them, healed me.

No Adam they will refuse to listen, there is none as blind as he who will not see, go home with my blessing, do no more, but wait for my further instruction.

Adam obeyed he left them with a heavy heart, He worried for Jesus and Mary as he had felt and sorely witnessed what the very leaders he had respected all his life would do to any human being who challenged their authority, they had torched him, beaten him, spit in his face, called him a liar, cut out part of his tongue, and threw him in the gutter to die.

Adam wanted nothing more to do with the synagogue He went home and told Eve, He now believed the leaders the phrases and the Sadducees were Evil as far from God as they could get, they never set foot in the synagogue again.

Jesus Mary, and his small band of followers walked back to the governor's house in silence.

Pontus looked at Jesus and said, thank you my Lord, because of you I am the happiest Man alive, by the way, how did the meeting with the Jews go, My Lord is something troubling you?

Jesus said we will talk later, tonight we will enjoy your good company and celebrate your New life with you.

They left to get ready for the evening meal. Pontus turned to James tell me what happened at the synagogue. James told Pontus of the day's proceedings. It was as Pontus feared, He knew how arrogant the Leaders could be, He knew there would be trouble ahead.

At supper that evening Pontius asked Jesus if He would accompany him to Babylon He had received a massage from the Great King Herod, who had heard of Jesus and the great upheaval caused in the Jewish community, The King asked that Jesus be presented to him as He saw similarities to their God known as Marduk who was the chief God of the old Mesopotamian Gods of which the whole of Babylonia and beyond.

Pontius explained, every year they held a great 12-day festival with endless prayers and processions, The People recited a long poem telling how Marduk created the world and how his Son Nabu arrived in splendour. The King visited Marduks sanctuary to gain the Gods approval for his Rule and also as Tiberius was the Concurring Ruler,

The Governor was received as guest of honour, where The King and Pontius Pilot as Cesar Tiberius's representative in the region, would walk to a shrine outside the city, where a special statue of Marduk was sanctified to let in the New year, after the sacrifice The King would be proclaimed as Maduks profit and leader of the Babylonians, and Macedonia it's a brilliant spectacle and as Herod the King has invited you personally, I believe it will be enjoyable and as we are both invited I thought it best to travel together.

Jesus listened with a wry smile. I would be most honoured to accompany you. Mary will enjoy seeing the great city, and this will give Luke a chance to document our visit.

Pontus replied, I am sending Solitous her Mother Sister and Children to our residence at Bethina I want her to remain calm whilst she is confined I worry that the journey would prove too much for her and we don't wish any harm to come to our Child, Mary and Miriam would be most welcome to accompany them.

Jesus laughed as he said well Pontius it seems you have everything organised, and I am indeed grateful however Mary and Miriam will be travelling with us, Solitous will be fine until we return so don't worry.

Pontius looked a bit ill at ease. Jesus said what is the matter Pontus, well you see my Lord this celebration as part of the proceedings many young Girls and Boys are presented to the king and his esteemed guests, Virgins who are offered as an honour, company to be enjoyed by the Kings favourites, it would be considered a great insult to refuse, and I don't think it would be acceptable for Mary or Miriam, Jesus stopped him by raising his hand in protest.

Pontus I will not take solace or molest any other woman or poor Child that is offered to me, and neither will you, I will not subject any female to this injustice or abuse, and if I bear witness to this happening I will offer my displeasure to the King himself, do not worry Pontius I will not embarrass you, but I will not condone this behaviour even if the young woman sees it as an honour, I suspect they will have been told it is an honour by the very People they love and trust.

Forgive me Pontius but How can we teach our future Children to hold in esteem and reverence our womenfolk when we degrade them, offering them to bad minded Men in this way, those Men who seek to monopolize on their goodness love and beauty, they degrade and wound their precious souls by these fiendish practices, by acting as a miscreation they put in danger their own souls as well. Women are not Men's property to be broken as bread and shared as men see fit.

All Women should be free to fall in love with the Man of their choosing for if she should choose you, you are blessed indeed, subsequently if a Man hurts or displeases her, then God help him. It is up to the Man to show his love, cherish her beyond all others and she will return his love and blessings tenfold, this is fundamentally what makes a Man happy. If only he could see this. He would not risk the beautiful bird he holds in his hand for the two smaller ones in the bush.

There are no secrets between us, Mary and Miriam will accompany us.

Alright my Lord but I must express caution on going against culture and beliefs, may I remind you that King Herod is the very Person who less than a year ago had John the Baptists head served on a platter for the pleasure of his wife and Brothers Daughter, who as gossip will have it is also pleasing him in his bed they are hardly a monogamous lot.

I also have it as good gossip that Herod has expressed concern at your arrival, saying that you may be John the Baptist reincarnation and as such may be out to assassinate him. Jesus threw back his head and laughed, Oh Pontus he laughed, he would be worried if he only knew who I really was.

Jesus said thoughtfully. OH, what a web we weave when we practice to deceive, unfortunately Herodias will go down in history known as the whore of Babylon, history will be unkind to her for they will not see the abuse she has had to endure in her own poor life, or the injustices She has had to bear.

Sadly, future generations will only see her as the well shod whore that cut off the head of John the Baptist, Lust is a two-faced wretch, and time will not forgive her, but it is not her fault she is as much at the mercy of Men as any slave is to her Master.

I am sorry my Lord I did not mean to displease you Pontus replied, there are many traditions and cultures that if not taken up or acted upon will result in the hosts taking great offence Wars have been known to start for less, culture can become a tinderbox in these troubled times,

One has to be very careful and diplomatic, not to do or say anything that can cause offence. I am merely pointing out these differences of belief and what will be expected of you.

Jesus replied you have not displeased me Pontus, I must point out to you that I do not adhere to any Religions Laws or Traditions of Culture, I do not follow those Laws made by Men, I intend to inspire the thinking of Men and write some laws of my own.

The two Men were so lost in talks that they suddenly became aware of a great deal of merriment Mary and Miriam had dressed Luke as a Woman dancer and he was busy pirouetting across the room to much laughter calls and whoops,

Jesus strained to look rubbing his eyes in fayed disbelief, joining the others laughter as Luke started a belly dance, everyone enjoyed the impromptu show some laughing until they cried Solitous had to be helped to her rooms by her Mother as She laughed so much she developed a stitch in her side.

Jesus quipped I always said He was a beautiful Girl, the revelry went on for some time, Luke pleased everyone with a great show, eventually retiring still laughing after spending the evening in good and entertaining company.

The next day Pontus was busy with planning the journey into Babylonia, He usually would only take one garrison as escort, this time he was planning on taking his finest three garrisons, just in case?

Jesus Mary Miriam James Mark and Jude had taken a walk to the local market, The ladies wanted to buy material for the trip, It was a hot bright day the city was busy, they enjoyed looking at the wares it seemed they came from all over the known world silks from china spices and material in bright colours from India, locally caught fish, vegetables, leather work carpets chickens goats sheep, exotic monkeys from Africa and intricately carved wooden ornaments, handmade jewellery of which Mary and Miriam were particularly admiring each holding the pieces up to their necks or dangling the earrings to see how each would look before making their purchases.

Excited shouts stopped them a young woman was running through the market the Men chasing her throwing stones shouting instructions stop her adulterer, she must be punished, kill her, whore and many other curses they ranted at her.

They caught up with her and she fell to the ground right in front of Jesus, she looked up, crying Terrified, please help me, Jesus made to help her up, the men misinterpreting his intentions cried thanks for stopping her we will take her. Jesus put his hand up to stop them and asked, what has this woman done.

The Men agitated and angry, said She has shamed her family, She is a whore lying with men for money, she also lies with solders, She is our Sister we sold her, this man paid good money for her she shamed us by stealing his full purse, and running off, She is no good ruined and we want rid of her.

Jesus lifted the poor girl to her feet and investigated her face, why he stated She is only a child, is it true what they say, the girl nodded her head and lifted the purse up to Jesus who promptly threw it to the man complaining of being robbed.

The two brothers moved forward to take hold of the Girl, Jesus stopped them and asked what will you do with her, She is of no further use to us, we were selling her, do you not have any care or love for your Sister, No she is spoiled no one will want her now, She is a whore, She will be stoned as is the time honoured way set by the synagogue.

I will take your Sister with me Jesus said, OH no you won't, only if you give us the pieces of silver we can get if we sell her, Jesus replied were you not having her stoned a moment ago, how much would She be worth to you as a corpse.

The brothers moved forward to grab the girl, she is our property either buy her or we take her to be stoned, Jesus said, you have no right to take this girls life from her, you are ignorant of the ways of true men, let he who is without sin cast the first stone.

The Brothers started to back away from Jesus as the crowd gathered, some saying its Jesus the new rabbi, from God, you know, gave them what for in the temple, pharisees were well shown up, lives at the governor's palace, and the murmuring went on, the brothers pricked up their ears and changed tone.

Well Jesus you can take our sister do what you will with her, sneering just give us a few dockets and we will go on our way.

Jesus said No I don't think so, this is what I propose, You do not deserve to have a sister as precious as this, She is not your slave or property to be abused by you two or anyone else, You do not know the meaning of Love or of Family, turn away, walk away and I will let you continue to see the world you are in.

The two men hesitated for a moment egged on by not wanting to lose face in front of the onlookers said threateningly who the hell are you to tell us what to do with our property.

Jesus said is that your final answer, the men replied gesturing arrogantly with a shrug of the shoulder, and presentation of their index finger. Duu.!!

Before they had got the last utterance out of their mouths, the men cried I can't see, I can't see, and Jesus said and so be it, this was your choice.

Jesus calmly told Mary and the others to continue Shopping to buy whatever they wished, he was going to talk to the young woman, and he would join them presently.

The onlookers were completely taken up by the men screaming hysterically they could not see, that they didn't notice Jesus take the young woman by the hand and lead her to a quiet area where he sat her down wiped the tears from her stained face gave her a drink of cool water and waited until the sobbing stopped.

Presently the girl looked up, What are you going to do with me now my lord, Jesus smiled into her face, Why sell you of course, the girl gave a sharp intake of breath and stared wide eyed back at him, He gave a little chuckle I am joking with you Ruth, Now tell me all about yourself.

The Girl asked how did he know her name was Ruth, Jesus smiled at her and said I will tell you after you tell me all about yourself, Ruth had never before been asked to talk about herself once she started she couldn't stop, time passed as if by an instant.

She told him all about her life being a gypsy, travelling with her Father and Mother and older Brothers, they moved around mending things gathering crops, entertaining people in rural communities and cities, performing an act with six pure white Horses, Her Father was a master

IN THE BEGINNING

horseman and had bred them himself for their cleverness and beauty, they lived well and mostly happily until they were set upon by robbers, they murdered her Mother, and Father her older brothers ran away and the thieves took their precious horses with them.

She told him how they had raped and beaten her, leaving her for dead at the side of the road, her Brothers returned looking for anything they could salvage, the older Brother wanted to leave her but her younger Brother said that their Mother and Father would never forgive them if they left her.

They buried their Parents, put her into the back of their mobile home, pulling it along to the next town, as they pulled the wagon She could hear them talking and realised that her Brothers did not love her, and only saved her so that She would look after them, then they could marry her off or sell her, then she remembered what her mother had told her about some money she had hidden, she showed her where it was, with the promise that she should never tell her Father or Brothers where it was.

The Robbers didn't find it either, She kept it well hidden, She was ten years old at the time and couldn't remember much about it, She cooked and cleaned, looked after her Brothers until She was thirteen, and was going to be married to a man her brothers had chosen, he was a big fat smelly man and she didn't like him at all so she took the purse of money her Mother had cleverly hidden and ran away.

A very nice lady in Jerusalem took her in, and she had enough money to pay for a nice room buy herself some new clothes, in return she would clean keep house and run errands, She met a handsome centurion called Marcus Flaviouse and they both fell madly in love.

He was sent on a reconnaissance with his garrison and he gave Emily some money to let me stay with her until his return.

That was two months ago, and he hadn't returned yet, but he will soon, then no one will ever hurt her again.

She was shopping, when her Brothers spotted her following her back home, They were very mean and nasty to the Woman who had taken her in, calling her a whore and saying she was a harlott, they dragged her to the slave market to sell her, she pleaded with them, I was trying to tell them that I was engaged to be married, they wouldn't listen, that's when I grabbed the purse and ran like the devil was after me, I was lucky because I fell into you. Thank you for saving me.

Mary and the others had finished shopping and joined them, how are you dear Mary said brushing her hand gently across her face, OH much better thank you my lady.

Jesus asked Mary what shall we do with our little Ruth, do you think we have room for another sister Miriam, I think you had better ask Ruth what She wishes my lord, why yes of course Miriam what am I thinking, Ruth what do you want to do? I would like to go back to my friend's house she has always been very kind to me.

Alright Jesus replied we will escort you there madam just to make sure you are safe.

Ruth showed them the way to a poor part of the city, this is it She knocked on the door of a shady looking residence a Woman opened the door ever so slightly.

Emily it's me with some friends, Ruth oh my goodness she opened the door threw her arms around the girl, the Woman had received a black eye which was badly swollen and closing, along with a split lip, and broken nose.

What happened to you, I tried to follow but your Brother hit me so hard I felt dazed and look at me I won't be able to work for weeks, it's alright Emily these kind People saved me, so I came home.

My Brothers have more to think about than me, Emily replied, Ruth I am so sorry, but you can't stay here, People from the synagogue came they told me that I am exposed as a whore.

Your Brothers were taken there, they told them my profession and that you were working here also, I have to move out of the city by tomorrow or be taken outside of the city and be stoned to death, I don't know where I will go but if you are here they will give you the same fate.

Mary said well that settles it, looks like Pontius has some more guests, Jesus laughed yes it seems like these two ladies need Protection of the governor, and they shall have it, you both will come and stay with us, no one will dare take you from us.

Emily and Ruth walked to the governor's palace with Jesus and Mary, as they walked, they heard the whispers and scathing comments from the bystander's, Luke told the Ladies keep your heads held high you have nothing to reproach yourselves for and you have done nothing wrong.

On arriving back at the Palace they were met by Tiber Drusus, Ah Tiber, Jesus greeted him just the person I need to see do you know a young Centurion by the name of Marcus Flaviouse, No Sir but if you wish I will make enquiries, Yes please do that it is very important that we know of his wear a bouts, thank you.

Tiber Drusus said I have come to tell you that I am travelling to Rome immediately after our return from Babylonia am being presented with my diploma after all, it's happened just as you said it would I am to take my betrothed, marry and receive some lands, It appears that I am held in high esteem by Cesar himself and will be celebrated in front of the whole of Rome, which has made Maximus except me as Son in Law and Heir, as He has many Daughters and no Son.

I am to journey to Rome at the request of Cesar Tiberius himself, my lord I know that I have you to thank, I am eternally grateful and if I can do anything to repay all your goodness and kindness, please don't hesitate to ask. I am your servant. And as I can read and write my own letters thanks to Luke, I would like to invite you to my wedding.

That is very kind of you Tiber and if we can we would love to witness your marriage when the time comes, Jesus embraced Tiber Drusus together they walked into the residence, Jesus telling Tiber the reason why he needs to find the young Centurion.

Pontus and Solitous ran to greet them, We were getting worried about you I was just about to call Tiber Drusus to ready his troops, We are so relieved that you are safe and well, the market place is not safe its full of vagabonds, Yes Pontus, Jesus replied, we found this out for ourselves and on account of our adventure we have two more guests.

I hope you don't mind Pontus there was simply no other way these Women are in dire need of our help and protection, I know you are an honourable and good Man and would have come to their aid if you knew their circumstance.

Pontus Laughed out loud of course lets welcome all strays and people of no fixed abode into the Governors house, after all the crowds of thousands that arrive at his gates daily, two more are of no matter, If they are your Guest then they are mine, I look forward to hearing their story at dinner,

I don't know where we are going to put them to sleep, Miriam said if it pleases you they can stay with me my rooms are far too large for me I have plenty of room to share.

Mary was looking at Emilie's closed black and blue eyes, she beckoned her to come close to her with a gentle hand caressed her swollen disfigured Face, as her hand drew across her face, the injuries disappeared as if a clean cloth had rubbed them out, Emily was so amazed She stood with her mouth open no words would come out, Mary said it's alright Emily close your mouth or the flies will have a new home. Miriam let out a chuckle,

Ruth's eyes were so large with shock at what she had witnessed, she didn't dare utter a sound. Miriam said to Ruth you will have to get used to this sort of thing they do this all the time, Ruth still wide eyed whispered to Miriam who is She. Miriam still chuckling replied I will tell you everything later.

That's settled then, Pontus exclaimed, I hope you Ladies will enjoy your stay with us, now everyone goes and get ready for our evenings feast.

Miriam took the two ladies with her and everyone went their separate ways to get ready for Dinner and the evening's entertainment.

The next Day brought news of John the Baptist, A messenger from the Kings palace brought the news that John had been put to death, his head being served on a silver platter for the pleasure of Solomi King Harrods niece and step daughter.

Two days later they were on the journey to Babylon, Word of mouth travels fast, every town they came to people rushed towards them lining the streets to take a glimpse of the Couple.

They were the first Celebrities, Jesus and Mary stopped at every opportunity to preach to the crowds and heal the sick. Luke was very busy recording all the fascinating sights and individual accounts of People being healed.

Although the People loved them the Church elders, the Pharisees and Sacristies were very suspicious of them, they did not believe this was their God.

They felt that this man was here to set up a rival church taking their flock with him, and they would be ousted from their comfortable seats, Jesus did not give them the respect they felt they deserved nor appeared to follow the laws of the synagogue or respect the holy book, their jealousy was all consuming and so they decided to plot against him.

For now, they would have to play a compliant game remain quiet, whilst they hatched a deadly plan.

The progress was slow on the road to Babylon, Pontus was growing more annoyed at the length of time Jesus and Mary would take pandering to the hordes of sick disabled people, that appeared out of nowhere to stop their journey whilst they blessed and healed them all.

He joked that it would take a whole year to get to Babylon at the rate they were going, and he had some meetings to attend. Jesus suggested that he go on ahead, so it was decided that Pontus would go on with two garrisons and leave Jesus and Mary with Tibur Druses garrison as bodyguards, although Jesus pointed out this was not necessary Pontus insisted.

The large group split into two, Pontus going ahead at a faster pace Jesus and Marys group taking a more leisurely pace behind.

As they negotiated the stony road, a band of ragged people appeared to cross their path, they were walking in single file and one in front held on to the garments of the person behind which formed a curious procession, the leader was ringing a bell and shouting unclean.

Jesus dismounted and stepped forward, don't come any closer shouted the leader we are all unclean lepers we heard a man is heading this way who it is said brings light into this dark world, have you seen him on your travels.

Jesus said what have you heard, We were told that he is heading to Babylon we want to warn him that a large band of robbers are lying in wait, and have already been given the promise of a large purse of gold by holy men, who should know better to kill everyone Man Woman Servant and especially take the heads of the Man Jesus and his wife Mary.

We believe This would be a terrible loss to the world and although we are worthless lepers seek to warn them so they should take another route avoiding these evil men and their evil deeds.

Thank you my Friends I am the one they seek. Then Lord we beseech you Run away in the opposite direction find another road that will take you safely to Babylon, We got away to warn you only because we are lepers and they didn't wish to become like us by murdering us also, They are killing everyone journeying on this road, they are not far away.

Jesus beckoned to the waiting party to take a rest among the trees out of the hot Sun, He said to the leader We thank you, and ask you that you break some bread with us, come sit a while drink and eat with us.

No Sir are you not familiar with this terrible curse we suffer, you shall not be any nearer to us lest you become infected. Jesus said fear not my Friends and walked towards them.

No! No! please, the others started pleading with Jesus to keep away from them, He walked towards them, when he got an arm's length from them said, Why you look alright to me Jesus said, the leader looked down at his hands virtually ripping the bandages off them, then turned to another unfortunate and inspected a young boys face then ran to another and another finally it proved all too much for him and he collapsed sobbing to the ground lord this burden I have carried for so long and now we are whole again my whole tribe was stricken with this terrible curse these twenty are all that is left of us.

We resigned ourselves to die a pitiful death, and you have delivered us, praise be to the lord our king of kings. The band of lepers prayed beautiful prayers of deliverance thanking Jesus saying that it is true, God has come into the world to deliver them from evil.

After Jesus had quieted them down, the whole group ate with them, Jesus gave them a large purse of gold and silver, enough to set themselves up and enjoy a new beginning, as they parted company Jesus said to the leader this purse will never empty, you are rewarded for your belief and faith in me I will never forget the poor leper so shunned by all society that robbers wouldn't touch them, took such care and great compassion to find a stranger and warn him of the wicked deeds ahead.

There is true good in this world which is so worth preserving, bless you all, Tibor Drusus approached Jesus I think it would be better if we did find another way, from what these people tell me there is about two hundred waiting for us, I am thinking of the Women, I only have these twenty Men at my disposal we are greatly outnumbered I will not be able to guarantee their safety.

Jesus replied, Oh Tiber Drusus ye of little faith, have you still not worked it out yet, we will carry on this road I would like to meet our would-be assassins.

I want you to know Sir that this is against my better judgement, I am afraid for you and the Women Jesus replied Tiber Drusus you worry too much.

Three miles further, they were set upon by a large band of whooping screaming madmen brandishing their swords as they galloped towards them on horseback, Jesus sat and watched their approach with interest and just when the hordes were near enough to offer the first blows.

Jesus lifted his hand and the horses they were mounted on stopped abruptly then went completely berserk rearing bucking throwing the men in all directions, Then turning on them, appearing to trample over their owners, their ears back on their heads teeth barred, they galloped around knocking over the bandits, grabbing them by the scruff of the neck and shaking them until they were half unconscious.

The rest of the party watched in disbelief and then with great amusement at the punishment the horses were dealing out laughed uncontrollably even the soldiers couldn't keep the laughter under control.

Horses stamping, snorting chasing grabbing no man was safe some tried to hide, the horses found them one particular beautiful white filly had a bandit between its teeth and was having great fun kicking him up the bottom, it was hilarious the bandits tried to fend them off by brandishing their swords, the evil men couldn't get near them, as one horse kept them busy another ran from behind and kicked the swords out of their hands.

Eventually all the bandits were either rendered unconscious or fleeing on foot for their lives, Jesus shouted to the horses round them up my beauties, and they did dragging them back and dumping them at Jesuses feet, the White filly reluctantly gave up her bandit holding him in front of Jesus by the scruff of his neck. It turns out he was the leader, and She knew it, giving him a last sly kick in remembrance of seeing her beloved human family slaughtered by these wicked Men

He immediately started crying and begging for his life, as all bullies do, the Bandits were rounded up tied together and marched into Babylon to be judged and sentenced by King Herod himself.

The Women watched and laughed until their sides ached, Suddenly Ruth stopped laughing, muttered something under her breath, then jumped out of the Sudan running towards the horses shouting Faye Faya the beautiful white filly looked up dropping the bandit she was pulverising to the floor, ran towards the girl, their joy at seeing each other was heartwarming, the girl threw her arms around the horses neck buried her face in her mane and sobbed, Faya oh Faya my beautiful girl I never thought I would see you again, Faya threw her head in the air and let out a long whiney.

Immediately five more similar, magnificent looking horses came galloping towards Ruth, Dancer, Nacre, Bloom Bray, and Flower they circled Ruth through her tears of joy She hugged and kissed each one in turn, as Jesus walked towards them the horses appeared to stand quite still in line side by side, as he approached they bowed towards him front leg outstretched, head touching their hoof. Jesus laughed and said now you're just showing off.

Ruth, yes, my lord, you know these horses? yes Sir they are my Family these are the very bandits that killed my parents and stole them, they left me for dead and hurt me very badly.

These beauties obviously know you, so they must accompany us, they after all are your family. Oh, thank you thank you, with these clever horses I can put on great shows, they are worth a lot of money, but I could never sell them.

What about all the other horses, I am sure that over one hundred horses are left they can accompany us also, which if you sold them to good homes at Babylon would provide enough for your Baby and Emily to live well, don't you think? in the meantime let's turn our Roman Garrison into Cavalry.

The travelling band was growing in numbers fast, yet everyone had enough to eat even the captured Bandits were fed and watered, after resting, the day after the battle of the Horses they continued on their way to the great city, progress was slow at each small village Jesus insisted on stopping, walking hand in hand with Mary and talking to the People, hearing their stories of strife hardships and healing any sick, they took time to advise them and answer any questions, many hundreds of people were reached by this method and they always left them believing that they had been in the presence of the divine.

Well most people anyway there were always those that even bearing witness to miracles right before their eyes would still never believe because in their ignorance they didn't want to.

This exasperated Miriam, especially having overheard some local Men talking together denying Jesus as being God saying that He is just a magician using tricks to fool the people.

Mary merely said there is non- so blind as he who will not see, I know it's hard Miriam but there are those Humans who will hate our lord and us also for the goodness and love he gives.

They are very jealous men who are willing to commit any vile act to get wealth land and power over women, these men crave adoration, and the love of beautiful women, after setting themselves up as false kings using the sword and extreme violence, gaining what they say they want, they find they have no love, only worry, and at the last moments of their miserable existence realise they were despised, I must feel only pity for them because they will never feel the joy and rapture of life just by sharing company with our Lord and love for Family and each other.

Those Men will forever look over their shoulders with suspicion, will never trust anyone, because they know how disloyal and evil they are, they always fall in with like-minded others so one betrays the other, living in fear of being murdered, they murder innocents and each other, and so it is for generations. We can do nothing in the face of such barbarism. We can only wait until time washes clean.

If everyman could feel our Lords way, then this world will become the true paradise our dear lord wishes it to become, maybe not now but for future generations with knowledge and enlightenment this will be possible.

This is our hope for this world Miriam, but still there is none so blind as he who refuses to see.

Ruth and Emily were listening to Mary and Miriam as they travelled along, Ruth cried but Mary we believe don't we Emily and we love you both very much, it's as if you are my true Parents Mary smiled at her young companion gently stroking her face, Emily was crying, Why Emily whatever is the matter Miriam exclaimed.

I cannot put it into words I am grateful for everything you have done for us I understand how you can care for Ruth, but I feel wretched and so unworthy, I have done some terrible things in my life, watched as men stole and murdered, sold my body since I was ten years old there was nothing else I could do of any worth, I was orphaned so young that I do not remember my Mother and Father how can you and Jesus welcome me as you have, protect me as you have, when I am shunned by all society, Men who use me and Women who despise me for sleeping with their Husbands, I would have been stoned to death by the Rabbi's and women of the synagogue if you had not taken me with you, my life has been so lonely, and now I find family yes, more than friends, Family on a journey in a fine Sudan fit for a queen seeing with my own eyes extraordinary events witnessing miracles, yes I believe, and I love you and Jesus, with all my heart, Why do you love me so Mary.

Mary replied Because of all the things in life you have shared with us, because you saved and protected a young girl that needed your help, because you are loving and kind because your heart aches to be loved and because you are you, unique and magnificent.

In the years to come we will have need of your loving devotion I ask that in the distant future when you hear of us in need of you both, that you will come to us immediately, because I will need your presence to help give me courage to face a terrible inevitability.

Dearest Mother Mary you have our word, wherever we are we will come to you, Ruth and Emily became devoted Disciples on the journey to Babylon.

All four Women laid together and slept in the heat of the late afternoon.

It was late evening when they passed through the magnificent gates of the Gods, Called the Ishtar gate, Babylon was a magnificent city it stood on the banks of the River Euphrates, It was protected by walls so wide that two rows of four horse chariots could ride along the top, this grand entrance was decorated with brilliant blue tiles and figures of Bulls and Dragons.

Beyond the gate a wide avenue called the Processional Way Decorated with 120 Lions leading to the centre of the city and the Temple Ziggurat, dedicated to the chief God Marduk it rose a majestic 90m 300 ft. above the city,

Their destination was the great palace of Nebuchadnezzar known as the Marvel of Mankind It was incredibly luxurious, built around five courtyards, opulence enjoyed by kings or emissaries of Rome or the religious leaders of the day, a virtual army of slaves and servants was needed to provide service to the VIP Guests. Babylon, it seemed that every person in the great City came to welcome them a great fanfare lining the processional way.

Pontus pilot came to greet them at the entrance of the inner Palace, I was getting worried he said taking Jesus by the arm asked, what on earth happened?

How have you managed to capture the most notorious criminals in the world, when the palace guards could not, and where have all the horses come from?

Are they a gift for the King, Jesus replied no, I have already given them away elsewhere, If the King requires a gift, give him the criminals, they are his to pass whatever punishment he deems appropriate, Heaven knows they deserve it, The road to Babylon is free of their tyranie, and safe for good travellers.

However, I crave a meeting with them before they are sentenced, I have a wish to understand why their hearts are so black and why they are unremorseful of their evil deeds

Everyone marvelled at the Luxurious beauty of the Palace, Pontus gave orders for the Horses to be taken care of and the prisoners taken into custody by the royal guard and the centurions given leave to fall out to the soldier's barracks for rest and refreshment.

Jesus Mary and the rest of their group were shown to rooms reserved for them in the palace, where they could find great comfort and luxury, no expense was spared in the sumptuous rooms sweet meats, cold buffet and sweet wine, were waiting for them and a fragrant bath of perfume made from lotus and lily flowers, ready so the guests could wash away the heat and dust of the road, they were so grateful for the comfort, falling into each other's arms enveloped in the silk bed linen and an exhausted sleep, looking forward to the next day's adventure, in this amazing City.

Many servants and slaves were at the beck and call of the Kings guests, They performed all tasks quietly without any complaint or discussion, as ghosts working reverently in the background to ensure smooth running of the household, They were also to report to the King, any conversations that could be determined as a threat to the King or his Emissaries.

CHAPTER 5

The Servants attending Jesus and Mary were particularly skilled in unearthing subterfuge, listened intently to their conversations so that they would tell the King every detail of the couple's conversation, thereby securing rewards for themselves.

One of the Slaves, Nubia, so called because that is where She was captured and enslaved in Africa was very striking and beautiful, she was Tall and slender and although her skin was dark her eyes were the lightest blue, very unusual and greatly prized.

She was a particular favourite of the King, she lived well, and enjoyed many favours, but inside She Hated and despised everyone, especially the King and these so-called Men of God and so-called dignitaries.

This couple meant nothing to her, in her mind just two more hypocrites, she knew that The King was apprehensive at meeting them, He was paranoid to the point of promising to give Nubia her freedom, if She could provide him with evidence of their Heresy.

Nubians' story is a very sad one, She was captured from Africa when Slave Traders invaded her Masai village, She had never known such cruelty as these Men, She was a happy Teenager who adored her family, She was forced to watch her Father, and Brothers killed, She was chained with her Mother Brother and with others from her Clan, and some not from her clan, Her Father had often spoke about the White devils who take children and Women, they are never seen again, He warned Her to keep vigilant, if She ever saw these Strange Demons She must alert the villagers right away, by drumming the warning or Screaming for her Father.

IN THE BEGINNING

Nubia was determined to find anything that would give her Freedom, she decided that She would befriend the Woman's Servant, Miriam, she arranged to bump into her whilst carrying a large pitcher of Clean water begging forgiveness at being so clumsy as falling into Miriam.

Miriam took it in good grace telling her not to worry it was a complete accident, the report was now set and Nubia invited Miriam to take a walk with her and She would show her all the marvels of this great city, they arranged to meet later when they both had some free time.

Nubia was a wealth of knowledge, Miriam was enthralled at the tales Nubia told about the great King Nebuchadnezzar who loved his wife so much that he had special gardens made for her, they spent the afternoon walking and talking, Exploring the City, Nubia started asking questions about Jesus and Mary.

She asked, was it true that he was the King of the Jews. Good heavens No replied Miriam, where did you hear such nonsense Miriam had started to become suspicious of Nubians' questioning, would you like to meet them you can ask them anything you like.

What cried Nubia are you serious, they would clap them both in arms if it got out that slaves and servants presented themselves as equals to the elite and invited guests of The King, why we would be put to public death by beheading as an example.

So please do not suggest such a thing Nubia was becoming more aggravated and angrier at Miriam for suggesting this could be possible.

Miriam replied Oh please calm down Nubia, I am not a Slave or Servant for that matter I am a very free Woman and can please myself what I do or say, and Yes I can go to Mary and Jesus at any time and talk to them as easily and openly as I am talking to you right now.

Nubia was suddenly afraid, and threw herself to her knees in front of Miriam, oh please forgive me my lady for being so forward with you, I thought you were their servant, or like me a slave, that is why I have tried to befriend you, forgive my insolence.

Miriam gave a little chuckle to herself and gave her hands towards Nubia in an attempt to bring her back to her feet, Come now Nubia don't take on so, suppose it was an easy mistake to make as I am always fussing over them, you see Nubia I am with them because I love them unconditionally with all my heart and soul.

They are my Family, I am treated as a beloved Sister, they love me, and I am so grateful to be at their side I busy myself taking care of their every need, but I don't need to, they will still love me, and if I was ill or indisposed they would care for me in the same way, it is a relationship build on mutual trust and unconditional love, not on slave and master. I am so loved and am very happy, If I need anything I only must ask, and it will be given with love.

Nubia looked strained to understand, you mean you fetch and carry watch over them because you love them? And you say you do all the work you do and do not get paid, so therefore you are a servant or slave.

You know Nubia I am never going to win this argument with you, So I suggest we go back to the Palace and find my dear ones and you can put this very question to them yourself.

Oh please do not inform the King of this or I will be in the most terrible trouble, In fear of my life yes Miriam I would be put to death, even though Nubians' greatest fear could be realised She so badly wanted to meet these Special People who could command others to work for them for Love without paying them a single ducat.

In Nubians' world this was completely unheard of, She fully understood that a Master had every right to treat her as he willed, to take her body and use her as he seemed fit, to beat her without mercy if she angered him in any way, and kill her if she did not please him, or sell her if it pleased him, She knew that even if She was granted her freedom She would have nowhere else to go, and would simply carry on with the duties of serving her Masters for bed and food.

Come on cried Miriam taking her by the hand and running quickly in the shadows towards the Palace. Come and hear it for yourself, I promise you after meeting with my beloved ones your life will never be the same again.

Jesus looked at his beloved Mary while She lay sleeping, He found a great marvel in her, he marvelled at her Beauty the richness of her golden Hair, the shape of her eyes and lips in a perfect pout irresistible to both man and God.

He found his eyes tearing at the emotion of the profound love he felt for her, and also because he knew that in the distant future this Mother of Mothers Queen of Woman and Men, would have to endure the horrific heartbreak so bad that no ordinary Human being could withstand the pain and desolation that the great betrayal would bring them.

He thought to Kiss those bountiful tasteful lips, then changed his mind deciding to let her sleep longer, enjoy the peace before the celebrations started in earnest this evening, He shook off his thoughts deciding to leave tomorrow to itself and deal with the present, with this in mind he arose silently dressed ate a substantial breakfast, left a message with the attending servant for Mary that he would return soon.

She should enjoy the rest. and set off towards the Sentinel Guard House, He wanted to talk to Barabbas the leader of the bandits.

Celebrations in the mall had already begun, acrobats dancing bears, Music loud and whirling dancers Children excited at the spectacles before them clapping and laughing at the entertainers, it was a very noisy and exciting Time.

He walked on and passed a large building where young girls where being taken by their Mothers, but these Girls some as young as nine years old were crying afraid and begging their guardians not to leave them.

Jesus noticed that some of the Guardians and Mothers came out of the building also weeping, one of these mothers was so bereft sobbing as if her heart had been broken, by the very act of leaving her Child, she ran into Jesus, He caught her in his arms and said Dear Mother what on earth is the matter, why do you weep so, is your Child being held against her will.

I am sorry Sir, you must be a stranger here and not aware of our customs, it is a great honour that We leave our Children in the care of the Matriarchs, they will be preparing them for the night's festivities.

They are the Children in White, Pure and unsullied, They will make up the procession tomorrow carrying candles, They have been chosen for their Beauty and chastity, afterwards they will be given to the holy men and guests of the King, some will only keep them for the evening, others will take them with them, and some Mothers will never see their Children again.

I was once chosen, the night held such depravity and pain that I could not stand it I screamed and the Holy Man had me flogged and thrown into the street, at least he did not Kill me, unlike some of my Friends. Although the Matriarchs will try to prepare the Children, nothing can prepare them for what they will suffer, so you see Sir, this is why I weep,

There is no solace, I know we are told that this is a great honour and will not stand in our way of a making a good Marriage, indeed some Girls are offered Marriage by the Men that take their innocence. I go now to pray to Maduk that I will see my Child again.

The poor Woman was so distraught she suddenly became aware of her ramblings. And looked up into the face of the Man that had caught her, in a moment she realised that She had said to much in her distress, and tried to free herself from his grasp, saying I am Sorry Sir it is a great honour please forgive the tears of an over protective Mother.

She looked up into Jesuses eyes, and he said dearest Mother, I promise you that your Child will be returned to you without any harm on her, Be present at the ceremony, enjoy the festivities you do not need to weep, and flay yourself before Maduk, he has already heard you.

The poor Woman seamed to stand in shock unable to speak or move, still focused on Jesuses eyes, she spoke in a calmer softer voice, you are Him are you not.

He that we were told would be attending our celebrations some call you the living God, that you heal the hearts bodies and minds of Men and Women,

She sank to her knees before Jesus, My dearest Lord please forgive me for I have sinned and am not worthy. Jesus lifted her up to her feet, Dearest Mother whose love for her child is the most pure, nearest to god's love for you than any Man of wealth could understand, be blessed in your home your family and your Child returned without harm.

He kissed her on the forehead and carried on his journey to the guard's enclosure. Jesus noticed that there was a lot of activity in the centurion's quarters, Soldiers seemed to be running around falling in to be inspected by their commanding officer, and Jesus stood by and watched the proceedings with interest.

They fell in to the beat of drums, in seconds every soldier was ready lined up in a great long assembly it looked like thousands of troops had joined together, each Garrison about one thousand strong in perfectly formed formation stood to attention in the morning heat.

The General arrived with pomp and ceremony, horns sounded his arrival with his Garrison trotting behind him.

IN THE BEGINNING

This was an important Man, a Soldier a lawyer and personal advisor to the emperor Cesar himself, riding an immaculate black steed in full battle dress, with his famous red plumbed helmet he looked a fearsome sight.

Gaius Plinius Secundus was his name a giant of a man standing over six feet and with head dress six foot five. He rode the lines of the troops declaring that all was well and ready.

With that, a great cheer went up by the troops and they started to disperse to take up their stations defending the city.

The great Gaius Plinius was being helped from his horse, although showing no outward signs of injury whilst seating on his steed, it was very apparent that as he was being helped, he was trying to hold himself erect in great pain, which made him extremely bad tempered, shouting out Mordechai where the hell is the bloody Doctor.

A man carrying a gourd ran forward and gave the gourd to Gaius and instructed him to drink as much as possible as it would help with pain, he drank long and hard finishing by throwing the gourd back at Dr Mordechai with great force almost knocking him of his feet and winding him.

Mordechai, you said that this would be healed by now, its bloody well worse, what are you going to do about it, I swear Mordechai I will kill you if you don't make this wound better.

Mordechai looked crest fallen He was a good Doctor He had tried everything he knew, Gaius refused to follow his advice to rest and apply a poultice to the infected wound, He knew that there wasn't much he could do, the infection was too far gone the stench coming from the general, told him that the black gangrene had already taken over it was just a matter of time before he would face his death, Mordechai also knew that his patient was terrified of death, he could not mention disease, he feared his Patient would take him with him, just so he could berate him in death as much as life.

Mordecai stood looking awkward at the floor, eventually saying, maybe we should take you into your quarters and look at the wounds again.

Two centurions supported the general and gently walked him into his bedroom.

Jesus followed them into the quarters and stood watching as Dr Mordecai helped his patient out of his army uniform his hands shook as he unbuckled his body armour, the smell was becoming overwhelming and he was beginning to feel sick himself when he noticed Jesus, Can I help you?

Jesus replied yes, I am looking for Doctor Mordechai, I am a Doctor myself of sorts, and wish to introduce myself to him, oh well in that case you may be able to help me with this patient Dr Mordechai stated, have a look at him, and tell me what you think, I am going to fetch my bag and gather some herbs I will be back presently in the meantime, you inspect his wounds and when I return you can give me your opinion.

Jesus turned to Gaius, I think Gaius that you do not have long in this world, this infection has become far to advance to save your life, even Dr Mordechai can't help you now I think you should say your prayers to your Gods, what do you believe Gaius.

I believe in nothing, I have seen so much death, and can tell you it isn't noble. I have never seen any God or believe in anything in death, I would rather escape the reaper if I can, so as doctors do your job and help me heal this god forsaken wound.

Jesus lifted Gaius's tunic so he could have a good look at the wound, It was the worst thing he had ever seen the whole of his right side from ankle to shoulder was black and riddled with puss oozing out everywhere it stank of rotting flesh he was decaying before their eyes, Jesus said, with this wound you should be already dead, You must have a great spirit that does not wish to go.

Gaius replied sadly I fear no Man, but I admit I fear Death, sometimes I wish I could believe in the gods or a better place, but I don't, I think death is the end of me.

I heard that a new rabbi who healed everyone he touches is attending the ceremony to Maduk, I was hoping to live long enough to ask him to heal me, and if he did, I would also believe in the living God, as this has been told to me at every town I came through, that this Jesus is the living God on this earth.

Jesus replied Yes Gaius it is true. I will heal you if you wish, and give you more years on this earth on two conditions, that you gain discharge from your commission, swear to me that you will never hurt another in battle and become a writer a lawyer and Scholler.

That you will preach to everyone you meet with that you have walked with the living God, He healed you, that now you believe in Jesus Christ and Mary the Mother of Man.

The second condition is that you pardon out of the army a young centurion called Marcus Flavio's, I believe he serves under your command, Yes I know him if I had a Son I would wish it to be him, a fine Soldier, not only will you pardon him, but you will let him go with a purse of gold, and Diploma.

Do this after tonight's rituals ask him to come and help you off your horse, OH yes I nearly forgot, when you see a lovely lady called Emily, you must promise to marry her, and look after her with all the love in your heart.

She is a beautiful disciple of God, she needs a good Man to comfort her and protect her, she is a gifted Sister, treat her well, as your Wife, she will repay you with the most passionate wonderful love, do you agree Gaius.

Gaius reached for Jesuses hand, My Lord if you are who you say, and you can heal me, and give me more time, and a new and beautiful Wife, If you can achieve all this, I will work the rest of my life for you, for thou truly are the God I have heard talked about, It is amazing to me, That you are with me to comfort me in my hour of need.

Jesus laid his hand on his head and blessed him, Close your eyes Gaius and when you open them you will be healed, go to sleep now, when you wake I will have gone, remember your promise and we will meet again soon.

Jesus walked outside and left Gaius sleeping; He saw Tibur Drusus and called out to him immediately Tibur responded with a wave of his arm and ran over to Jesus.

Lord what brings you here, Good to see you Tibur, and you Sir replied Tibur Drusus, I came to meet with Barabbas would you show me where he is being held, Yes of course follow me, Tibur escorted Jesus to the holding pen and explained that all the prisoners would be tried and possibly put to death this afternoon, at the Kings pleasure.

Our orders are to get them ready for the trial and escort them through the city so that the people can see them being tried.

Tibur explained that some of the prisoners appeared like wild animals caged, they scream and curse, they are a frightening site to all who approach them as they attack even each other, the Leader Barabbas is the worst of them all, I don't know if you will be able to get much sense out of any of them, and also I beg to accompany you with my sword drawn, these are dangerous and evil men, I would have no conscious at dispatching them, as they have the look of the Devil himself on them.

That won't be necessary Tibur thank you for your concern please leave me to talk to these men I will be alright alone.

Tibur reluctantly let Jesus into the inner courtyard, yet still hung back with drawn sword if he heard one sound against the Lord then; he waited to act swiftly if Jesus needed Him.

Jesus walked the two-reed distance to the inner holding cells, He found that Barabbas was waiting for him leaning on the gate calling to him for all his companions to hear.

Oh, hear he is the bloody Lord and Master, What the Hell would you want with us, haven't you done enough to us already.

Jesus replied, Barabbas I come not to talk with you but with the Dark entity you hold in your heart and body. Barabbas laughed a loud defiant sound.

Jesus said come out oh miscreant, come and face me as you have taken over these souls to do your bidding. Come out and face The Father of Man and show me the Evil, I command you to come forward out of these Men, born of Woman as innocent Children, I know your name Beelzebub come out Now.

Suddenly there appeared three Angels standing around the Lord they each were magnificent in their presentation wearing white and gold tunics, one was dressed as a centurion, each held a long staff and one a sword drawn, as if to protect the lord.

Barabbas started to fit and contort his body in unnatural jerking movements spittle flying from his mouth, some of the other prisoners were behaving in the same way, screaming for mercy.

Then the prisoners seemed to be sick spewing forth a strange and ugly form from their mouths, as the prisoners laid motionless on the ground, a very terrible site stood before them, creatures not of this world with forms and smells to repugnant to describe, stood before Jesus and the Angels.

The Devil spoke Why do you call us forth you do not have dominion over me or my Followers, This Black earth is ours, our sport and purpose is to persecute every Man and Woman, We are free to quench our lust in whatever way we see fit, So Fuck you, Lord King of Kings, Fuck you crosskicking Angels you are powerless before us.

Jesus held out his hand be quiet abomination shut up, be quiet, His words seemed to cut the Devils and they fell to the floor screaming, blasphemy spewing out of their mouths, A few trying desperately to go back into their human hosts and failing.

The good Angels have come to take you to your rightful place, in the pit of tar, where all things dark and Evil come from.

You have had dominion over Man, and this earth, far too long, It is my command that you leave know this that wherever I find a Human soul so inflicted with your presence, I promise you, that I will cast you back into your prime evil slime were you belong, In the name of the Living God I cast you out.

The Devil cried out There are legions of us present in Human beings, we are legion hundreds and thousands quake at our feet and are rightly afraid, they worship us, we are in all bad thoughts murder war and vice, compelling evil acts.

You cannot keep us out of this world because they invite us in, with their beliefs, and so called religions, they crave our presence, let the battle commence, we are legion we will always win over pious hypocrites, So Fuck off you perfect beautiful bastards. We go back to creation just like you will.

With a nod of Jesuses' head, the Angels move forward striking each devil with their staffs, striking them down they writhed on the floor as if electricity was flowing through them, the most senior devil Beelzebub stood facing the Angel who sported both staff and sword.

Arc Angel Michael set his steely eyes on the evil thing before him, the devil as all bullies do when confronted with higher powers, threw himself at his feet asking to be merciful, Michael struck the devil with both sword and staff saying I will show you as much mercy you gave to the human beings you tormented.

All the Devils immediately disappeared.

The prisoners slowly started to come around. Jesus waited patiently for their full return to consciousness, when their senses returned, Jesus ask of them, why they lived to bring havoc cruelty, and murder to this beautiful world.

The leader Barabbas spoke, because of what was taken from us, my Family butchered by the Romans it's a similar story for us all, if we cannot earn it, we simply take it from those who have whatever we crave.

This world is about kill or be killed, I preferred to be a killer rather than a victim, I know that I will pay for my deeds at the hands of the hypocrites, who have stolen and killed more than I could ever fit into my short life, will you be judging them also.

Yes, Barabbas I will, but this is not about judgement, I came to talk with you and hopefully absolve you of your many sins before you are judged.

Lord will it make any difference, the outcome will still be my death and of my confederates here with me, however I will say this that the horrible anger and feelings to do murder, has gone from me I believe I no longer have the need or stomach to fight and hurt the world, therefore, would you please bless us before we welcome our deaths, at that moment the prisoners bore witness to the Angels appearing and surrounding the Lord, they were taken a back with shock falling to their knees begged forgiveness for their great and numerous sins.

Jesus said I will not absolve you, or forgive all your sins, that will be up to the many victims you have made by your actions, I will bless you, and tell you that my Angels will be with you when your end comes on earth, you will feel no pain, and they will escort your soul to a waiting area where you will rest and recuperate.

Lord are you saying that after our deaths we will survive, you see we turned our backs on religion we believed that we will burn in hell or at best be a nothingness or a long sleep.

I for one do not believe in the Jewish way, it is full of hypocrites and Men in high places that feel superior to anyone.

full of their own self-importance sitting in harsh judgement of everyone, and the People are like Sheep to the slaughter, I am happy to embrace Death I am sick of living in this Place, and I am sorry for the pain and hurt I caused to the innocent.

Do you promise me this that you will bless us and by your blessing set us free?

Jesus replied yes, but mind yourself because you propose nothing in the sight of God, I am not judging you for the choices you made, as you were under an evil influence, it will be up to you to judge yourself, and yes, I do have some empathy about the establishment that for many generations it has proved to house evil and corruption, and will probably do so for many other generations.

I leave you with this promise, in future generations when the time is right, there will come a pale rider from the west mounted on a white horse breathing fire, He comes from the House of eagles.

He will bring with him Fire, Honesty, and forthright truth, He will live to write all the wrongs done in the name of the so-called establishment, the world will become a better place for he will be given his place by the beloved Children of God.

He will lead the Children of God, exposing everyone as they are, in their lies and corruptions, they may believe that in their arrogance they are above the law, God hears sees and watches, no one is above God, believe me I Have a plan for this world, hear this when the time is right remembering, Truth Rightfulness under Maduk Prevails, in the Times yet to come.

Barabbas says, we go to our Deaths and you give us a riddle? No absolution for us then? Well thank you Lord of Lords King of Kings, before he could utter another word one of the Angels moved forward and gave him a jolt with his staff.

Rafael spoke to him, You are evil men, who deserve to be punished until the end of days, yet my good and beautiful Lord has still taken time to bless you, to understand you better, stay on your knees before him, Barabbas you are just as arrogant as the Men in powerful positions, except responsibility for all your crimes against Good Human Beings, do not dare to blame our Good and just God, Jesus the living God, has spoken words of great truth and spared you from the horror of the great primeval ooze.

All this he has done for you where you not employed, paid to take the living Gods life.

That would have been your fate if our beloved God did not intervene on your behalf sending only the evil Devils residing in you to that terrible place, what say you now Barabbas.

Barabbas threw himself at the feet of Jesus (who was also Maduk) my lord I am sorry for my actions and my ungrateful behaviour.

Please forgive us lord, thank you for preparing a place for us to rest, the other prisoner's move forward praising Jesus the living God to have mercy on them. Jesus gave them all his blessing and was turning to walk away when something caught his eye.

Ariel please bring that Child to me the ark angel Ariel, moved swiftly and giving the Child his hand brought him to Jesus, I am not bad said the boy, I don't think that I have done anything wrong.

If I have, I am sorry I do not remember, this Child looked at about five or six years old, Jesus knelt to the Childs level, tell me What is your name, and Why are you here with these Men.

My Name is Daniel I am all alone, my Parents were killed and my sister carried off, I have been trying to find her for many months, but since the loss of my dear Mother I found that I could not speak a word, nor hear what any man asked of me, I don't know how I came to be here.

Barabbas answered if you please my lord this child was already here when we were imprisoned, he hasn't spoken a word to any of us.

Jesus said This Child is far too young and without Sin to be incarcerated, therefore I will take him with me and act as his guardian until other provision can be made, suffer little children to come unto me, be blessed Daniel, will you walk with me, yes sir but what of these strange Men with wings are they your Friends,

Yes, Daniel they are, will they help me find my Sister, we will try, in the meantime will you stay with me and my wife, we will look after you.

OH, yes sir thank you I was very afraid on my own, people hit me, threw stones and cast me out, they said I was a child of the Devil so I acted as if I was one, and scared them, and they usually left me alone, the funny thing is that I became one, that didn't speak or hear anything, I just could not talk or ask for bread, so I took it and that I think, is why I was thrown into that awful cruel place.

I prayed so hard that someone would save me and find my Sister, and now Maduk himself is helping me Lord I am so happy I know in my heart that you are kind and true.

Jesus lifted the boy up into his arms and the child immediately fell fast asleep, this poor child was so afraid that he dared not to sleep. Jesus saw how pitifully thin he was so light just skin and bones.

Tibur Drusus walked towards Jesus, My Lord have you finished with these miscreants. Yes, Tibur I have, please open the outer gate and let us through, Tibur then noticed the Child in Jesuses arms my lord I think this Boy is to be tried for stealing along with Barabbas and his Men.

Tibur this Child is without Sin, He should be cared for, not locked up with the vilest criminals awaiting sentence for taking a loaf of bread, Tibur you have seen nothing, I will take the boy with me and that is final, Tibur knew it was futile to object, he shrugged his shoulders and said alright if that is your wish Lord.

Jesus carried the boy back to the palace.

Mary waited patiently for Jesuses return, she knew if he left without her, he was busy attending to his business and would return soon.

A faint knock on the door came and Mary called out to enter, Miriam came in with Nubia, Mary dearest I have brought my friend Nubia to meet and talk with you, She has many questions, She is here as a Slave of the King and is trying to find something incriminating against You and Jesus, by doing this she hopes to gain her freedom.

Nubia's mouth fell open as she heard this from Miriam, she had thought that Miriam was not aware of her true intentions and now she stands before Mary aghast and exposed.

Nubia didn't know what to say, So She threw herself down begging Mary to forgive her and not to tell the King She had been found out, this would mean Nubians' death for certain.

Mary held out her hand to Nubia She said come, sit here with me I wish to know you and your life, how did you become a Slave.

Nubia told Mary how her family has been killed and how she had to leave her Mother and Little Brother dying at the side of the road, How she was sold at the Slave Market, brought to this Palace, and had served the king in every way he demanded, He had promised to give her anything she wished if She could find out who Jesus really was.

That is why She befriended Miriam to get information, She confessed that if She could not find any legitimate information then She would have made something up, the King would take credit for exposing Mary and Jesus after the celebration as frauds, thereby gaining the reasons to have you both arrested.

Nubia started to sob uncontrollably, she looked up at Mary and found that she was weeping as well, Nubia stopped sobbing and said, Dear lady why do you cry, Mary replied, I Cry for you dear Nubia and for all the other poor Children captured by tyranny, made to suffer unimaginable horrors at the hands of greedy and unscrupulous Men.

I am sorry for you and for the generations of my Children who will have to live and survive by any means possible when there are such wicked Men and Woman living in this domain.

Mary wiped Nubians' tear strained face with her veil, now dear, Jesus will be here any moment, I will introduce you and we will talk together and see what we can do to make your heart, and load in life lighter.

What is your dearest wish above all things, Nubia replied Freedom I wish this with all my heart, and soul, although I do not know what I would do with it, I cannot go back to my home and tribe as they are all lost?

I would like to know exactly what happened to my dear Mother and brother she carried Him so bravely, He was only a Baby they were left for dead at the side of the road, although in my dreams I see them saved, Happy and smiling waiting for me to find them again.

Dearest Mary I must leave now, My Master will be furious that I have taken so long, what should I tell him. Mary replied, the truth as you see it my Dear Nubia.

Nubia ran as fast as she could to Harrods personal apartments, She had no idea what to say to him, he fully expects her to find the evidence that would condemn them, her mind was still reeling with this when she fell into the apartment's tripping and falling at the feet of Harrods himself, Who was being groomed by a small army of servants.

Ah Nubia where have you bean, I missed you, tell me have you some good information for me he said slyly, Nubia stood in front of the King feeling very ill at ease, looking at the floor.

Herod signalled to his guards and they stood at either side of Nubia.

Come now tell me, what have you witnessed. My Lord, I did not see the man named Jesus, I spent the whole day with Miriam who I believed was there Slave, I tried to get her to tell me the gossip about Jesus and Mary It turns out I was misinformed.

Miriam is a much beloved Sister to them both neither Slave or Servant, She looks after them because she loves them, adding quickly as devoted to them as I am to you Sir, She dared not look up into the face of her tormentor, She saw the look that meant any moment he would erupt in a violent rage, one that she had been at the receiving end on many occasions bearing the bruises for days.

She shuddered in fear knowing what was coming closing her eyes and waited, Yes well go on, did they mention Me at any time, Did they say that they were bound to take over the throne from the great Harrod, did they mention the name John, Come on now Nubia what was witnessed.

Lord could your spies have got it wrong, Mary seems very sincere, she said nothing that would incriminate them or anyone, she was kind and courteous towards me, and to everyone that attended her, she just knew things.

Things, things! what are you talking about girl, what are they about, what are there politics, I honestly don't know my lord, may I carry on with my duties.

Oh, yes, I can tell you about your duty's madam, tomorrow will be the procession to Marduk, this year there is going to be a special sacrifice, you, guards! take her away she displeases me, make her ready for the great sacrifice.

Jesus arrived back at their apartments carrying the Child, just as Luke Jude and James arrived Mary immediately taking the little boy from him holding him in her arms the child slept on, Oh Darling what has happened Jesus told Mary Miriam Luke Jude Mark and James of his adventures that day, ending with that is how it came to pass, that we have our first Child meet Daniel.

The Child awoke considering the loving eyes of Mary, his small hand reached up touching Marys face and the little boy whispers are you my Mother, Yes Darling I will be your Mother until we find your very own Family, Mary considered the little boy's eyes and declared I have seen the same colour of blue eyes twice today, what do you think Miriam, Yes Nubia has similar looking eyes.

Miriam then told them about how she had spent her day with Nubia and felt concerned as to what She would say to Harrod about them all.

Jesus replied that she couldn't have said much because the Kings guards had not arrived to arrest them all, James suggested that they carry on going to watch all the amusing acrobat's, dancers and revelry, as they had planned, Luke was preoccupied trying to write down the stories from today's adventures, so everyone agreed with James.

Mary and Miriam busied themselves caring for Daniel whilst getting ready for the evening. Servants arrived with a sumptuous cold platter of meat salad with warm bread and fruit. Daniel had never seen as much food, yet he showed reserve and resisted the urge to throw himself head first mouth open into the platter.

Mary said to Daniel are you hungry my little one, Daniel nodded his head so much they joked it would come off if he didn't stop, so for the first time in his little life he ate everything he could, as if it would be his last.

Mary asked Miriam if she would go down to the plaza and find Daniel some suitable clothes, and fresh milk, Jesus gave her a purse of money and bid her to hurry. Mary took Daniel to have a bath, She assumed that Daniel was dark skinned because of the dirt he had lived in.

She realised that this Child was dark skinned, pitiful thin with malnutrition, strangely the bluest eyes she had ever seen, and the whitest teeth, Mary looked at her Son declaring, Daniel you are so beautiful.

Miriam came dashing into the room out of breath from running, waving a variety of clothing she wheezed trying to catch her breath, blurted out saw Nubia being escorted with soldiers, she has been imprisoned.

They all agreed that it was even more important that they all go out to find out what had happened to Nubia, as everyone was ready and they were about to leave,

A knock came on the door James opened it to see a Roman legionnaire and six escort's, Greetings from King Herod and Pontius pilot we come to escort Jesus and Mary his wife to the celebrations as their esteemed guests.

Thank you, Jesus, said we would be honoured indeed, Mary gave the child Daniel to Miriam calming him by saying don't worry little one I will be back soon, Miriam Mark, and James will look after you. Mary took Jesuses arm and walked with him, the others walked towards the sounds of merriment in the main street.

Oh, what a wondrous site, was before them Market stalls with bangles clothing confection breads food from every continent, silks spices acrobats whirling sword swallowers, Elephants with People riding on their backs, dancers with great plumbs on their heads, exotic Animals making the strangest procession.

This was the Peoples evening, merriment wine and fabulous memories for all the common people, whilst the elite watched the revelries from the balconies and collaides of the great Palace, congratulating themselves on being able to have the greatest show on earth this year, because of the fabulous harvest's best grapes for the sweetest wines being reserved for the most prestigious of guests.

The procession starts with a fanfare of trumpets marking the beginning of the procession Roman Legions marching headed by the great Master himself Gaius Plinius Secundus.

followed the Chariots, each with six identical sets of beautiful Horses and golden chariots, these would be racing each other in the coming days, for now they posed an awesome spectacle then came the Elephants Great beasts carrying People on their backs, beautifully decorated they appeared to shake their heads and dance to the exotic music, following them Giraffe, tall majestic beautiful, greatly prized, and the property of the King himself, striding tall with their keepers once or twice the Animals appeared over excited, jumping up into the air, pulling their keepers off their feet.

To the great delight of the crowd

Then came the lions again on strong chains led by their keepers, not so well behaved, there was talk in the crowd that the lions had attacked and killed some of the keepers earlier that day.

As they passed by Miriam was observing one of the keepers of Lions, and she gestured to Luke and Jude to look at his eyes then pointed at Daniel, they took the lead and looked at the very large man trying to control an equally impressive lion, as the light flashed in their eyes, they saw what Miriam was gesturing about, his eyes looked the same colour of blue as Daniels and Nubia.

Miriam concluded that as they were greatly prized and rare in this part of the world, their appearance must mean that they share a family or clan resemblance.

Nubira may not be the last of her kind as she thought.

The whole spectacle was jaw dropping, after the lions came the Bears walking upright standing at least ten feet in the air, majestic animals being made to dance for their supper, acrobat's dancers and drummers then the music maker's trumpets drums tambourines flutes.

Dancers whose head dresses and scant clothing and amazing ability to shimmy their bodies, they enthralled everyone, lovely Maidens who danced erotically with scarves.

Then came the dancers who danced with snakes of all things.

The next splendid spectacle stopped them in their tracks, Ruth is that our Ruth, standing on the back of six beautiful pure white horses, driving them without fear or care for safety, every few hundred meter they broke formation and gave an incredible performance, standing on hind legs dancing as gracefully as any hand maiden, cumulating in Ruth dressed exquisitely in white Gold and purple with a matching plumbed headdress, coordinated in perfect harmony from girl to Horse.

So, Miriam exclaimed, that is what our Ruth and Emily have been up to, I wondered where they were, just then Emily came running towards the friends, she was so excited saying isn't She spectacular.

we've been getting the horses ready, since selling most of the others this morning in the market I would never have believed what a horsewoman Ruth is, She only has to show them once what She wants of them and they do it, She doesn't have to whip them or make them, it's as if they do what she asked because they love her, isn't She adorable.

Miriam agreed but then a realisation came over her as she said but Emily she's pregnant what of the baby, Well She says she is perfectly alright and the Baby will get used to riding and horsepower before its born, therefore will show no fear and become an expert horseman as a baby, indeed he will Mark exclaimed.

Jesus and Mary stood on the wide balcony at Nebuchadnezzar Palace with Pontus and many other VIP Guests, overlooking the grand peoples procession, they also marvelled at the sites enjoyed by their Friends bellow, then came Ruth with her wonderful horses, stopping outside the palace, putting on their incredible show for the King and guests.

She saved this performance for just this moment she performed the most impossible twists turns and throws high in the air always being caught by the next horse as if they were playing a ball game with Ruth playing the ball,

The whoops and Ahhhs of the crowd told her that they were impressed.

On the grand finish, Ruth rose high above the crowd performing a multi over swing. landing without effort on the balcony in front of Jesus and Mary she curtsied low to them and the horses below bowed extending their front leg and holding their mussel onto hoof.

Hello Ruth had a good day Mary said, Jesus looked over the balcony at the Horses and said laughing now all of you are just showing off, Ruth kissed them both saying thank you so very much this performance is in your honour, and I hope to see you both later if that is OK with you, Of course it is Dear, before you go just a little thing, look for the Garrison leader he may have a surprise for you, Alright Lord I will do that.

The Crowd went wild cheering Ruth and the clever horses, they didn't move until Ruth jumped back from the balcony landing on the flank of the largest Horse feet first, the group carried on thrilling the rest of the observers with their fabulous performance until reaching the end of the great mall, where the stables provided a much-needed rest and refreshment for the Horses and all the other Animals in the procession.

Ruth was elated the first performance went much better than She could have hoped for, she was telling her beloved Horses how much She Loved appreciated them, and how proud She was of them, whilst giving them hey. water and corn.

When She remembered what Jesus had told her, Look out for the leader of the Garrison, She walked outside of the stables to look around, and there she noticed the Garrison leader being helped off his horse, She trotted over to Him and recognised the young Man helping the Leader off his Horse.

Marcus, she called is that you, the young Man turned around in an instant they were in each other's arms kissing and holding each other, slowly they came out of their initial rapture.

Marcus suddenly remembered the Garrison leader Gaius Plinius Secundus who was watching and waiting patiently for Marcus to help him out of his dress armour, Marcus wheeled round sorry Sir I will attend you presently this is my intended Wife, I did not know She was here, and haven't seen each other for two months.

Ah now I understand what and why I had to ask Marcus to help me dismount, come here Young lady what is your name, Ruth Sir, a beautiful name for a beautiful Lady, now Marcus when do you intend to marry this young lady, Marcus replied while helping Gaius off with his armour, as soon as I can earn my diploma and be let out of serving Sir.

OK Marcus, suppose I was to give you your pardon out of service, diploma and of course a purse of gold to set you up in married life.

Sir how can this be, why would you do such a thing its unheard of. I asked if this would be what you wanted, well yes of course if I was free, I would Marry Ruth immediately and become a family Man, buy a farm raise horses, work the Fields and live well in civvies street.

I have the power to do just this and from this moment you can have all you wish, How, could I ever repay you Sir, OH believe me I do this under instruction from my benefactor who came to me and healed Me.

Ruth stepped forward I know the Man, He is my benefactor also, Jesus and his beloved wife Mary, They are living Gods, it is because of them that I am here, alive with a wonderful life in front of me I have Hope, so do I, said Marcus reaching out to hold Ruthe's hand.

Gaius Plinius Secundus observed the young couple in front of him what did Ruth say, I have hope, and so do I Gaius thought.

Marcus tomorrow morning come to my rooms, I will have the necessary diploma ready for you, for now take your intended, and go enjoy the celebrations, I believe Maduk is nearer then anyone will ever know.

Ruth and Marcus turned to leave, I have an awful lot to tell you my darling I want to show you my Family returned to me by Jesus and Mary, just then Emily came skipping up to them positively gushing you were wonderful Ruth, everyone is talking about you and your Incredible Horses.

Emily, Marcus is here, He will be demobbed tomorrow and we can begin our life together, well below me down, that's a bit of a miracle exclaimed Emily, and who is the handsome gentleman, Is it his Father, no he is Gaius Plinius Secundus the garrison commander, oh will you introduce me, Marcus took Emily's hand I would be honoured, Ruth and Marcus left Gaius and Emily chatting, Ruth led Marcus into the Stables to meet the Horses.

Marcus did not witness the procession he was driving the chariots in the procession under direction of his Commander He was full of questions, how did she get to Babylon, how did She know He was there, What Horses Emily mentioned. My Darling I will answer all your questions one at a time, first I want you to meet my beautiful Girls, the finest Horses in the World, and to tell you I am a Woman of means owning many Horses as well as her prized White wonders.

The King watched Jesus and Mary enjoy the celebrations and noted that the Animals especially the white horses and the young woman in

IN THE BEGINNING

keeping of them, directed their performances towards them and not the King.

Herod was notoriously paranoid at the best of times he saw assassins everywhere, He felt very ill at ease, His conscience was forever making him Angry, he had let his wife have her way with John the Baptist having him beheaded.

Before his death he was forever shouting about, He who will come after him a true God, and shouting up through the holding cells, calling his Wife an evil seductress who plotted her husband's downfall.

John was a loose cannon, She was beside herself with fury that Herod had not put him to death much sooner, she conspired with her Daughter Salome who She knew Harrods lusted over, to Dance for Him and ask for Johns head to be served her on a silver platter as a reward for giving him such pleasure,

His wife Herodias, a very beautiful Woman, who was his brother's wife before him, secretly hated her first husband and wasn't very keen on Harrod, it was surprisingly easy to seduce Harrod, She saw Harrod as the lesser of two evils, Her first Husband sealed his fate when he was abusive striking her for no reason, other than his jealousy, which came out in droves when the wine flowed.

She knew that Harrod had always loved her and coveted her from his Brother, it was easy to get Men all Men to do her bidding, she had no conscience. however, they were both true narcissists', seeing the slightest verbal and nonverbal messages as threats to their kingdom, they believed themselves to be Gods residing over the whole of Macedonia Babylon and beyond.

Harrod remembered his Father also called Harrod, He heard of a special child had been born from the soothsayers and profits they predicted that this Child would bring about change in the Jewish traditions would bring about the Kings demise and become spokes Man for the Jewish nation.

This Harrod was consumed with fear and paranoid to the point of distraction, He ordered the killing of all boy Children under one years old in the region, However after a short time He succumbed to a heart attack, Herod Antipas watched his Father clutch his chest and fall to the ground Dead.

He did not see fit to help his Father as He would be declared King on his death, as a true psychopath and Narcissist He was ready to take his crown, like his Father would Kill anyone even Babies if they stood in his way.

Harrod ruled with great cruelty, yet in truth he was only a token king being allowed to rule by the Cesar Augustus Tiberius, He had to be careful Pontus Pilot was the representative of Rome, He would have to be very careful in exposing Jesus and Mary as imposters and heretics against Rome.

Firstly, he had to get their confidence he would honour them with a private meeting. He called a servant over to him and whispered his command.

The Servant immediately ran over to where Jesus and Mary stood, King Harrod askes for your attendance at his Table, to experience His hospitality, and banquet after the procession this evening.

Jesus turned towards the young Man, thank you we are honoured and look forward to being in the Great Kings presence.

Mary took Jesuses arm and whispered to him, I would rather find the others, Jesus replied yes my Darling so would I but I think it wise to talk with Harrod if he so wishes, after all he is our host and we don't want to cause any embarrassment for Pontus Pilot, Mary replied yes Dear you are right and we may find out what happened to Nubia, they followed the young Man into the banquet Hall The young Servant gestured to the seating area, it was a lie down typical roman gathering.it was a beautiful sight lush soft pillows and couches seated around in a great circle where guests chatted in the middle was a fountain with flowing wine, guest could merely lean forward and fill their glasses, on tables in front of the lounging diners every kind of fruit was displayed, this was also where the evenings courses would be served.

When all the VIP Guests were seated a trumpet, horn blew which signified Harrods and Herodian was joining them, Harrod was feeling out of sorts which beset him after John the Baptists death, it made him bad tempered at the best of times. He was also suffering from gout his legs painful ulcers bleeding and oozing He wanted to ask Jesus if he could cure him but then he would have to acknowledge belief in him and the Jewish

Pharisees and Socrates would be furious, especially as the plot to kill them had backfired spectacularly.

Harrod had to judge those assassins and arrange their execution before any one of them exposed who had sent them, His role now was to discredit Jesus and Mary, hand them over to be judged and dealt with by the Elders of the synagogue, thus ensuring that they keep their status, wealth and congregation attending their religion, whereby Harrods is seen to keep peace and control, pacifying the Elders, Harrod was playing hard politics trying to keep all fractions happy including Rome.

Pontus Pilot was seated on Harrods right side Jesus and Mary on his left, The great feast of Maduk began with Servants bringing in the first course, there would be many courses that would last all evening a constant stream of servants bringing exotic food, fish and meat courses and providing bowls of warm lemon water to wash hands in-between courses, at the same moment the first entertainment Luverly Maidens dancing to beautiful layer and flutes music, then came the African Dancers with loud drumming acting out a hunt and kill of a lion, the dancing bears were next, followed by singers and layer players, after this there was an interval, so guests may toilet themselves, and get ready for the second part which was a comedy play.

Now, Harrod turned to Jesus and asked him if He was enjoying the feast for Maduk, Jesus replied that he was enjoying it very much, Harrod then asked him how was he able to subdue the Robbers without any blood being spilt, Jesus smiled and said by using the power of will, what do you mean by that Harrod said angrily, just that, tell me how do you use mere will to capture murderous thugs

Jesus replied by asking the Animals to help sometimes we all need help including you, we must learn how to ask for it, Harrod was clearly taken back he fell silent for a few moments contemplating what Jesus had just said to him.

Harrod stated arrogantly I have never asked for help and I don't need any help, Jesus replied, Is that so sir I wonder why you are so ill tempered and feeling ill especially with your poor legs being in such a state, Herrod stated Who told you this, Jesus replied no one I know you King Harrod probably better than you know yourself, Harrod was at a loss If anyone had spoken to him in such a manner he would have him put to the sword immediately, yet he reminded himself what John the Baptist had said to him, There will be one that comes after me who will change the world of Man, A King so powerful that the very earth and Animals in the field will yield to him.

Harrod felt vulnerable and just a little afraid remembering what had happened to John, Is this man here to do me harm for revenge of a mere profit, before he could utter another word Jesus says John has already forgiven you for his death, fear not Harrod I am here to save you I have no intention of doing you harm, Harrod could feel himself becoming week in Jesuses presence, are you a profit or healer he asked, Sort of both Jesus replied, can you truly heal me Harrod said almost pleading, that depends on you when you feel able to humble yourself and ask me for help.

At that moment, Mary returned and sat down at Jesuses side, the festivities resumed, the comedy drama was truly funny everyone enjoyed themselves laughing at the comic jokes and rude humour, all the time more courses were served, Harrod remained stony faced as if he wasn't paying attention he seemed miles away deep in thought.

The evenings revelry drew to a close, Jesus and Mary stood to say thank you and take their leave, until the next day, Herod said I would like a private meeting with you Jesus tomorrow, I will send an escort, tomorrow is a special day in the celebrations, the procession of Maduk, I hope you sleep well and I will talk with you tomorrow, Pontus Pilot also gave thanks and said he was going to retire as he felt tired.

Harrod fixed him with a look, Pontus are you not staying for the orgy, as I remember you always enjoyed the private and intimate party, I have the most beautiful Girls and boys they are virgins or so I am told, many of my guests can't wait until tomorrow they wish to taste some of the delights now, he gave Pontus a little push with his arm.

Pilot looked directly at Jesus and gave his excuse for not taking part, Jesus smiled at him and nodded in understanding, they walked out together happily chatting about the sights and sounds of the evening, Mary stopped and said oh no I forgot to ask about Nubia, its alright Mary it was not the right time Jesus said, we will all know in due course, She has not been harmed as yet, so don't worry my darling, Mary laid her head against his shoulder if you say all is well my dear then it is as it is, I will be patient until then.

IN THE BEGINNING

They walked back to their lodgings arm in arm chatting happily, Pontus exclaimed that he was worried Harrods would take offence at Him not joining in at the private revelries, Don't worry Pilot exclaimed Jesus there will be no taking of woman and girls tonight, those that lust after the innocent will find themselves overcome with illness being content to spend the night in the privies, the sickness will leave them wrenching all night, They will be in no state to do anything to the Children they will be sent home unused with great relief and happy hearts.

Miriam waited for Jesus and Mary to arrive back at their rooms, Daniel was fast asleep on the day bed, He so wanted to wait up so he could tell them about everything he had seen, He was so exhausted and Happy but sleep overcame him and he fell asleep in Miriam's arms.

Miriam had found out that Nubia was being held, imprisoned by the imperial guard in the deepest area of the Palace, no one was allowed entry to see her, Miriam was worried about Her and wanted to talk to Jesus and Mary about her fears for Nubia, She didn't have to wait long, Jesus and Mary arrived in good spirits Mary immediately went to check on Daniel, who was still fast asleep, Mary stroked his brow and kissed him goodnight, Miriam was talking to Jesus about her fears for Nubia.

Mary felt that She had let her friend down by forgetting to ask Harrods about Nubia and joined them as Jesus was pointing out to Miriam that She had to be patient as tonight was not the right time to intervein, Tomorrow at the ceremony for Maduk is when he will champion for Nubia, in the meantime Miriam must remain patient and trust him that She will be freed at the right time.

Miriam replied that of course She would trust to her Lord for Nubians' deliverance, she bade them goodnight kissing each one She left for her own room, she still felt heavy hearted thinking of poor Nubia being imprisoned and alone in a dark dungeon.

The following morning Jesus and Mary was woken by an exuberant Daniel, he jumped onto their bed chatting about everything he saw last night calling Mary Mother.

He exclaimed what a wonderful feeling he had saying, Mother so he said it a few more times because he said that it sounded so good, and Father turning to Jesus, they laughed and chatted like any Family, Daniel suddenly fell quiet, What's the matter Darling, Mary said Daniel looked up with big tears in his eyes, he placed his little hands on Marys face and said Will you never leave me, will you always love me, Mary gave him a big hug and said reassuring him of course I will never leave you and I will always love you.

Daniel replied Good because I think I just wet your bed, Jesus and Mary fell into each other laughing so much it brought tears to their eyes, Mary took Daniel to the toilet room, saying it wasn't his fault they should have shown him what to do, she was still laughing as She took the bed linen of their bed.

Breakfast was brought in to them delicious fresh warm bread with honey millet potage fresh figs, fruit and fresh milk, a lovely breakfast, Daniel ate heartily still talking amid mouthfuls of food, Miriam Jude, Mark, James and Luke arrived together to breakfast with them.

As they ate breakfast, they talked about the last nights festivities how exciting, it was a wonderful experience and tonight is the most important part of the celebrations, the procession for Maduk,

James relayed to them what he had found out about the proceedings this night of conclusion, a great procession takes place starting from the beginning of the Mall, like last night's procession, headed by all the holy men priests of Madoc and Socrates, Pharisees and VIP s who have proved their allegiance to the King and Rome, behind them walk the virgins Children dressed in white tunics with garlands of flowers worn as crowns on their heads then come the Boys dressed the same way.

All the followers walk in silence holding a white candle the long walk starts from the beginning of the grand mall.

The ordinary citizens follow singing the praises of Maduk again holding white candles, after the orgeration of the King declaring him to be Maduk chief on earth for another year, there are celebrations Parties and the Virgin Children are taken into the palace for the night.

Miriam stated that She had talked to the guard holding Nubia taking him some cold meet and flagon of wine to help the conversation she says sweetly, The Guard told her that Nubia is OK with instructions not to beat her or bruise her in any way, He told her that Herod had stated handmaidens will come and wash and dress her, they will give her a large portion of Valerian Root to keep her subdued, When I asked him why? He just said it was the orders off the King himself and that the King had said that he had a special sacrifice instead of the usual sheep Goats and doves, a sacrifice worthy of the highest God, Maduk,

So, make it of what you will, I haven't said anything said the Guard. Miriam ran to Jesus and exclaimed, Do you really think King Herod intends to sacrifice Nubia, Maybe said Jesus, we will wait and see, No No Lord you must stop Him cried Miriam in obvious distress, at that moment Mary joined them She had been washing and dressing Daniel, He was happily snuggled under Marys arm sitting on her hip, the usual ways that Mothers hold their small Children, Mary dashed to Miriam's side to comfort Her, Dearest little sister do not worry our Lord will not allow this terrible sacrifices isn't that right Dear, Of course not Miriam trust me Jesus said, I do my Lord but sometimes the bad in this world makes me afraid, All the others nodded in agreement.

An uneasy silence was interrupted by the arrival at their apartments of Pontus Pilot together with his body guard Centurions, Pontus said good morning to everyone, then turned to Jesus, and said King Harrod has asked me to intervein on his behalf he felt his conversation with you last night was misinterpreted, you may have misunderstood what he wanted to convey, and he humbly requests that you go to him immediately and heal him before this evenings activity.

Pontus my dear friend Jesus replied I task you to go back to King Harrod give him my regards and say unto him, I will heal him if he wishes, however this can only be after this evening's celebration.

Well Pontus replied I really think he wants you to attend him immediately and the many others of his guests who fell violently ill last night, The Gossips are doing their work well this morning, saying that the guests and the King himself may have been poisoned, all the servants and slaves are running their legs off trying to help, they all appear horribly out of sorts.

On hearing this, Jesus and everyone else started laughing, OH sorry Pontus I am not mocking you, it just gave me a vision of everyone running to the privy holes fighting each other, and what a horrid stench there must be at the Palace and you saying they are horribly out of sorts, with that Pontus got the same vision and he started to chuckle, saying yes your right it stinks in the palace.

Pontus my dear friend and brother will you take my message to the King for me, tell him I have business to attend to today, and with Madoc's blessing I will heal him tonight.

Pontus left to convey the message to the very out of sorts King Herod. Jesus turned his attention to his beloved group and asked what each one had planned for today.

Jesus and Mary both noticed how Mark looked at Miriam, it was a look of love and admiration, yet She was so busy looking after everyone that She noticed nothing, Mary suggested that Miriam with Mark as escort and protector, should take a little time off for herself and go and look around and buy something nice for herself, have a walk in the beautiful gardens anything She wished.

OH, alright she said if they didn't mind, do you want to come with me Mark, Of course I do, trying not to sound over enthusiastic.

That's settled then, go on you two go and enjoy yourselves Jesus said, Luke Jude and James have you got any plans for today, well said James I would like to see where Emily and Ruth are, Jesus stated they are at the stables at the other end of the grand mall.

Do you mind Lord if I go to find them, Not at all give them my love and blessings, and that leaves, Luke and Jude what do you wish to do for today, Luke and Jude had been talking together with much excitement, about writing and illustrating a special scrolled documenting the magnificent spectacle they witnessed last night Jude was a brilliant painter, he would illustrate it with pictures and Luke would scribe.

What a wonderful idea Mary said. you two are so clever, Darling are you going to give them a purse so that they can buy the parchment and ink, of course here you are happy shopping That's settled everyone is having a day off Jesus exclaimed shooing them out of the door, don't come back until you have enjoyed yourselves.

Mary looked at Jesus with a side gaze, and exclaimed what are you up to, what do you mean said Jesus indignantly and made a move to catch Mary in his arms, she was too fast for him and Jesus started chasing Mary, they were laughing so much acting silly they forgot about little Daniel Jesus had caught Mary and was kissing her when a little voice exclaimed clapping his little hands oooh goody can I play kiss catch to.

They ran around catching and kissing each other, which culminated in Mary and Jesus catching Daniel all falling together in a laughing and kissing heap, the picture was of a happy and contented Family.

They spent the rest of the day exploring the city with Daniel they marvelled at his great smile and laugh, this Child who only a day ago was in such terrible danger, was the happiest little boy in the world.

Daniel wanted to see where the Animals were kept, they walked through the great crowds and markets buying trinkets along the way, little presents for the others, and some beautiful earrings and necklace for Mary,

She said, they would be perfect for the evening, as they neared the stables they could hear the whinnies and brays of the Animals, amidst of all this noise a great Roar went up, Men came running panic ridden Shouts of hese loose run for your lives run run, they fled past the little family.

Daniel was starting to become afraid, Mary comforted him, He still would not let go of Mary he buried his head in her neck and held on to her for dear life, Mother please lets go back I changed my mind I don't want to see the Animals now.

I have a bad feeling something going to happen, before he finished uttering the words an enormous lion stood right in their path, Roaring angry like he wanted to take on the world, He had broken his chains, he was enormous and magnificent, the poor Animal only desired his freedom, He was unconcerned about the people fleeing terrified, His only concern was to find his keeper and gain his freedom.

He moved slowly towards them menacing growling showing a great sneer and even greater teeth he stepped in front of Mary and Daniel confronting the beast

The great lion, seemed to hesitate then to everyone's amazement lied down and rolled over in a submissive way so that Jesus could tickle his belly, which he obliged of course and at the same time found out what was happening.

Jesus talked to the Lion as He continued to rub the lion's tummy, who appeared in ecstasy when his keeper ran unto the mayhem. Kinta what have you been up to, I can't leave you alone for one second.

He started issuing instructions to Jesus, saying Sir remain calm He is a good and friendly lion just back away slowly toward Me.

Jesus stopped massaging the great beast, stood up and turned towards the keeper, The Lion stood up He appeared to stand taller than most Men He was so large that Jesus looked small in comparison, He stood looking at his keeper Kinta, Jesus and the Lion walked side by side towards Kinta Jesus held on to his main, everyone was dumb struck, although there was so many people around them no one uttered a sound it was as if everyone was holding their breath.

Jesus stood in front of a very large muscular black Man, He stood well over six feet tall, his arms were so large rippling with muscle as was his whole body but the most striking thing about him was not how tall or the muscle or the gleaming of black skin it was his eyes, vermillion blue just like Daniels, Kinta I presume quipped Jesus.

Yes Sir I apologise for my Friend. He doesn't like it when I leave him, We have been together since we were both captured as children to become Slaves, He can be very fierce, and also very gentle when He wishes, Look at Him now it's as if He loves you as much as I love Him, He has always been my protector and I his, I have never known him to behave in such a quiet way not even with me, by the way Lord how do you know my name.

OH I know you well Kinta, I know you could have escaped many times on your own, but you would never leave your Friend here, He tells me He was going to escape but could not leave without you, He risked being killed until he found you.

He knows that now He will have to go back to his cell, as long as you are with him, He doesn't mind at all.

Kinta where have you been Jesus asked, Well err its quite a delicate matter replied Kinta, come let's sit over here and you can tell me your story, and there is someone I want to introduce you to, Jesus beckoned Mary to come to his side, This is my adorable wife Mary and hiding himself in her robe is our adopted Son Daniel, Come out now Daniel there is someone here I want you to meet, Daniel slowly turned his face towards Jesus.

Kinta took a sharp inhale of breath when he saw Daniel for the first time, OH my days he said This child is of my own race, look at his eyes only the Masa are blessed with the sign of God in their blue eyes.

Yes, Kinta you are right, this Child was abused and badly treated the only reason he was not killed was because of his unusual blue eyes' superstition, can be a good thing sometimes, isn't that so Kinta.

IN THE BEGINNING

Yes Lord its kept me from being killed on many occasion and the friendship of my great lion kurta kintea as I named him, it means stay put in our African language, So we both stayed put, but what of Daniel how did he find his way here, Kinta reached out and took Daniel into his arms.

Jesus replied, Daniel will tell you the whole of his story when he is ready to, Kinta looked fondly at Daniel I thought that I would never again see a Child of my likeness and race, I am so blessed and Happy to meet you Daniel would you like to meet the lion he will do you no harm, gently Kinta sat down beside the great lion and gingerly Daniel stretched his arm towards the Big Cat Kunta sniffed at Daniels arm then gave him the biggest cat lick, Daniel moved forward and put his little arms around the lions great mane.

Kunti gave a great sigh then closed his eyes and the great lion wept, Kinta immediately dropped to his knees in front of his great friend, for a moment all three wept for the Families that had been so cruelly taken from them, they held each other, neither wanted to let go of the other for fear that they would never meet again.

Kinta lifted Daniel away and said I am sorry I have never wept I don't know what came over me.Thats alright Mary said taking Daniel back into Her arms, sometimes the soul bears such great sorrow that the only way to express it is by weeping it clean.

It is a good thing, but don't dwell too long there are others that need you Kinta, Jesus said there is so much injustice and evil in this world I think it time to undo what has happened to these precious People, however there is much to do.

Daniel looked puzzled at Kinta, I smell you and I remember home, how do you mean little one asked Kinta, I don't know but it's like I know you and the big kitty, you make me feel as safe as my Mother here, we look the same except I am much smaller, our skin is the same our eyes are the same, oh my! have you seen my Sister.

No little one I don't know anyone else who looks like us, err except the reason why I had to leave Kunti alone today, please tell us Mary said, well please try not to judge me but I had seen this girl everyday walking to the market, going about her day and work She is so beautiful Tall and slender with dark skin and brightest bluest eyes I have ever seen just the sight of her makes my heart beat so fast, She never sees me, but I love to watch her, I thought that She must be a lady of high standing to look so lovely, I watched her and another Lady walking through the gardens and followed them back to lodgings within the palace grounds.

I saw her run out towards the palace itself and She was weeping, I only wished to comfort her but She moved so fast I lost sight of her, and didn't get the chance to catch up, I was still some distance away, so I made up my mind to wait for her and get up enough courage to stop and talk to her, but I had to go back to Kunter He would be needing to eat, He gets very tetchy when he is hungry, but as I turned to leave I saw the guards dragging her towards the holding cells, I didn't know what to do how to help her, I watched them move through the building making mental note of where they had taken her, then I went back to feed Kunter.

I have been watching every day since, today I was able to see her through the air vents, she heard me I said don't worry I will help her, but I really don't know how.

Mary looked up at Jesus. Hese talking about Nubia, Jesus replied yes my dear, What we need is a plan of action, However before we do that I want to ask Kinta some questions, Kinta if we can help Nubia would you want to be with her as Man and Wife, OH yes with all my heart, but She would not look at me let alone marry me, I have nothing to give her, would you help her by giving your life for hers if you had to, Yes Lord I would, would you take Daniel as your Son and travel with your new Family, why yes but Daniel is your Son.

He will always be my Son, but his place is with his own kind, and there will be no other more fitting than you and Kunter to guard and keep him safe, Nubia is a slave like you Kinta, we must be in a position to save Nubia, you. and Kunter freed by your owner Harrod himself, this must be done publicly so that Harrod cannot change his mind, do you agree, Yes Yes of course but why do you care about us, why are you willing to help us?

I love an impossible situation replied Jesus and you are my beloved Son as is Nubia and Daniel all beloved by God although you do not know it, well Sir you are right there Kinta said, not understanding a word, it is an impossible task, how do we do it without getting killed, ok Kinta you need to be in position right at the front of the ceremony with Kunta, you must stand behind the alter to Maduk then leave the rest to us.

They said their goodbyes until the evening celebrations.

Jesus looked at Mary he became immediately concerned She looked ashen and ill, He quickly moved to her side held her up and helped her to their rooms, Little Daniel started to cry, are you ill Mamma Mary replied no Darling I am alright nevertheless She gave him over to Jesus.

Will you walk now Daniel and help me to bring Mother to our rooms, Yes Father I will help to hold her from this side and you hold her up on the other, Jesus smiled at Daniel good boy, his attention went back to Mary my darling what is the matter I have never seen you look so ill, I am alright my dearest just a little sick and faint I will be fine after a rest.

Jesus laid her down on the bed placing cushions around her for her comfort, He was just about to say he would send for Miriam when she came rushing into the room, one of the servants had told her that Mary had been taken ill, she rushed to Marys side taking her hand, my dear Mary how do you feel, I am alright Miriam, would you please just hand me some water, Miriam ran off to get a cool pitcher of water.

Jesus sat at Marys side and gently stroked her forehead, Daniel cuddled up to her holding on to her as if he would never let go, He was silently sobbing He remembered His other Dear mother He held on to her for a very long time praying that She would live.

She went very cold and Daniel knew he had lost her, the pain he felt was unbearable, Still he held on for days, until a passing Camel train saw him, took pity on him, they brought him with them to Babylon, He was still a Baby, The grief and loss was so unbearable that his little mind had completely blocked the memory out until now.

Mary said I feel much better now, Darling I have something to share with you, Yes my love what is it, I think we are going to have a child like Solidus and Pontus, We are going to be able to share our happy news with them very soon but not yet.

I wanted to go to Babylon with you, I was going to wait until we return to tell you, Jesus said my dearest darling love I already knew, I was simply waiting for you to tell me. I will be at your side you will have nothing to fear, we will love our First born on this earth with all our hearts.

Poor Daniel looked crestfallen and began to sob, what is the matter Daniel Mary said gently, Daniel sobbed, You are going to have your own Baby and then you will not want me anymore, OH dearest Child, I will always love and want you, but I must tell you that very shortly if all goes to plan, you will have your own Family and I fear that you will no longer want Me as your Mother, That is alright Daniel as long as you are loved cared for and happy with your Family, I will stand my own heartbreak at losing you, because I love you so much, I will let you go, I will always love you.

So to help me bear this pain I know I will feel, I am to have another Child not to take your place in my heart, because that place is yours and could never be filled with another, but to help me and comfort me, so that I can let go of my beautiful Daniel, as you had to let go of your Mother, do you understand Daniel, Yes yes Mother I think I do, Mary kissed Him and held him to her heart, as only a Mother can, Daniel felt comforted and loved by his foster parents, He decided to wait and see.

Jesus was visibly moved by Marys declaration of love and how well She explained things to Daniel in a language He fully understood, he was wiping a tear from his own eyes as he marvelled at her ability to address the most difficult feelings so that little Daniel could understand and except the changes that had so quickly overcome him.

Miriam came hurrying back into the room armed with a large pitcher of water and various cloths she wet one and placed it on Marys forehead poured her a large tumbler of water, then stopped and looked from one to the other, OH you know then, they all burst out laughing.

Mary was soon back to herself again, Jesus was particularly loving and attentive towards her, and she felt at ease happy and content with the confinement.

The others in their group of Friends came bursting into their Rooms, Is Mary unwell we just heard it from a servant, Jesus greeted them and said She will be alright, We are going to have a child, Happy news and congratulations all round, Jesus asked the others to go and get themselves ready for the evening's festivities before they did He had to give the Men their instructions for the evening, they left in high spirits, and Jesus went back to Mary and Daniel, they had both drifted into sleep and Jesus watched over them for a few moments before shutting the door and leaving them to sleep peacefully until the time they had to get ready,

Jesus sat meditating in the other room he wished to convey his arrangements to Angels and give them their instructions for the evening He requested the Ark Angels Michael, Rafael and Arial they were ecstatic to be of service to their Lord, they listened intently as Jesus explained their role at the evenings proceedings.

They were disturbed by Servants bringing refreshments, the Angels immediately disappeared, and Jesus awoke Mary and Daniel, so they could have something to eat before getting ready for the evening's celebrations, Daniel ate heartily as always, chattering on about the big lion and the great big black man.

Mary moved to get ready, she wore a white slip and purple head and shoulder wrap, the jewellery She bought at the market was perfect complimenting the outfit, she looked every bit a Queen herself Jesus remarked at her beauty and Daniel let out a low breath and said Wow no one in the world had a more beautiful Mother than him.

Mary said thank you to her admirers, Daniel I have placed your outfit on the bed go bathe and get ready, Miriam and the others arrived.

The Men seemed to be in deep talks with Jesus so Mary and Miriam went to help Daniel, Miriam asked Mary how She was feeling and if there was anything She could do for her, Mary replied that She was much better and thanked Miriam for her concern, She asked how her Day went with Mark, Miriam blushed and said yes they had a lovely day, Mark was a very good body guard, Mary asked if Miriam liked Mark, well yes of course I do, and do you think that Mark likes you, well yes I think so, ahh then you must go out together more often Mary quipped, OH stop it Miriam laughed you are playing matchmaker aren't you, Yes I suppose I am, we have noticed how Mark looks at you, He is obviously in love with you, there is only you who doesn't notice Miriam.

I don't know about that, He hasn't said as much to me, Mary replied Well let's wait and see, let nature take its course eh Miriam, giving her companion a hug.

They joined the others, just as Pontus arrived with his Centurion body guards, King Herod has asked for your party to join him walking the mall to the meeting place of Maduk, The King is always the last in the great procession, only after everyone is in their place will the King be presented to be blessed as Maduk's appointed.

They Walked together to join the King at the start of the great Mall, what an incredible site awaited them Hundreds of Children boys and Girls dressed in white with fresh flowers adorning their pretty heads each holding a lit candle, followed by all the townsfolk hundreds of the Kings subjects moving slowly up the grand mall, each holding a candle the lights of which shone in the darkness lighting up the night sky an awesome spectacle, everyone was singing praises to Maduk.

King Harrod and Haroda followed held high by a platform and many foot slaves holding the King and Queen in their thrones above the crowds, they were dressed in the finest of garments, garlands of fresh flowers lined the platform.

The Holy Men followed immediately behind the King each wearing the robes of office, from the Jews to the Priests of Maduk, sang their prayers and blessings as they walked.

Pontus Jesus Mary and the others walked just in front of the King surrounded by the garrison armed guards designed to protect Pontus and His guests and to prove a show of force as the emissaries of Rome, and so the procession moved forward toward the meeting place.

When they arrived after the long walk at their destination, they were astonished at the great statue of Maduk dressed in garland of fresh flowers and gold apparel, they looked up and standing between two stone pillars in front of the great statue was Nubia, chained and stretched between them, she could not move as the chains held her at the wrists and ankles.

Immediately below Nubia were the criminals condemned to death, bound by their hands behind their backs, and kneeling before the pillars that held Nubia.

The King and Queen were manovered into place so that he could be seen by everyone attending and address his subjects, Each Priest knew their place and took them, as silence fell, and each awaited the Kings address.

Harrod stood up from his thrown and stretched his hands wide above his head and cried God of all Madoc if it pleases you I King Harrod am offering in sacrifice this prized Slave and known criminals, let their blood be a most fitting offering, far more in favour than the usual offerings of goats, and Animals, OH mighty Maduk I am your Servant on this earth I ask that you favour My people with well born Children a good harvest, strong livestock, and deliverance from our enemies.

I summon you to take these offerings, The priests moved forward and each stood behind each persons that were being offered as sacrifice, The Priest of Maduk moving towards Nubia with his ceremonial dagger making ready to slit her throat, each of the Men being put to death in the same way, Had a hooded Figure, A Priest standing behind them, ready to take the moment of sacrificial death from the direction of the High Priest, All of the sacrifices would have their throats slit at the same time.

Harrod was about to give the sign when there appeared three Angels, everyone was taken back a loud gasp from the crowds, Herod stood for a moment in shock, then the largest and what looked like the most fearsome, He looked like a Roman Gladiator dressed in Gold armour with rippling muscles, and sporting a large gold sword which he had unsheathed and ready for any action, even the Centurions were impressed by his fearful countenance, secretly hoping they would not be given the command to challenge him, Here Me He commanded. I come with great news and all people hear me, I am Angel Michael sent by Maduk to watch over the ceremony There will be no blood shed on this sacred ground, tonight or any other night or day.

Maduk has no need of this sacrifice in the blood of human beings.

This Girl is being set free as a slave along with Members of her blood family, enough gold must be given to them to aid their new life Harrod you will see to this out of your own purse, and they must have a lion that belongs only to them, this is to be your sacrifice in the face of Maduk and once you give your word in the spirit of Maduk it cannot be broken, release the chains that hold her.

Just a moment cried Harrod looking down at Jesus and Mary, how do I know you are sent from Maduk, what shouted the Angel Michael, you deny Maduk and suddenly the Angels appeared to grow People were beginning to be very afraid screams could be heard. NO! NO! OF course I believe you what was I thinking replied Harrod.

The Angels grew, standing at about thirty feet high. Every Man Woman and Child fell to their knees praising God, priests and Holy men fell to their knees praising Maduk, trembling at the proposed wrath of the messengers, Ariel Beautiful Angel of light and mercy, spoke next to them who so ever takes one of these children for their own selfish lust shall perish in flames, every Child is to be escorted home to their Mothers and the practice of defiling the innocent must stop for evermore.

Rafael dressed in white and Gold another beautiful being who appeared with the most magnificent wings joined in blood sacrifice must stop, you are only wise to take enough to eat, give your prayers to Maduk for the life of the Animals you kill for food, do not shed blood in the name of Maduk as a sacrifice, Never take a life in sport, be it as small as a bird or tall as the tallest and largest Animal on earth for all these are Holy in God's presence.

Ariel stated All Slaves and Servants must be treated well until being set free with dowries which will be three times the amount paid for them, on the Death of their Masters, anyone beating whipping or using violence against less privileged people will burn for eternity.

Anyone using violence in any way against any other, will find the same fate, however Maduk states that there will be arguments and injustice so every dispute will be heard and judged by a person who will be placed in the office of adjudicator by vote of the people they will swear to protect the rights of the innocent and punish the guilty.

These words and instructions from our Holy and greater God Maduk will be the laws that every man woman or child will adhere to from this day forth.

The three Angels turned towards the Men being put to death, instantly there appeared other Angels one for each Man being put to death, they placed their hands on each of the condemned Men's shoulders, Michael said take them for judgement from Maduk himself, immediately they vanished.

The Angels then turned again to Harrod, Ariel stepped forward the light around her was so strong that Harrod had to shield his eyes, Ariel spoke, King Harrod you have much to atone for, but if you will follow Maduk's instruction for the next year, you are granted another year in your kingdom, which will bring great blessing for your People, will you put Gods Laws into action.

I will, I promise I will, then rise up King Harrod greet your People, and start to put into practice all we have told you, firstly by untying the slave Nubia.

Michael shouted for Kinta, he walked into the light with Kunti the lion at his side, they both bowed low to the Angels, we are here Sir.

Untie Nubia, Kinta ran forward jumping on to the large rock, reaching Nubia he set about untying her from her bonds, a great chain was holding her fast Rafael shot a bolt of lightning from the staff he was carrying, and the chain instantly disappeared.

Nubia fainted, Kinta held her fast in his arms and spoke softly to her, it's alright my darling I will never let anyone hurt you again, he lifted her up in his arms as she was coming back to consciousness she put her arms around his neck, and whispered I dreamed about you, I knew you would come for me.

Little Daniel was standing with Miriam, He looked at Nubia in disbelief rubbing his eyes in case he wasn't seeing right then screamed at the top of his voice, Sister Sister here I am and ran forward to Nubia and Kinta, Nubia saw him and ran towards him falling into each other's arms they hugged each other kissed and cried and held on to each other, a great sigh went up as the People witnessed this scene of a Sister and Brother reunited, Mary brushed tears from her eyes She knew little Daniel had to leave her and She was sorrowful for that but also so happy for Daniel and Nubians reunion, Jesus smiled at her knowing what her and His heart felt.

Rafael turned to look at Harrod, and the purse, Harrod gestured to one of his Priests, bring me some gold he instructed, But Sir I only have a few coins with me, Harrod commanded all the priests Holy Men VIP Guests to contribute, being scared out of their wits obliged, willingly handing over gold coins, bracelets rings anything they had on them being valuable.

The collection was more than enough however Rafael noticed the jewels adorning Harrod and Heronia from your own wealth give them also, Heronia reluctantly gave over her jewels, Herod seemed glad to hand his over, gushing with yes yes of course, here they are take them with my blessing.

And, you must sign this partition which gives freedom to Nubia Kinta and Kunti for all time, and that a tithe be given with freedom of slaves on the death of their said original owners, Slaves cannot be passed on as a bequest on Death. let no man overturn this judgement made in the presence of Maduk.

The collection was done documents signed and placed into bags the Donkeys use to carry heavy loads, Kinta placed these on the back of Kunti, Rafael leaned over to whisper something in Kinta's ear and He nodded in reply, People moved away to make a road through the sea of bodies everyone silently watching the little Family walk away.

No one issued a sound as everyone now turned towards King Harrod and the three Angels as they appeared to bow to the King, in reality they were bowing in respect to Mary and Jesus who still stood in front of the Kings platform, In an instant they vanished as fast as they had arrived, everyone stood in absolute stunned silence not knowing how to react.

After a few moments, the chief priest of Maduk shouted Praise be to the King, sing hosanna to the King, the large throng of People obliged singing hosanna to the King as if their very existence depended on it.

The Kings platform moved now to the front to lead the procession back along the great mall towards the palace, King Harrod was visibly shaken his face was white with great beds of perspiration, Heronia and Salome looked stone faced, not a hint of a smile touched their faces, it was a great relief to be transported back to the palace, and the privacy of the royal chambers. Harrod and Herodos felt that they had been mugged by Maduk Angels, and in truth they were right.

And so, it came to pass that the people and Herod lived with those laws given on the evening of the Kings orientation, lessons of that night lived on in the hearts and minds of all the People that gave witness to the spectacle witnessed when Angels visited their celebrations.

The age-old practice of Animal or Human sacrifice was forever stopped, only the Jewish groups who did not recognise Madoc as the one true God when they knew that Yahweh or Jehovah was the only true God, and other cults carried on with the practice.

The excitement of the evening gave way too many parties the People sang drank and loved, the Children returned to them, the mood was very happy, celebrations carried on for seven nights.

After the Royal party was delivered back to the Palace, Jesus Mary and their party walked on back to their chambers'.

At first they walked slowly with dignity then faster until they ran laughing whooping with joy Mark and Miriam danced together skipping along with James, Look and Jude jumping into the air whirling around laughing, We do love it when a plan comes together, they burst into their rooms and there stood Nubia, Kinta, Kunti lying on the bed with Daniel.

Mother he cried and rushed into Marys arms he sobbed as He said I don't want to leave you, Mary held and soothed the Child It's alright Daniel don't take on so my Darling, you are reunited with your Sister, who will become your Mother as loving as only a Mother can be, You have a strong and Good Father in Kinta, he will look after you as his own Son, and the biggest kitten you could possibly want Daniel laugh at the silliness of Kunti being a kitten, as everyone else did, Nubia and Kinta moved forward and knelt in front of Jesus and Mary.

How can we ever thank you we know it is you who is Maduk, you gave us a miracle when everything was lost, you gave us hope, you reunited us as a family, you gave us so many blessings already and we had to say thank you before we left, although it doesn't seem enough just to say thank you, would you bless our union, this act of devotion to love for life before the one true living God would mean more to us than all the gold collected.

Jesus and Mary placed their hands on their heads and Jesus said will you promise to love, honour and care for each other and Daniel for the rest of your lives, the couple looked at each other smiled and said OH YES, then go with our blessing go out in the world and find your home, go with our love to hold you in testing times and remember us at your celebrations. light a candle and tell us of your life, ask us for help and help will be with you.

Mary was still holding Daniel, Mother it hurts my heart so much to leave you, I know darling it hurts mine to, but you have your Family they need you too, and you need them, it is your duty to look after them as they will you, Familly is very important and needs as much love as you have in your dear heart, so please don't cry my little Man, when you need me I will be there for you, you will feel me with you and gradually as your love grows for your Nubia and Kinta, you won't remember.

OH NO MOTHER I WILL NEVER EVER FORGET YOU. And neither will I most precious of Mothers, said Nubia, Maybe embraced both her Children, promise me that you will never again become separated look after each other, listen to Kinta, He will protect you and Kunti will protect you all, that is his mission, Mary talked as She gathered the clothes bought for Daniel placing them in the treasure bags she also gathered food, cold meets fruit and flat bread in case they got hungry on their journey, Nubia turned to Miriam dearest Sister how was I to know that you would help me make all my dreams come true, I came to you as a false friend wanting to use you to dishonour Mary and Jesus.

I am so ashamed can you ever forgive me, Mirium replied to err is human to forgive Devine, of course I had already forgiven you, you were never a false friend you did not betray them, isn't it strange how this has worked out today I stand a free woman, with the Husband of my dreams and return of my little birth, Mirium replied live with us a while and you will come to believe that strange and miracles are part of everyday life, the women laughed and embraced as Sisters.

Nubia turned to Jesus and Mary, I feel I must warn you Herod conspired with those so called Holy Men to Kill you on your journey to Babylon, when this did not happen He was very angry, He was trying to get something on you to discredit you, that is why I came to you through Miriam, I was supposed to listen in to your conversations and find any words that would prove you to be heretics.

He was going to publicly try you both and find you guilty, then he could put you to death, please be very careful now you are walking this earth there is great trouble and evil, I think that the Devil himself has taken over Harrod, when I said I had found nothing to condemn you He was beside himself with anger, his face was so contorted He looked like an evil devil, so he condemned me to die as a sacrifice.

James said its time to go friends, you must be out of the city and well on your journey before first light Herod is unpredictable, when he realises, He has just let valuable Slaves free, changing a legal ruling in favour of releasing slaves.

He just may change his mind and send his Soldiers after you, I will walk with you until you are out of the city, Mark said, I will go with you Miriam said I want to walk with you to. Jude and Luke agreed also to walk with them until they were sure of their safety outside of the City. Jesus asked Kinta if they would journey back to Africa, Kinta replied that he had not discussed it yet with Nubia and Daniel but felt that there was nothing for them there only bad memories, and their new life must start fresh, they had great hope for a wonderful future wherever they found their home.

The Friends set off, Mary and Jesus waved them away and watched them walk into the night. Mary was exhausted and went to bed, Jesus held Her in his arms and felt her sob, He understood that a loving Mother had let her Child go into the dark night and her heart had broken, She had to

IN THE BEGINNING

Show such unconditional love to let go, so that her Son would make his life good and Happy without her.

The morning came to soon, Mary and Jesus awoke with a start at pounding on the door, Jesus immediately got up and opened the door a centurion in full battle dress was standing in the doorway, King Herod wants to see you immediately we are your escort.

OK Jesus said, just wait a moment while I dress appropriately, where is Pontus Pilot, He is resting we were given instruction to bring only you.

Jesus dressed quickly and kissed Mary, I won't be long my Darling please try to rest, Mary was a little concerned She had that knowing feeling something wasn't quite right She told Jesus her concerns and said I must come with you, I could not bear to be alone when I know you will face the devil himself.

She quickly dressed, hand in hand they walked out of the room, the Centurion stated we were told to bring only you, Jesus replied my wife and I are one, we go together or not at all, the centurion conceded preferring to deliver them to Harrod as quickly as possible rather than involve himself in any argument.

King Harrod sat propped up in bed being attended to by the Doctors, Hello Mordechai Jesus said the young Doctor seemed nervous and preoccupied mixing some concoction in a mortar and pestle looked up at Jesus

Oh, oh it's you, Yes Mordechai I believe I am Me, quipped Jesus, this is the Doctor I was talking about said Mordechai to Harrod, He healed the garrison leader of a terrible wound.

Well thank you for coming to my aid, Harrods tone was sarcastic, I need your services as a Doctor replied Harrod I believe you heal people, Yes replied Jesus only when they ask us with humble reverence and true need will we heal them, Mary had moved towards Harrod and stood at the side of the bed, Please show Mary what ails you. What cried Harrod a mere Woman have you lost your mind Harrod screamed.

I need a Healer, what can this Woman do for me, Jesus replied She is a greater healer than I, she will attend you, but first I want you to be contrite, be as humble as your loyal servants and ask her gently to heal you.

Everyone gets out shouted Harrod. immediately everyone left the room, leaving Jesus and Mary alone with the King.

Harrod addressed Jesus more calmly I am sorry I shouted at you, I have many enemies who would kill me or take my throne if they could it's not easy being Harrod, He looked up at Mary and said in a quiet voice, My dear I would give you a whole fortune if you heal me, Mary replied I do not want your fortune, just your promise that you will keep to Maddux's laws given to you last night, and you say please and thank you, in our presence and to your servants who look after you so diligently.

If you give your word of honour that you will be fair and always show manners and gratitude for Maduk and your household, then I will heal you. Harrod stared at Mary, then he began to laugh is that it, so simple a task you give me? Yes, that is all I want replied Mary, then Please Mary and Jesus will you heal me, Yes Mary replied, first there is something we must take from you, their lives within you a diabolical an evil presence that must be cast out,

What cried Harrod, You act as if you do not know who I am, I am your King, Why do you displease me, how dare you insinuate that I am possessed, Jesus held out his hands and said be quiet and come out of him, Harrod started to writhe and shake he looked like He was having a fit He foamed at the mouth, and he started to wretch, sicking out of his mouth a horrendous creature.

Jesus and Mary stood fast facing the creature, who was shouting all kinds of obscenities, Jesus called upon an Angel Lucifer to come and claim the beast immediately a Black Angel appeared, He took hold of the creature and said what do you want me to do with it My Lord, Jesus replied take it to the black ooze where all its kind should dwell.

The Angel and creature instantly disappeared, Mary moved forward to Harrod who was starting to come around She placed her hand on his forehead and said gently be calm you are healed.

Jesus and Mary turned and started to walk to the door, their work was done for Harrod, as they walked through the door many people were waiting outside including Malachi the Doctor, Jesus turned to him go to Harrod, He needs to sleep he will be better when he wakes, Malichai bowed to Jesus and Mary thank you I believe I would have been put to death, you saved me, thank you He promptly left to attend Harrod followed by Harrods trusted Servants.

Jesus and Mary turned to leave again, excuse me a man approached them wringing his hands and obviously distressed, He was hovering about as if he wanted to say something to them, it was as if He just couldn't bring himself forward to address Jesus and Mary, Jesus saw him and said Is there something we can help you with.

The Man came forward and said, I am lord Chaffe chief accountant and advisor to the king, I have a very difficult problem my Wife Simone is very sick I fear that any moment She will be taken from me would you please be so kind to see her, and God willing heal her, She is near death, I am willing to pay any amount you ask, if you would help us.

Nothing has helped her, She started experiencing terrible headaches took to her bed, She has remained bed ridden for six months, She is growing very week I don't know how to help her, I am a very rich Man, I will pay you anything you ask if you would come to my Rooms and heal her, Mary said take us to Her We don't want your money.

Lord Chaffe led the way, their rooms were beautiful, decorated in gold and white, He led them into a bedroom that was very dark, Simone He spoke softly are you alright, I have brought the couple who has healed Harrod.

A week voice replied, Yes dear I am here, Jesus suggested that they open the heavy drapes that blocked out the sunlight, Lord Chaffe was reluctant, Simone called out No please don't let the light in, my eyes can't stand the light, I am in terrible pain, Mary was at her side by the bed it's alright Simone Mary said taking her hand, you will feel better in a few moments, Mary placed her hands on Simones head, Immediately She felt a large tumour in her brain.

She could also feel that a Cancer had taken over her body, Mary turned to Jesus Darling please come over here I have need of you to send out these diabolical, Jesus commanded come out of this Woman, Simone fainted, then from out of her mouth, ears, nose everywhere on her poor body came what looked like black smoke, It rose towards the ceiling it sounded like many voices talking all at once we are legion we are many, who dares call us forth.

I do replied Jesus in a loud commanding tone, and as quick as a flash they shot out through the open windows, Mary placed her hands again on Simones head, She was not moving or breathing, Lord Chaffe was beside himself oh no She is dead, what have you done to her, Jesus said Sir, let Mary continue, your wife will be well after She heals her, let her get on with the task, the poor man was grief stricken sank to the floor and wept for he loved his wife above everything, and said I cannot live without her.

Suddenly Simone gave a big breath and sat bolt upright, She grabbed Marys hand Thank you you have delivered me from the very brink of death She kissed Marys hand, Her husband had gained his composure, ran to Simone he wrapped her in his arms, I am so happy your back with me my dearest darling I thought for a moment I had lost you.

Jesus and Mary stood holding hands patiently waiting until they could address them, Chaffe calmed down and turned towards them, How can I ever repay you, first let in the light and open your heart Simone is chosen to now be able to heal others as we have healed her, how She wishes to do this is up to her, others who are in pain and ill will seek her out, She is destined to be one of the living Gods chosen disciples, Will you except your destiny with free will Jesus said.

Simone held out her hands to both of them, with all my heart I will follow you until the end of days, Jesus and Mary sat on either side of the bed still holding Simones hands as if She did not want to let them go, If you except, then we have much to tell you about, the origins of Man and why we have come to walk this earth, Jesus told Simone and Chaffe the teachings.

He had already given to the other disciples; they spend the rest of the day with them answering Their questions and talking together.

It was early evening when they left their new Friends, Chaffe walked them to the doors of their apartments, as He left them, He whispered quietly looking around to check that no one was listening.

He said Jesus be mindful of Mary, I have overheard talks that the Cesar himself wants her for himself, Harrod hoped to gain favour with the Cesar by having you killed and sending Mary to be his concubine.

We will be leaving Babylon tomorrow for our palace at Galilee you would be very welcome to us, we would be honoured if you would stay with us, Jesús replied thank you We would love to come and visit you, We will do just that soon, for now we must return to Jerusalem We have work to do for a dear Friend, Chaffe hugged Mary thank you so much, He turned and bowed to Jesus and left them.

Jesus and Mary walked back towards their rooms, holding hands as always, their Friends were already waiting for them with Ruth and Emily,

We are so happy to see you, we became a bit worried about you, being with King Harrod, we are so relieved cried Miriam, why are you worried Jesus says, if you possess great faith and the knowledge you know to be true in your lives, simply trust God and all will be well with you.

So, my Dear Friends what has happened with you.

Ruth started with her story first, telling them how She bumped into her intended and his commanding officer after the procession ended, she told them about her plans to buy a horse breeding farm with her husband.

Her happiness would be complete if Mary and Jesus would bless their union and attend their wedding, Emily cried that would be a double wedding because the Commanding Officer asked Her to marry him, they would be travelling to Crete His ancestral home in a few days, we would be thrilled if Mary and Jesus would merry and bless them before they travelled.

Mary exclaimed of course we will be happy to bless you both and your partners, however if we are going to have a celebration Party for both of you, we must do this within the next two days because we will have to leave for Jerusalem.

At that moment Pontus arrived and added, I am leaving for Jerusalem this afternoon and came to ask you to accompany me, I am getting a little worried about Solitous She is very near to giving Birth to our Child.

Jesus replied don't worry we will be with you in a few days She will be well until then, we have time to marry off our Daughters and Sons, Pontus looked sadly disappointed and as he turned to walk away added, then please come directly to our summer palace at Bethesda, Tibur Drusus is to accompany you.

His instructions are to deliver you both safely back with us Oh yes there is something else whatever did you do to King Harrod, He keeps hugging Servants and thanking them, Heronas thinks He has become possessed and has locked herself away in her private apartments, demanding that Chaff take her with them to the Palace at Galilee

Harrod was dancing singing and appears in the best of moods, He says He wants to be a kind and humble King from now on, it remains to be seen how long He can keep this up, so hurry back to us as soon as you can. I bid you farewell my Friends.

As Jesus and Mary said goodbye to Pontus, promising to be with Him and Solitous in a few days, they turned towards their entourage who immediately burst in to roicherouse laughter, with Jesus and Mary joining in with comments like Well I believe that went well, on calming down Jesus stated lets now plan the ceremonies of marriage and blessings for our friends, this must happen tomorrow because we must be with Pontus and Solitous when their Child is born.

The rest of the day was taken up with arrangements for the double blessing, which turned out to be one of the best Weddings possible, born out of such short notice, the brides looked beautiful in white silk adorned at their heads with garlands of fresh flowers.

The grooms being military Men were given a garrison of armed guards forming a column by which the wedding procession passed through, the Grooms looked very handsome in their dressage, They had decided to marry at the very place of Maduk in ordination of Harrod which seemed for everyone attending a fitting place.

Walking behind the Brides acting as ladies in waiting were the beautiful six white horses, Ruth and Emily walked together, hand in hand and looked very happy with beaming smiles, as they walked to join their husbands at the front of the wedding party, Jesus and Mary stood together waiting the Brides arrival.

Jesus spoke first, everyone in attendance became hushed as they listened and bore witness to the wedding blessing, do you Ruth and Emily promise to love honour and take care of the needs of your life partners in sickness and in health, honouring Him with your Body and honour His until Death, We Do, Mary then turned to the Grooms Gaius Plinius Secundus and Marcus Flavorous, do you both promise to love honour and Keep Her in sickness and health as long as you both live, Do you also promise to live as equals until death, honour their bodies and your own as long as you both shall live, Protect and keep her happy, never beat her or abuse her in any way, We Do.

The promises you make today is binding on earth and in the celestial realm, let no Man or Woman put asunder in the name of God, we bless you and your union and especially your Children to come. Jesus then pronounced them Man and Wife to live as one.

A great party was scheduled immediately after the blessing, some of the acrobats and musicians were to provide the entertainment, It proved to be a great day with much dancing singing and feasting, there were only a couple of constraints one being the head priest of Maduk who felt He should have affiliated and legally bound the brides to their husbands as the age old tradition commanded.

It was only the interference of Tibur Drusus who pointed his sword at the priest and stated that this was a Roman wedding and the priest of Maduk had no duristiction. The.

The priest informed them that the ground was Maduk, and as he was ordained as Maduk representative, He deemed they must pay for its use; However, He quickly changed his mind on feeling Tibur's dagger at his nose.

The second was when the owners of the street tavern who were hired to provide the wedding banquet, informed the couples that there was no more wine, Jesus being merry making and enjoying the celebrations told them to fill the wine pitchers with water, and then pour the water into the drinking vessals, they did as instructed, became dumfounded when the purist delicious wine poured out.

Jesus had turned water into wine he wanted this day to be very special, and it was, for everyone who attended which turned out to be many hundreds of People as more and more became enticed in by the noise of Happy celebrations, everyone was invited in who wished to join the happy couples blessed Day.

The revelling went on through the night, It was early morning when Mary said She was feeling tired and had to go to bed, as they started to move to leave, Ruth and Emily came to them, they hugged them and said you have made this miracle happen how could we ever thank you for all the joy you have given us.

Mary said just be happy and blessed, When your first Child is born and your last child tell them you met the living God when life was truly bountiful and happy, tell them everything we have shown you, above all show them unconditional love, You are the truest disciples as is your Husbands, they are taxed with watching over you keeping you safe, You will find in time that you also possess the ability to see and feel the future, heal the sick and weary, understand other tongues, and be able to preach the word of God remember the lessens well, your Children will grow and spread throughout the world, that is our legacy to you.

Emily said I cannot find the words to thank you again and again, but my dearest Mary I and my dear Husband are no longer young, I believe I could never bear a Child at this late stage, Mary smiled and gave her a heartfelt hug, My dearest Emily You can and will bear Children, your body has healed of any reason you could not conceive, but Mary I have had many Men when I tell my Husband I fear he will not love me anymore and reject me.

CHAPTER 6

Mary said, Emily don't tell him, that was an unhappy past life you have been forgiven by God you are as pure of heart as any virgin Bride, today is the start of your life with your Husband, do not talk of the past, only your future is important not your past, If God has forgiven you why can you not forgive yourself, because you have done no wrong, Mary held her hands on Emily's head blessing her now, go in peace and love forevermore Amen.

Jesus approached them, sorry to break you two up, but Tiber Drusus is waiting impatiently to accompany us back to Jerusalem, I think it's time to go I fear we are needed there, Yes Darling, Mary took Jesuses hand and walked towards Tibur Drusus who was holding the rains to their Horses.

The rest of their entourage were already sitting on their Horses ready for the long journey to Jerusalem Ruth kissed them farewell, told them that these Horses are yours, I am giving them to you as you gave them to me, I wish you a good and speedy journey, Before giving them to you I ask them who would like to accompany you on a very important journey, these Horses came forward and I could understand them, especially this beautiful white lady who wished with all her heart to become Marys own Horse, She loved you so much that She said She would give her life to protect you on this and other journeys, So I granted her wish and She is very happy to lead you to Jerusalem,

Likewise this beautiful black stallion requested He be your mount Jesus, and as no other Man has been able to mount him, because of his hate and distrust of them, I believe him when he told me he would only ever allow Jesus to mount him, He will only ever serve him, thereby I believe him to be devoted to you as we all are.

These beautiful Animals Love you as we do and will serve you all their days if you will except them.

Thank you, Ruth, Jesus and Mary, said, turning to their New companions, each Horse moved forward and offered bowed heads to them, Marys whispered something into Her Horses ear, and Jesus did the same with his stallion, everyone bore witness to the horses whinnying acceptance and obvious Joy, they held still why Mary and Jesus mounted and set off at a slow canter towards Jerusalem.

They moved at a fast pace, Mary scarcely remembered how tired She felt as they witnessed the start of a beautiful day. they were not held back because of the early start they were spared the usual crowds waiting for them on route, the day passed quickly with many miles behind them, they rode without stopping, until Tibur suggested that they rest for the evening as his Men were showing tiredness, Jesus said yes of course Tibur.

Mary must be exhausted, we must stop at the next crossroads where refreshments will be waiting, sure enough a few hundred yards along the road brought them to travelling tents that seemed to be waiting for them, a few men and Women waited for them to unmount and the Women ran forward to take Mary into the first tent, the Men beckoned the Solders towards another tent where they were being served a stew and soft fresh bread. James Mark and Jude joined them

Jesus took his and Marys horses to water, thanking them for carrying them so diligently and stroking and petting them in turn, a Man approached them and bowing low to Jesus said do you want me to see to your horses Lord, the others are in a corral enjoying fresh grass and barley, yes thank you, please make sure they are well provided for, I will see you both in the morning.

He walked slowly towards the tent Mary and Miriam were so expertly spirited into, He suddenly felt very tired, He stood for a moment to look at the glorious night sky, then turned and walked into the tent, a hot stew awaited with the fresh loaf of bread Mary and Miriam sat waiting for him, as soon as they had eaten they fell back onto the cushions exhausted, sleep came immediately and neither moved until morning.

They arose at day break fully refreshed they ate a light breakfast, the Men and Horses were waiting for them mounted and ready to ride, Mary and Jesus took time to greet their Horses, mount with the aid of one of the Men who waited on them so well, they thanked them for the comfort they had provided and again set of at a slow canter with Tibur and his men following.

They made such great progress that they made the journey in two days, as they approached the Summer palace at Bethesda it was late evening, they were greeted by Solitouses Mother who appeared weeping saying to Mary oh thank God you are here Solitous is very ill.

Pontus is with her as is the Doctors, She collapsed yesterday and hasn't moved since, the Doctors want to take the child from her body as they fear She will be dead by morning, Please help her, Mary comforted the poor distraught Mother and bade her take them to Solitous.

She led them to Pontus and Solitous private rooms and there lying completely still they found her, Pontus was beside himself and clutched onto Jesuses arms sobbing.

Thank God you are here I was so afraid She would be gone before you came please help her, and if you can't then tell death to take me instead of her, so that my wife and Child may live.

Jesus held Pontus and said dear friend why would I not hold you in your hour of great need, do not worry everything will be good, Mary immediately ran to Solitous, Mary asked the Doctor attending to her tell me what happened.

I think She is already gone I tried to tell Pontus but he was in such a state I was afraid to tell him, I can't find any sign left that She is still with us, Mary held Solitouses hand, She is still with us although only just, She has a high fever her poor body has become septic Miriam tell the servants get a bath full of hot water, hot water and salt, after placing Solitous in the bath, Mary ordered everyone out of the room.

Including Pontus and Jesus, the next hours were taken up with Mary and Miriam working to bring Solitous back, and delivering the baby, Mary skilfully brought the baby out of Solitouses body a beautiful Boy large and perfect, then Mary saw movement in the poor mother's body quickly realising that there was another Baby a much smaller and rather sickly-looking Girl. TWINS shouted Miriam.

Miriam and a wet nurse attended the babies while Mary worked on healing Solitous immediately as the baby girl was born Solitous started to haemorrhage blood, it came fast and without warning turning the bath water into a fierce red, Mary worked diligently with her hands on Solitouses body.

Then She opened her eyes, Mary I am so happy you came I need you to help me to birth my Child I am afraid I can't do it without you, Mary replied don't worry my dear friend your babies are alright and have been delivered safely.

Mary instructed the servants to lift their mistress out of the water, then to bring the babies to their mother, Solitous was crying tears of happiness as she held her twins, Mary and Miriam took time to wash all three, then instructed Solitous in putting the babies to her breast, they suckled immediately Mary praised Solitous at what a Wonderful mother she was, We will get you ready to receive your Husband.

Pontus was walking around wringing his hands, muttering incoherent prayers Solitouses Mother was sobbing, the Doctor was trying to comfort Her as best he could, knowing as he did that Solitous had already passed, Jesus said come and sit down Pontus, your Wife and Child are in the best of hands, hours passed then Miriam approached them, Sir your Wife has delivered your Son and Daughter, She is ready for you to meet your Family, Pontus and Solitouses Mother ran into the rooms, everyone was sobbing especially Pontus, He held his Son while Solitouses Mother held the beautiful little Girl, Tears became euphoric laughter and Joy, Pontus held His Wife telling her that She had made him the happiest Man on earth, and He loved her even more, He marvelled at her great beauty and looking so well after giving birth to the Twins.

Jesus and Mary held hands and watched the Family come together, they shared their Joy and felt the Love in the room, Jesus spoke to Mary My darling you have made this happen, she replied We have made this wonderful scene possible, they believed in us, Loved us as part of their own Family, they deserve this happy beginning above everything, isn't it wonderful that We are witnessing the joy in birth of this Family, and we are going to be blessed with our own Child, Jesus kissed her tenderly.

Solitous called to Mary as She said I am so blessed to have the best midwifes in Mary and Miriam, I don't remember anything about giving birth, the last moment I remember was feeling a little light headed and then nothing until Mary called me back.

IN THE BEGINNING

Pontus said what do you mean called you back from where, I really don't know, she said it was as if I was in a dark place, then Mary was there, taking my hand, and then I awoke feeling better.

Then She tells me that I am delivered of two Children, I am so blessed my heart is so full of love for our Children, Thank you Mary, Jesus and Miriam, I really think that I could not have done it without you, I would like to name our Daughter Mary Miriam Solitous Pilot and our Son of course after his father Pontus Jesus Pilot, is that all right with you my dearest Husband yes my Darling I suppose it is laughed Pontus Pilot, err well, you do know that Jesus is a Hebrew name my dear, it may not go well with Rome or Cesar, alright then said Solitous, determined to have her way, how about Pontus Tiberius Jesus Pilot, Yes my dear I believe that would be acceptable replied Pontus.

Over the coming months the Babies grew into strong little children full of mischief and fun, everyone loved them even the Servants smiled as they attended them, they loved their Parents and Mary Miriam and Jesus.

As Mary was expecting her baby it was decided that they would stay with Pontus and Solitous at the Jerusalem palace where Mary would be looked after in comfort and Jesus could go about the public and preach the way to live with the 7 levels of spiritual enlightenment, He would not attend the synagogue, even though the Elders sent many requests.

Pontus tried to persuade Jesus to go to the synagogue as he felt it was dangerous to antagonise the Pharisees, Jesus would only say I am not in those large cold buildings, I have nothing or anyone to answer to.

Nevertheless the Synagogues were not doing well, droves of people had left the Faith and way of life preferring to spend the Saturday holy day following Jesus and his Disciples listening to him preach, Time travelled onward, it was at such a meeting of the faithful to God, that proceedings were interrupted by a servant of Pontus who ran forward to Jesus much out of breath to say that Mary needed him, Jesus and disciples ran quickly back to the palace.

Mary was in the last stages of delivering her Child the most painful part of the process of giving birth Miriam and Solitous were at her side when Jesus burst into the room.

He went immediately to her side Darling why did you not ask me to stay with you today, I thought I would be able to handle it myself, my darling help me Mary pleaded, the pain has become unbearable, Jesus took her hands in his you will feel no pain now we are together.

The babies came very quickly after Jesus took her hand, Miriam attended the Babies in turn, saying with great glee Oh they are so beautiful, as she looked up, she saw Jesus looking very pail with beads of sweat on his forehead.

Mary also saw the pallor, and distressed look on Jesuses face, My dearest, Mary cried are you alright because you were right I didn't feel any pain when you took my hand, I know darling I took the pain from you and put it on myself, it's a pity all Men can't feel birth as I have, how wonderful and brave you Women are.

I think I will be alright in a moment, the pains have gone now, let's introduce ourselves to our Girls, Yes Miriam declared two of the most beautiful Girls, Jesus held the twins one on each arm, He began to weep, Miriam stood in shock She had never seen Him weep before, Mary held her arms open Jesus and their Children fell into those loving Arms, and they shared the tears and overwhelming Joy together.

Later Mary asked him, what made you weep when you held the Girls, He replied it was the overwhelming love He felt for them, He now understood for the first time how overpowering that feeling of unconditional love a parent has for a child.

All he could think of was am I worthy of feeling such great emotion, such fabulous Love and protection, He experienced a light going on in his mind and he wanted to protect them and be an exceptional Father and husband, He understood complex human feelings it overwhelmed him and he wept.

They named their Daughters Star and Moon, under the loving and watchful eyes of their Parents and loving Aunty Miriam, they brought great love and pleasure to everyone who was lucky enough to meet them, They looked very different from the other children having blond hair and large blue eyes, their beauty astonished People, before long the world knew of their beauty even the house of the Cesar Tiberius learned of them, Pontus expressed concern to Jesus that he had received messages directly from Tiberius himself enquiring about them, and sending his regards to Jesus and Mary inviting them all to visit him as his esteemed guests.

Jesus asked Pontus to make their apologies as they would not be able to journey it would be too strenuous at the present time, Pontus did as he bade him but expressed his fears to Jesus, Tiberius was a force to be reckoned with when he appeared to be reaching out in friendship he was at his most deadly, he would not be repeatedly refused and at some time in the future he will demand both their presences in Rome, then it would be impossible to refuse him, Pontus pointed out that Tiberius would have many spies reporting back to him on all aspects of his Families lives.

Jesus understood that their presence in Pontus pilot's palace could be putting his dearest friend and his Family in danger, so he put it to Pontus that he felt it would be a clever idea for Jesus and Family to move out of the palace into suitable lodgings, Pontus reluctantly agreed as Jesus pointed out that it would be very difficult and emberacing for Pontus to remain in his protection in the future.

Pontus sadly agreed and told Jesus that he would set about immediately finding a suitable home near enough to them so that He, Solitous, Children and rest of his family could visit them whenever they wished, He expressed his sorrow at missing them all and that his cheerful home would feel very empty without them.

In the next day's Pontus found a perfect home, a beautiful villa near the gardens of gethsemane still within Jerusalem walls, the Roman owners were leaving for Rome, however the villa was also home for a wealthy merchant Joseph of Arimathea, He owned most of the Ships used to transport goods from the silk road, spices and colourful material from India.

He was a wealthy and well-known celebrity, when he was in Jerusalem he always enjoyed living in his splendid apartments at the villa. The owners asked Jesus and Mary if they would allow Joseph to keep his apartments, if they agreed, they would happily let the Family stay there.

Jesus immediately agreed, within a week they had moved into the villa, it was the first time Jesus Mary and company had seen the villa, they were pleasantly amazed, it was the most lovely home richly decorated with painted freezes, the most beautiful rooms, overlooked the inner quad with a swimming pool with flowing water and fountain, the Children loved playing in it, they all enjoyed swimming in the cool water, the villa was fortunately situated over a well of spring water which was also pump up to the kitchens and bathhouses, this was a modern happy home Mary and Miriam were delighted, as were James, Luke, Jude and Mark, Jesus watched his Family Happy laughing content faces, and he was filled with love for all of them.

Joseph of Arimathea arrived as they were enjoying a family meal, He approached them a little awkwardly as he did not know what to expect from this new family, he had no need to fear, Mary immediately got to her feet and greeted him like a long-lost Brother, Jesus bade him to enter and enjoy the meal with them, they made him feel completely at home.

Jesus and all his household received an invitation to attend the wedding of Tibur Drusus and Sevilla Maximillian's wedding was to take place in Pompei, which was the home of His Brides Family, it was also the Port of Rome, handling the distribution of goods coming from Egypt, Indian spices, silk roads and Jerusalem.

Pompei was a metropolitan city, it was full and colourful, the popular place for Romans to enjoy the seaside and indulge themselves, with a multi-cultural population. Jesus and Mary were discussing the invitation with the whole household when Joseph joined them, just in time, to hear Miriam say it's too far away, how will we get to Pompei with everyone, it will take weeks of traveling to get there.

Joseph interrupted, there is a way you could get there and back within a few days. And how's that going to happen retorted Miriam, Mary smiled her knowing smile as she turned to Joseph, by sea our Joseph has Ships, I certainly do my dear Lady.

I came to tell you I am going to Pompei myself leaving tomorrow, I would love you all to be my guests on board, it may be a bit cramp but my ship will get you there without effort, when is this wedding, Jesus said in five days, Plenty of time said Joseph, if the weather is good we should arrive in three days.

I have a house, so there would be no problem in finding somewhere to stay. Mary turned to Jesus shall we go, Tibur Drusus is our most loyal and good Son, Jesus spoke yes, we must, I think Tibur had need of us.

Before daybreak they assembled at the dock, Joseph escorted them to one of his merchant Ships, the mariners on board were getting ready the Sails, as the light dawned on a new day they set off on yet another adventure, the going was good they made good time. They made the crossing without incident and they were joined by a school of Dolphins who delighted everyone by jumping out of the water and swimming at the bow playing a game by quickly moving from side to side of the ship.

Miriam hadn't forgotten to bring with her the food bag, that never ran out of food, so everyone including the mariners ate well, they arrived in Pompei with a day to spare, they were glad to get off the boat some had felt very sea sick, nevertheless they were all were in good spirits.

Mary Miriam and Children went to Josephs house, Jesus and the other Men collected the gifts and went loaded to find the wedding venue, and Tibur Drusus.

They didn't have to search far, Jesus seemed to know exactly where he was going, the others followed looking around them astonished, at the goings on in this city of many colours, before long they came upon a courtyard that was dressed up in garlands of flowers.

Jesus stated this is it, Tibur Drusus was talking to one of the servants, as soon as he saw them he practically bounded over to them throwing his arms around Jesus, Lord you came, he cried you came for me, I didn't think you would come, I didn't think the letter would arrive on time, I am so happy to see you, but what of Mary, Jesus replied She is well Tibur and here also.

As if this day could not get any better than this, I am to see the whole Family, just as he finished the sentence a Man approached them, he said what's this Tibur, you told us that you had no Family.

Tibur replied that he had stated that he had no Family who would be coming to the wedding, Jesus interrupted what Tibur! you didn't tell them about your Father, Mother Sisters, Aunties Uncles that are all here waiting to look upon your lovely Bride and wish you well.

Tibur just stood there and all he could utter was ERRRR, No matter, Jesus beckoned with his hand, he turned to the Man and said Mr Maximillia's Its so good to meet you at long last, He said shaking his hand, Oh yes? well he replied? what is your Family Name, Jesus replied Jesus and Mary Drusus Father and Mother of our wonderful Son Tibur Druses.

Maximus replied Jesus! is that not a Jewish name, immediately turning angrily on Tibur you didn't tell us you are Jewish, if this is true, I would never have agreed to this marriage, Jesus said we are not Jewish.

Then what deity do you worship, NON, Jesus replied and don't assume anything, it's very insulting when all we have come for is to bear witness to our brave sons marage, bringing gifts of gold and silks for the happy couple, and the Bride's Family.

Jesus appeared to lose patience with him raising his voice to match the Mans in volume, what if my name was Camelsarse Drusus would you seriously take the same offence, how dare you assume so much on my name.

How would your other guests view your standing, at the way you have received you proposed Son in Laws Family, is this the way you treat your Son in Law with prejudice and intimidation, is He an unwelcome addition to your large and greedy Family, Is it a shock to you to realise that your future Son in laws Family have more riches and connections than you, the whole room fell silent as they contemplated the reply.

Mr Maximillia was clearly in shock He appeared to stagger. Tibur rushed to take his arm and help him to sit down, giving him a cup of water, He sat for a few moments sipping the water and in deep thought after a few moments he regained his composure.

I am very sorry Tibur your Father speaks great truth, I ask humbly for forgiveness, they will be welcomed into our Family, I admit I did not want you to marry Savillaone I had what I thought much better propositions, it was only because Sevilla threw many tantrums, refused food, behaved in ways that was not her nature, whenever I had set up meetings with possible suitors, It was Cesar Tiberius that forced my decision, when you received your diploma and discharge.

I was directed by the Cesar himself to allow you to Marry my Daughter, I was unhappy with her choice until today, I believed that you had no good Family, that you were worthless, I am sorry I have given you such a hard time, I can only add that today I am a very Happy man that you have chosen my Daughter, and from now on, will prove to you that I have excepted you as my Son, as I sincerely hope your Father will except our precious Daughter into your Family.

Jesus I am made humble before you, would you please forgive a stupid old Man, Jesus held his gaze looked into the Man's eyes and very soul, shall we start again Jesus said, wonderful to meet you Mr Maximillia.

Maximillia left them as he stated that he had some business to attend to, as soon as he was out of ear shot Tibur turned to Jesus and said shrugging his shoulders, what just happened? Everyone started laughing, the servants took the gifts.

Tibur instructed them that provision to be made for his Family, Tibur took Jesus to one side dearest Father how did you know I was having difficulty fitting in to the Maximillia Family, they have repeatedly cancelled the dates for our Marriage, I was waiting for them to cancel any minute, we only arranged this day because Sevilla had one of her wonderful screaming fits, She always knows how to get her own way, She is so funny, you must meet her.

She is the most beautiful Girl in the world and very clever, I prayed that you would come as I knew you would know what to do, and here you are, its unbelievable, you and Mary taking me as your Son, I couldn't be more happy.

The wedding was a wonderful affair Sevilla virtually screamed with joy when she saw the silk it was of such quality, She wanted to wear a gown made out of it for her wedding, unfortunately as this was the eve of the wedding there wasn't enough time, however She was so taken by the beauty of the twins insisted that Tibur's little sisters walk in front of her as flower girls.

In the morning of the wedding Sevilla woke, as her eyes gained focus, saw before her the most beautiful silk garment She had ever seen, it was complete with beautiful head dress and the softest shoes.

She shouted to her entourage waking everyone, they came dashing to her room, everyone expressed shock and amazement at where it came from, only last night it was a whole realm of silk, this morning it turned into a fabulous gown, no one owned up to making it, it fitted perfectly She was so happy, Mary and Miriam glanced at each other and smiled a knowing smile, Mary embraced Sevilla welcome to the Family Sevilla.

The wedding went ahead smoothly, the party was unforgettable for everyone attending, new friendships and Family, found and formed, everyone was sad it ended, however everyone commented at how much love the young couple had for each other, Jesus and Mary blessed them both with kisses and told them that they must come and visit soon as good Parents do, with sad goodbyes they set off back to Jerusalem.

Over the next five years, Jesus preached, healed the sick, and answered questions through debate Joseph was amazed at the amount of people that came to the villa, Rich and poor seeking enlightenment and resolution, Joseph asked if he could join the debates over time He became one of Jesuses closest friends and disciple.

On one of many private conversations Joseph confessed to Jesus that He would never be happy despite the riches he possessed and the high standing he enjoyed that his dark moods were the result of losing his wife and Baby as She gave birth.

He was away on trade business when it happened, he blamed himself for not getting back on time to help her, this happened in the house they stayed in in Pompei and that is why he preferred to stay in the Villa, and why he was unmarried.

it was a painful reminder every time he visited Pompei, he felt haunted by the memories and great sadness, He hoped He didn't show it when they stayed there, and he confessed that seeing the little Girls run around and play always brought him to sobbing alone in his room.

He knew he wouldn't find anyone who loved him like his dear Felicity, so He wasn't interested in looking, Jesus pointed out to Joseph that he will never get over this terrible loss until he forgave himself, even though it wasn't his fault it happened, he asked Joseph how was your Wife before you left on the business trip.

Joseph replied She was radiant very happy so pleased to be having their child, So that's what you gave her, concentrate on that every time you feel the sad blackness of your depression and one day you will understand there are worse things in this life than death, She felt great, passion, unconditional love and belonging, what is worse, is never feeling that in life, that really is worse than Death.

Joseph had many conversations with Jesus, still, this did help Him, he could not get the pain of grief in control, He couldn't let go of the past and therefore could see no future.

Mary suggested that he try walking, not to go anywhere just for pleasure around the hills of Jerusalem, so that is precisely what he did, he came to enjoy his private walks, it was when he was on such a walk that he fell upon a situation.

A horse had bolted with its rider screaming for help, the offending Animal became even more spooked when Joseph appeared right in front of it stopping dead and rearing in fear.

The poor animal became lost in flight frenzy, set off again at full gallop the poor rider clinging on in terror, they let go of the rains and fell into a ravine, the Horse galloped on, Joseph ran as fast as he could to help the rider, climbing down the ravine he realised that the rider had become lodged on a ledge just a few feet away.

He could reach them, Joseph was a strong Man but it took all his strength to reach the casualty who was obviously seriously injured and unconscious, on reaching the casualty he realised that it was a young woman, Josephs protective instinct came on in full steam, He gingerly climbed onto the ledge bending over the casualty listening if her heart was still pumping and realising it was, drew his attention to her face which was swollen and bloody on the left side, He looked at her head which had a large gash he ripped his tabard to form a bandage which he applied to the wound to stop it bleeding.

She had started to moan and Joseph hoped that She was returning to consciousness, He held her in his arms and noticed for the first time her face, She had a lovely a face perfect but for the blood, She was beautiful, with dark hair a smooth complexion perfect features, as he sat studying her face he heard shouts coming from above, he was just about to start shouting back to get help, when he overheard what the voices were saying, CAN YOU SEE HER, ILL KILL HER IF MY HORSE IS INJURED, BLOODY NO GOOD BITCH.

Joseph froze as the shouting ran past and into the distance, he looked down at what looked to him the picture of innocence, He noticed that She had no shoes, her feet were bloody and her wrists were tied, there appeared to be more to her story than a runaway Horse, it was getting late, night tends to fall fast, within a few moments it was pitch dark, Joseph gently undid her bonds and was taken back when he saw the deep welts where the rope had dug into her skin, Poor Poor girl he caught himself saying.

I have to get her home to Mary she and Miriam would be able to help her, he checked that the coast was clear, then picked the Girl up, was surprised at how light she was, it was easy to Put her over His shoulder and climb out of the ravine, He knew he was only about a mile from home, but it was hard going carrying the girl. He was nearly home when he heard running footsteps behind him, quickly He dived into the ditch at the side of the road just in time as several Men ran past still shouting ARE YOU SURE SHE CAME THIS WAY ONE MAN SHOUTED, NO IM NOT BLOODY WELL SURE, LETS GO BACK THE OTHER WAY AGAIN, I SWEAR IM GOING TO SLIT HER THROAT, STUCK UP LITTLE WHORE.

The three Men stopped turned around and ran back along the track, unfortunately the young woman started to come round and Joseph had to put his hand over her mouth to keep her from screaming out, the poor Girl fainted back into unconsciousness, Joseph was frantic he thought he had killed her by smothering her cries, it was now imperative he got her to Jesus and Mary.

He picked the Girl up again, put her over his shoulder and ran full pelt towards Home and safety, Joseph was out of breath when he finally reached the doors of the villa quickly dashed inside and shouted for Mary and Jesus, everyone heard him and ran to help, joseph had just enough breath left to say HELP HER MARY, then passed out himself it had taken a superhuman effort to save the Girl, and Joseph was spent.

Joseph came round in Jesuses arms, well my Friend looks like you had an adventure, They both started to laugh then Joseph realised, got up with a start, Where is She, Jesus replied don't worry Joseph, Mary and Miriam are tending to her, I am tending to you my dear friend.

Oh thank God she is safe, Joseph told Jesus what had happened, as he finished his story Miriam came towards them, It was very lucky you got her here, the poor girl was badly beaten and she suffered a terrible blow to her head we have mended the outward wounds, but She is very traumatized, Mary says that She is so psychologically damaged that She doesn't think that She will recover fully, we have fixed the damage to her body, but the mind is a strange thing, She is awake but her mind is somewhere else She does not respond She is lying there staring at the ceiling, I have never seen such shock before, She must have endured something terrible, you Joseph are our Hero that saved her life, I only did what most people would do in the same circumstances replied Joseph.

Mary joined them and said, no Joseph most people would have ran away, you didn't, We are so proud of you Well done, however the task is not finished yet, She hasn't spoken a word we don't know her name, hopefully in the coming days she will wake from the coma what we need is someone willing to sit with her and talk until She wakes up, Joseph stated I will do that, I will camp in her room and be there when She decides to join us, I will not leave her alone.

Joseph was true to his word, He sat at her side for days talking reading sonnet's confiding in her in a way he had never been able to do with anyone, he would tell her how beautiful She is, that She had everything to live for, in a strange way supporting this Woman became healing for Him as well as Her.

Although She was a complete Stranger and he hadn't even heard her voice, He was developing a bond that was very strong, He hadn't felt the darkness depression come over him while He was with her, protecting Her, loving Her, After seven days She woke up with a start, NO NO PLEASE LEAVE ME ALONE SHE SCREEMED, Josef calmed her, talking softly and kindly, telling Her it was alright and She was safe, the poor Girl looked terrified.

Mary came to bring fresh food and water and check on their Guest, She saw the look on the Girls Face, immediately She was at the girls side stroking Her hair telling her She really was safe, no one would ever harm her, Mary held her in her arms as any mother would and wept with the poor Girl because She knew the trauma the poor girl had endured, Mary felt her pain.

After a little while, Mary wiped their tears and asked what is your name sweet child, the Girl looked puzzled for a moment and then said Joanna yes my name is Joanna, but I don't remember anything or how I came to be here, Mary said Not to worry about that for now, the memories will come back in time, you have our Dear Joseph to tell you how he saved your life, and brought you here, Do you wish to join us for breakfast or you may stay here if you wish.

No I would like to see the sun and breath fresh air I would love to join you for breakfast outside, Joseph will help you, you have been in this bed for over one week, so your balance will be off, lean on Joseph and come and meet the rest of the Family, Mary was right She did feel out of balance her legs seemed wobbly slow to respond, She leaned on Josef and gently and slowly He helped Her to walk, out of her room into the most beautiful atrium, fresh flowers were everywhere opening up into a most lovely bathing pool.

She was taken back when a beautiful black stallion trotted past them followed by an equally striking white Mare, OH don't mind them Joseph said, they always come to breakfast, they are Mary and Jesuses Horses, they are free to come and go as they please, they spend a lot of time grazing outside I think Breakfast is the best time for them, that's when they are closer to Mary and Jesus, they love them very much, as we all do, all the family sat at a large round table chatting and laughing.

Mark and James immediately jumped to their feet to make a place on the cushions for Joanna and Joseph, everyone introduced themselves, just before they were to give thanks for the abundant table, Jesus joined them, the two little Girls shouted Daddy launching themselves at him, he caught them both kissing them, turning them upside down saying has anyone seen Moon or Stars, Mary laughed at the antics, so did everyone else even Joanne smiled a little, Jesus settled the Children down and gave thanks to the universe for the table, and Joanna's deliverance, the chatter and light banter started again as everyone ate breakfast, Miriam was busy giving two large buckets of bran molasses and vegetables to the horses who were excitingly waiting their breakfast.

There you go beauties that will make your coat shine, then She settled down at the table for her breakfast. Are you feeling better Joanne, Miriam asked, Yes thank you, but I am very confused and can't remember anything?

Jesus said unfortunately you will, the memory will return, but for now concentrate on your Family, Parents, or are you married with Children, try to think of these things and that memory will come back to you, you have nothing to fear here we will protect you, until you can tell us who your family is so that we can return you to them.

Thank you for your kindness, I would like to sit in the garden and if you would be so kind Joseph, tell me how you found me, It would be an honour Joseph replied, Just then Solitous the children Her mother Sister and older boys arrived, a whole lot of chatter greetings laughter the Ladies took off the Berker they used as a disguise so that they would not be recognised on their daily walk, Luke and Jude had already started to set an area as a classroom.

Mary interrupted the Children who wanted to go immediately in the pool and start playing, No Darlings you must have your lessons first, all of you go with Luke and Jude, it is very important that you learn to read and write and count.

And learn music, OOOH Alright Mother, said Star come on Moony all the Children followed the little bossy ones, Joseph and Joanne walked towards the Gardens and sat at the side of the pool.

Joseph held her hand while he told her what had happened, When he finished She said She still could not remember anything, She felt very tired, Joseph suggested She lie back on to the cushions and have a nap, Yes alright She said but you won't leave me, Joseph promised that he would not leave her on her own but he needed to go to the toilet room, then I will come with you I need to know where it is myself, don't look so worried Joseph I don't want to go in with you, I will wait outside well there is a ladies only room, that may suit you better.

Thank you Joseph She said as they began their walk for everything you have done for me, you are truly a good friend, I have never felt so at ease with anyone as I do You, I think that I have never spoken so freely in my life to anyone, And your Family are adorable, He was about to say they are not my family when he stopped and said, yes they are all remarkable.

Joseph asked her how old do you think you are, twenty one she instantly replied, well She said in amazement don't know where that came from, but I must be right, how old are you Joseph ahh about twenty seven, and are you married, no are you, I really don't know for sure but I think not, hopefully your memory returns soon, joseph said and then everything will come clear to you, if not then you're going to be stuck with me I am afraid. that's not so bad replied Joanne, I am very content with the Man that saved my life, I can feel that you are a good Man Joseph of Amnethea.

They talked about everything that afternoon they were healing both their hearts and didn't know it, all they knew was how good each felt in their own company after the evening meal which was the same as breakfast lots of chatter, this meal lasted a long way into the evening where the children would sing and play games bedtime would be announced by Miriam.

The Girls saying, they were not tired, even though their eyes were closing, after kissing everyone goodnight twice, Miriam and Mary took the Girls to bed, Joanne excused herself saying she felt very tired, Joseph walked her to her room, said goodnight and for the first time in a week slept in his own bed.

However, at about three in the morning a blood curdling scream went up as if someone was being murdered. Joseph immediately shot out of bed his only thought was of Joanne, and sure enough that was the sauce of the mayhem, Jesus Jude Mark and James came running from all sides towards the heart rendering screams followed by Mary and Miriam, Joseph reached her first She was crouched up in the corner of the room screaming and sobbing I REMEMBER OH GOD I REMEMBER.

Her eyes were wide and full of terror, Mary went immediately to her and she fell into her arms sobbing, do you want to talk about it now Mary asked, No not now where is Joseph I am here don't leave me joseph, no I will never leave you alone I promise, Mary and Joseph lifted her on to her bed Jesus stepped forward and laid his hand gently on her head She immediately fell into a deep healing sleep, She will be alright now, I suggest we all go back to bed and in the morning we will hear her story.

Joseph stayed and held her hand whilst She slept, He stayed with her and was the first thing She saw when She awoke, goodmorning my friend She said smiling at joseph, have you stayed with me all night, yes you asked me not to leave you so I stayed.

Thank you now I am ready and fully remember, We will go to breakfast together and I am ready to tell everyone my story, they went to breakfast hand in hand as they approached the usual good humoured chatter stopped and all eyes were set on Joanne. Good morning, she said to everyone Jesus said come and sit here by myself and Mary I believe you have quite a story to tell.

Yes Joanne made herself comfortable on the cushions and began, to tell her story everyone was very quiet, I belong to a very wealthy Family who deal in diamonds precious stones and Amber, My Family have provided fabulous jewellery for a hundred years to wealthy people and Royalty from Spain France Italy and Gaul, Kings and Queens of every part of the world have commissioned my Fathers work, our Family home is in Assyria.

We lived in great splendour surrounded by fertile fields, rich harvest and happy people who are our servants, My Parents are good people they

IN THE BEGINNING

made a terrible mistake, they gave me in marriage to a truly evil man although they did not know this at the time.

I was 13 years old and although carried away by the attention, marriage day and all the gifts I gave my consent to the marriage, It was of my own free will, I did not know what horrible abuse awaited me, this Man was ten years my senior I came to hate him, his very touch made my skin crawl, and He stunk like a pig, He made me understand what a man wanted from his wife and was raped and brutalised daily.

He had a large household I was his second wife, His first wife had given him five Girl children, and had given her last, so I was expected to give up a son, his Mother ruled the household with an iron fist she would tell lies, say to her son was that I had answered her back, or refused to do something then my husband would beat me showing no mercy.

I was kept away from my Family, I had no support, If I could have got a message to them, they would have insisted on seeing me.

I fell pregnant but the baby miscarried at 7 months the pain was terrible to bear I wanted my Mother, they didn't even tell them I was pregnant, I wanted to die, I fell pregnant again and again miscarried, At 15 I did have a Son.

I thought he would now leave me alone, but he didn't he said he needed at least 2 sons, I felt that I could not bear another day with these awful people. All I felt was misery, pain and torment, my only reason to carry on was my Son who I loved so much, I gladly devoted my life to him, excepted the awful life I had, and carried on, I could never take my Son away He was my Husbands property as was I, until death.

Such was my, and babies fate, I prayed to god to help us but we were never heard, or so I believed, one day my husband was taken ill and died of his fever, secretly I was elated I thought this meant I could go home back to my loving Parents, His Mother informed us that we were now the property of her other son who was on his way to claim his birth right.

Then all the Children and my sister wife fell ill with same symptoms, They were dropping like flies, then I saw my Mother in law stirring something she kept cackling and mumbling, then she served up a soup for everyone Sister wife children my son and myself were all given a bowl of this broth to eat, I poured mine into the others bowls when no one was looking, then she took my son from me and started to feed him the broth.

I made some excuse that I felt a little sick and He needed his pants changing so I could whisk him away, She only objected a little, I ran out of the house into the temple, where I asked to see the elders on a very important matter. I told them I believed my Mother in law was Mad, poisoning her family, at first, they did not believe me, then they decided that some of the Men would go and look, they found everyone Dead, apart from my Manic mother in law who appeared possessed.

That night I left, taking my son with me, I was so happy to be going home with my son, I gave thanks for my deliverance as I walked, however my son appeared to get heavier and heavier it was very dark and believing my son to be asleep I lied down with him, cuddled up put my arms around him to keep him warm and fell fast asleep.

I was exhausted, I awoke at daybreak and called to my son come on sleepy head wake up, then panic took over me, He did not stare OH NO NOOOOO MY BABY MY BEAUTIFUL SON WAS DEAD. The old Hag had done her wicked deed on my only reason to live.

I picked him up and carried on, my heart broken I don't remember the walk but I kept going day and night until I was at home again, it must have been a terrible shock for my parents to be confronted with a distraught Daughter holding a dead two year old in her arms.

The next thing I remember was waking up in my old room in my soft comfortable bed with my Dear Mother and father at my side, I wept and wept and then my parents wept when I told them everything of my horrific life, and the child I would not let go of, was their Grandchild, they had already buried him in the family vault.

They promised me that they would never arrange another marriage for me ever again, and that I could live with them at home and help run the home with my mother, and so it was, I was beginning to live again, even though I spent a lot of time at the family crypt talking to my son, I was trying to find something good in every day, I surmised that if I could find one thing good then these days would eventually come together and my life would become bearable, if I had dreams aspiration and dared to hope.

I was now over 20, past the time when anyone would want to marry me, I praised God that no one would want to marry me ever again.

On this day I was walking in the gardens it was a beautiful day the birds were particularly happy chirping away I was picking fresh flowers, when I saw a group of riders with a coach and four horses coming up the drive, this was very unusual my brothers would ride up and wave to me I knew this was not them, something in my mind started to feel afraid.

I walked back towards the house and listened at the open window, I heard my brother shout OVER MY DEAD BODY WILL YOU TAKE HER, My Mother knew I was listening so said in a loud clear voice that She feared her daughter had become feebleminded over the deaths of the Family and especially over her Son, She was not the same gentle and loving Daughter, She had taken to screaming and attacking strangers carrying on so much that they had to tie her in bed for her own safety, Her mind was permanently damaged from the loss of her family and young Son, which your Mother in her madness had taken all from her.

My Father gave my Mother a strange inquisitive look, She raised her eyes to the window, He got it immediately, Yes he said it has been very difficult and sad time, we are saddened by the loss of your family, and ours, it must have been difficult to be told that your Mother was responsible and more so that She had been stoned to death for the crimes of genocide on her Family.

The Man then said yes I suppose it was, that has no bearing on the fact that your daughter is now my property, and I have come to take her as my second wife, I had also hoped to take my nephew but as you say he is dead then that is out of my hands, nevertheless I must see Joanne now.

Father spoke to James Joanne's Brother, would you go and get her, James looked at his parents with distain his mother seemed to wink her eye at him which he thought a bit odd but nevertheless he stormed out of the room in search of his sister, finding her at the front door he whispered quiet shhhh, your husbands brother has come to stake his claim on you.

He says you are to go with him, Joanne replied whispering Mother has told me what I must do I will play as I am in a deep state of shock, just bear with me go along with everything as if it were true, alright I will escort you into the room, James came back into the room holding Joanne by the arm.

She had purposely ruffled her hair so that She looked dishevelled, there you are Dear, Mother said, immediately Joanne started screaming and lunged at her Brother in law, Father distracted her just in time She was drooling and father said, are you not going to kiss our guest Joanne, She screamed like a banshee then kept looking upwards and shaking her hands and moaning as brother in law decided to make an exit.

Before he left he suggested that the family may want to compensate him for all the trouble he went to, to find Joanne, coming away empty handed was not his intention, so Father gave him some gold coins as long as he signed a parchment receding all hold he would have had making her a free woman, James drew up the document and both parties signed it, then he left them, they waited until he was at the bottom of the road and far away from the villa so that he didn't hear a single cheer go up at last they are free of these terrible evil people.

I was really starting to be happy again even celebrated my 21 birthday with my brothers and their families it felt wonderful to be home, and nothing would take me away again, how wrong I was, my past brother in law decided that my Family should compensate him further and sent a servant with a letter informing the family he would be taking Joanne after all. Father sent a letter back reminding him of the contract he signed and thought that we would hear no more from the greedy beggar.

Not so, a few weeks later I was taking my usual walk to the Family cript, when three men set upon me throwing a blanket over my head the bungled me into a closed carriage and set off at a fast pace I recognised my brother in laws voice and heard him say to the other criminal, did you leave the ransom note in plane site, another Man said of course I did.

Hey can I have a go at this he said, kicking Joanne, wrapped tightly in the blanket, be my guest I don't want her She is feebleminded you know, best put her out of her misery if you ask me, are you going to give her back when they pay the ransom, Ha Ha what do you think said the brother in law. Make sure the ropes are very tight on her, she goes off like a bucking bull, keep her covered, after hearing their conversations I was terrified.

I knew my Father and Brothers would look for me and would pay a ransom, I believed that they had no intention of giving me back to my Parents that they would kill me without a second thought, if I was going to get away it would have to be up to myself to make it happen, the movement of the carriage made me fall asleep, when I woke up the carriage had stopped I wriggled out of the blanket only to find that I had

IN THE BEGINNING

been bound hands and feet, I tried to listen then the door opened and the carrier criminal was looking right at me.

brought you some wine little lady you be nice to me and I will be nice to you, he was drunk and smelled even worse than my husband, now I will give you a little drink he held the wine gourd up to my lips then grabbed the back of my head and forced me to drink, I had to drink an awful lot before he let me go chuckling to himself, now what about a little kiss he tried to catch my lips but I kept dodging him until he grabbed my hair and forced his lips on mine, it was revolting so I bit him hard He went berserk, hitting me in the face with his fist I thought I had lost my teeth and was sure my nose was broken.

I fell into unconsciousness when I next awoke my Brother-in-law was in the carriage and he was pulling the blanket from around me, he said sit up girl, I sat up as he pulled the blanket from me, he looked at me with a startled look, He said bloody hell, what have you done to her you idiot we can't sell her in Jerusalem's slave market, he got mad at the other evil one and started hitting him, cursing him and shouting she's bloody worthless, no buyer will pay anything for her when she has got so much damage.

And that is when I saw the horse the brother in law had untied my feet checking if I had any other injuries Then the two men started arguing and fighting each other, I could not see the third one around, so I lept from the carriage, right on to the horses back he was so startled that he set of at full Gallup, I could have kept this pace up all the way back home then all of a sudden the horse starts rearing set off again and somehow I fell off. The rest of the story you already know bringing us to this moment.

Everyone was very quiet and thoughtful, Mary said you poor child she promptly put her arms around the Girl, Jesus retorted, Joanne I promise you, I will watch over you, we will protect you and get you back to your Family if you wish.

Firstly Mary and I need to work with you, to heal your wounds in your body and your spirit, would you give us consent to work with you, Yes please, I feel so much pain and sadness replied Joanne I don't know if anyone can help me, Joseph said, Joanne go with Mary and Jesus they will help you like no other can, believe me.

Mary helped Joanne to her feet and left with Jesus and Joanne, they went into one of the private rooms and spent the hours healing Joanne and telling her of the important work She will do on behalf of the living Gods, She eventually became one of the most influential Disciples teaching the seven stages of enlightenment.

Joseph waited patiently outside deep in thought about how Joanne had suffered, He had already f alen in love with Her, He felt Anger at the evil Men who abused her, he desperately wanted to protect her, She is so beautiful, She would never look at me as a possible husband, He wouldn't blame Her if She hated mankind and never trust a Man as long as She lived, He started to pace up and down deep in his own thoughts and anguish.

He came suddenly out of his thinking when he heard the whinnying of a Horse, He walked through the entrance of the villa and looked out over the field, He saw three Men who had already tied ropes around the White Mare, She was trying to break free, the Men worked to tire her and overpower Her, She looked desperate and terrified calling for help, the black Stallion was pawing the ground ready to fight for his beloved Mare, He reared and kicked one of the Men to the ground trampling on him to get to the other Man at the other side of the Mare, the third Man had made a lasso was readying himself to throw it around the Stallions neck, He wasn't quick enough, the stallion caught him reared up, with a stunning blow knocking him senseless.

Joseph ran shouting to the men of the household to come quick Mark was the first followed by James and Jude they ran up to Joseph Look he cried those Men are trying to steel Marys Horse.

The men ran as fast as they could towards the villains ready to fight the Men, however The Black Stallion was victorious in fending the Men off their prize, when Joseph and the others reached them the Men were already beaten cowering away from the Black beauty, Shouting to anyone who would listen Help, Help, the Horse is mad.

The Stallion was unconcerned his beautiful Mare was all he cared for, he stood now quiet and placid nuzzling the Mare, Joseph reached them first, I saw what you were doing steeling the Mare.

How dare you! by Jerusalem law anyone steeling a Horse is punishable by death, The Men pleaded, we were only going to borrow the mare until we found our Horse which was stolen.

IN THE BEGINNING

We can't pull our wagon ourselves, please forgive us and let us go, James held fast to one of the villains who was pleading for mercy, the other was still unconscious, we had better get some help for your friend called Jude.

He appears to be in a bad way, James and Joseph made the Men carry their friend back to the Villa, whilst they walked they talked and asked questions, I've never seen an animal so vicious cried one of the villains it should be put down it's a dangerous Animal, the other agreed can't do anything with a mad stallion its unridable, who lives in this villa, who are you, the questions were nonstop.

Joseph and the other good Men said nothing but wait and see, it's not our fault we lost our Horse, a servant stole it, If I ever see her again I will kill her for her insolence, I am an important Man of good standing, I swear to god that I will find her, She will be cast out and killed for her treachery.

The disciples stopped dead in their tracks James said what did you say a servant? Was her name Joanne, in a flash Joseph had the man by his shirt, throwing him on to the floor, Mark and Jude restrained their friend saying.

Stop Joseph, only Jesus and Mary have the right to hear and condemn these wicked Men, wait Joseph quiet, until they are told of the situation. Joseph regained his composure, let the Villain go who started to rant about being treated so badly, when he was a man of high standing knowing the governor Pontus Pilot as a good friend, who would have them thrown into jail and crucified for the way they had been received and treated with such distain.

They arrived at the villa, and shown into the vegetable store room, they tied the wicked Men together so they could not escape, Mark and Jude were given the task of watching them, Joseph and James went to tell Jesus and Mary about the prisoners, finding them in deep conversation with Joanne who was completely restored, radiant and beautiful, the site of her made Josephs heart beat much faster than it did apprehending the villans, James led the conversation because Joseph appeared to be struck dumb by the site of Joanne's beauty.

He told them all about the situation, and that these Men may be the very Men who had hurt Joanne so badly, She would know who they were, Joanne looked afraid, Mary held her hand and felt it trembling, be brave she said to Joanne, Jesus has told you that He will never allow anyone to hurt you ever again, you must believe in him.

These Men have no power anymore you must identify them as your abductors, I promise that they will never hurt another person or you ever again, Joanne nodded yes in reply, however She still held fast onto Marys hand, they followed James out to the vegetable store as they crossed the quad the Horses greeted them.

Mary greeted and stroked the Mare and felt her distress, she was trembling, Mary placed her forehead on the mares She could see and feel what the mare suffered, Mary spoke to the Mare well done my brave girl now be calmed these bad Men will never hurt you again.

Jesus was in the throes of listening to the account from The black stallion he was snorting stomping pawing with his front leg then neighing to show his anger at the attack on His Mare, Jesus calmed him down patted him calling him his brave defender, Jesus did the same as Mary, placing his forehead onto the stallions who obeyed his master with such gentleness.

Then Jesus went to the Mare to console, comfort her, Mary went to the stallion and thanked him for his bravery and for defending her dear princess, Marys pet names for them Princess and Prince.

Joanne watched in amazement as She witnessed the Horses respond to Mary and Jesus with such love giving and receiving their fears and feelings, She had never seen this behaviour in Horses, when they finished talking to them, the Horses gave a bow and walked behind them towards the vegetable store, Mary took Joanne's hand again as they opened the door to confront the villains, Jesus spoke first, Joanne are these the Miscreants that abducted you and damaged your face and defiled your body.

Joanne stepped forward, looked at the Men and said, yes, this Man here was my Brother in law, this Man is the one that hurt me, and this man who had just regained consciousness, tied me up gagged me, and drove the cart.

Thank you Joanne, Jesus turned addressing the Men, can you defend your actions, The brother in law started his defence by attacking the virtue of Joanna, saying that She was a known whore, then placing the blame for their actions on Her, in trying to borrow the Horses, because She stole their Horse, and lost it, they had been looking for it and Her for days, She had caused them nothing but trouble, He believed she was cursed, all he wanted to do was to provide her with a home and was willing to take the place of her husband in his duties.

As for taking money from Her Parents that was a lie, but he did ask them to contribute towards the cost of keeping their Daughter.

The tying her up and beating was the other men's doing, which made the other villain gawf and say it was you, who told us to do it, He said she was mad and it would be a good thing to beat her and even kill her to put her out of the misery of madness.

He said he wasn't bothered about her; he just wanted the money Her parents would pay to get Her back. SHUT UP shouted the brother in law you idiot.

Joseph stood listening to this his fists clenched He wanted to kill them, they were guilty and should be punished, Mary looked towards Him and saw the emotion, she gently placed her finger on her lips and made the gesture shhhhh.

Joseph understood and relaxed, taking hold of Joanne's hand to indicate his support for her, Joanne looked up at Joseph with tears running down her face, He so wanted to take her in his Arms and comfort her, but He was afraid She may reject him thinking He was like these evil Men.

Jesus addressed the men saying are you sorry for your crimes, the brother in law attacked by brazening it out, he said I have nothing to be sorry for, She is my property, I can do with my property what I wish, how bloody dare you tell me different.

I am a personal friend of Pontus Pilot the governor, Jesus started to smile, Oh really well it just so happens that Pontus is a dearer friend of ours as well, should we send for him, Mark would you be so kind as to ask Pontus Pilot to join us.

The brother in law started to stammer no, no, mino we don't want to put him to any trouble, surely, we can come to a resolution as Men of the world without bothering the governor of Judea.

Your crimes are many Jesus said, I will ask you once again, are you willing to take responsibility for your crimes against this Woman and my own dear Horses.

OH, come on said the Brother in law, this is ridiculous crimes about a used Woman, and Horses, there are no crimes to answer to, Jesus said I will ask you one more time before I commit you to creation are you sorry.

NO he replied, in that case you give me no choice I must commit this to someone who will fit your punishment to your crime, Jesus lifted his eyes to heaven and called out to the Angels, in the next moment an Angel appeared, Black as dark beautiful as the moon, complete with black wings, He immediately knelt before Jesus and Mary, my lord and lady you have called me I am here, ask of me anything, I will do your will, Jesus replied thank you Lucifer, these Men have committed crimes against a woman and will not admit their guilt, so I cannot give them Absolution, therefore I commit them to you, I ask that they be punished by you, until they admit and confess their crimes.

Jesus turned towards the guilty Men and said, Lucifer has always had a problem relating to the human race, He is very prejudice against Human Men, He is the only Angel that refuses outright to aid any human, I try to keep him away from human beings, however in this instance I believe he is the perfect judge.

He hates you and will show you no mercy. The Men were aghast with open mouths they had never seen such a creature, suddenly terror gripped them No No lord do not commit us to this abomination, we will admit our crimes we will even say sorry, Jesus looked at them reading their hearts, and for a moment said nothing, then he said Take them Lucifer, in a moment they were gone.

They walked out of the vegetable store into the sunshine, the Horses were still waiting for them as if they wanted to say something, Jesus addressed them both and then said of course you can, shall we have a little celebration tomorrow, then announced to everyone Prince our beautiful Stallion wishes to be with Princess as a family and want us to bless their union, tomorrow at one o clock we will bless their union, everyone prepare a feast for tomorrow.

Joanne and Joseph walked out behind the others, She said to Joseph what just happened, Jesus has made sure that those evil men are no longer in any position to hurt anyone else, but where did they go, Joseph relied I honestly don't know but I wouldn't want to be in their shoes, neither would

I, said Joanne both started laughing simutaniousely, they were trying to regain their composure as they walked out of the store.

They watched in amazement as Jesus and Mary announced that their Horses wanted to be married and blessed by Jesus and Mary. Tomorrow was declared day of celebration; Miriam was talking to Princess about getting her ready and Mark was discussing with Prince how to make his coat shine after all they must present themselves even more beautifully at their wedding day.

Jesus turned around to talk to Joanne and Joseph, now what can we do next for our Joanne, he declared, send her back home to her Family, Miriam shouted.

Is that what you wish Joanne, Yes lord if it pleases you, I would love to see my Parents and Brothers, So they won't worry and be distraught looking for me, I can only hope that they didn't pay a ransom, in that case Jesus said we will send you home after the wedding, after all I must ask the Bride and Groom if they will let you ride on their backs to take you home, Joseph would have to accompany you, we don't want anything else to happen to you, he will defend you with his life because He loves you so, Joanne blushed looking down, She thought how comfortable it was to be in Josephs company, but Love I hardly know him, and I never want to marry again, and He wouldn't want me as his wife I am damaged goods no one would want to marry me.

I am happy with that prospect, her thoughts were going round and round in her head, When Mary interrupted her concentration, are you comfortable with Josephs company on your return to your Family Joanne, we could send you with Miriam then Mark will insist on coming along He hates to be away from her, Mark and Miriam stood in stunned silence it was the truth, however neither had declared love for each other so they both shyly looked away and tried to pretend they hadn't heard Mary say anything, their secret was out they both felt embarrassed such was their nature so alike yet so in denial of their love for each other.

Joanne said I would like it if Joseph would accompany me home, it's a long journey I would be vulnerable on my own, I know my friend will get me home unscathed, if it's alright with Joseph, Of course it is replied Joseph I wouldn't have it any other way, It would be an honour to accompany you.

The following day was very busy everyone in the villa pulled together, Miriam fixed princess Main with plats and pink ribbons, her coat was shining she presented as a bride, beautiful.

Mark groomed Prince his coat was like gloss black, shining in the sun, then when everyone was ready Jesus and Mary called for quiet and stood before Prince and Princess, they blessed them and wished them happiness, the party commenced, a full afternoon celebrating the beloved horses happiness, joyful memories for everyone attending.

The day after the celebrations Jesus was talking to the Horses asking them if they would allow Joseph and Joanne to ride them to take Joanne home at first Prince was apprehensive, he had vowed that no one else would ever ride him again, but Jesus.

Princess felt the same, as She was Marys Horse, Jesus left them and returned with Mary, She spoke to both Horses asking again if they would be so kind as to allow Joseph and Joanne to ride them they would be back home with them again soon, Princess would always do anything Mary asked of her she agreed, Prince had no choice to except.

The following morning Jesus and Mary called Joseph and Joanne to them, they told them that they would let them ride their Horses to take Joanne home, Joanne was very happy and so they started their journey home, Jesus and Mary waved them off and Miriam gave them her bag of food that never ran out, So they wouldn't be hungry on the journey.

They made very good progress, Joannes family lived outside of Antioch in Syria, as they rode along they talked of the past in both their lives, Joseph listened intently and then he shared his story with her, they wept for each other, something happened as they rode, they felt themselves falling in love with each other.

The first night after leaving the Horses to graze, they ate out of Miriam's bag, it felt so right that they held each other to keep warm long after the fire went out, Joanne felt completely at ease with Joseph, and He with Her.

They made swift and good time, arrived within five and a half days at Joanne's home, Her Family were completely elated all burst into tears on seeing Her, thrilled to have her home with them Joanne told them what had happened to her, and about Jesus and Mary, Joseph took the Horses into the Stables fed and watered them then went to find Joanne.

He found her telling her parents and Brothers what had happened to her, They had found the ransom note but it did not contain any details on where to send the ransom they found themselves distraught, not knowing what to do next to get her back, Her Brothers conducted searches, still they were disappointed, the waiting wishing and prayed hoping they would let her go eventually had taken its toll over Her Mother and Father they were bereft at the loss of their Daughter, there were no words to express their gratitude to Joseph.

Joseph walked into the room He introduced himself, the Family returned introductions they then asked Joseph what he knew about Joanne's abduction, Joseph told them what happened to Joanne from the time he startled the Horse, also what had happened to Her abductors, They appeared transfixed at Josephs account.

later in the evening Joanne told them again about Jesus and Mary how they had healed the vicious wounds on Her body, and put her mind at peace, especially the part about Joanne becoming a Disciple of the living God, She wanted Her Family to meet them, She wanted their permission to start her work with Jesus and Mary, She knew that if their Family met them they would Believe as She believes in the living Gods and She felt it important to honour her Parents and Brothers viewpoint and at the same time give Her their blessing, even though it meant that Joanne would leave home a single woman, She could find herself in difficulty again or worse, murdered.

They talked for hours, her family could not come to a contentious of opinion, Her Mother brothers and Father expressed their concerns about her safety as they had already been through the agony of losing her twice.

They agreed that it would be acceptable if Joanne was married to someone who would ensure her safety, and status as a married woman, Joseph remained quiet, listening to their conversations, in his mind he was crying out to them and Joanne.

I want to marry you, I love you so much and I know your family would welcome me as another Son if only I had the guts to ask you to be my bride, Joanne was engrossed in the conversations, yet all the time not taking her eyes off Joseph in her mind She was crying out, Joseph don't you see me I want to be with you I love you, declare your love for me, ask me to be your Wife.

Sadly nothing was said or given away, Josephs mind started to fill with doubt, maybe She doesn't feel the same, If I asked her in front of her family and She rejects me, I couldn't bear it, Oh please, I wish Jesus and Mary were here, they would know what to do, everyone in the household went to bed to sleep on it, maybe a solution would be found in the morning.

Joseph felt exhausted he fell asleep immediately, He started to dream he was flying through the sky flying so fast he saw the villa, Jesus and Mary looking up towards Him, He called to them what should I do, Mary called back follow your Heart Tell Her how you feel, it will be alright, Joseph was flying again over mountains and pastureland back to Joanne.

In the morning Joseph joined the family at breakfast stated good morning to everyone, then turned to Joanne, after breakfast would you join me in a walk, Joanne said yes with enthusiasm She looked forward to spending time with Joseph showing him her grand home.

She found herself missing Him. This would be an opportunity to test the water before She lept towards making a fool of herself by declaring her feelings for him, she loved everything about him, she yearned to be taken in his arms, but for now She would remain quiet. She took him to where her Son was laid to rest The Family crypt.

They both prayed that the Child would be at peace. Joanne wept, she told Joseph that sometimes She missed him so much that She wanted to rip her own heart out and leave it here in this place of the dead and lie with her Baby forever.

They walked through the vin yards, Joanne telling Joseph about the delicious wine they produced, small talk to hide burning passion and love for Him, Joseph remained in quiet contemplation, Joanne chatted on, Joseph stopped suddenly turned to Joanne and said I love you.

Joanne stood in shock for a moment then She breathed out and declared, well thank God, I was beginning to think that you didn't care about me, and I love you so much I was afraid you didn't love me, in a flash Joseph enveloped Joanne in his arms, I love you more than my life please marry me, be at my side as my wife, I promise that no one will ever hurt you again, Joanne replied through tears of happiness, Oh my darling I will be your wife I am honoured to be by your side until the end of time.

They ran through the vin yard back to the beautiful grand villa, Joseph was ready to ask for Joanne's hand in marriage and sought out Her Father

IN THE BEGINNING

to ask him as was the custom, however Joanne's Parents had reservations about the marriage and before they would give their permission, they asked Joseph a series of personal questions.

Joanne's Father declared We don't know anything about you Joseph, why are you not married at your age, Joseph replied I was married, I lost my Wife and Child at childbirth, isn't something I want to discus, I have suffered much mentally since their loss, therefore I understand Joanne's Grief at the loss of her Child I can only promise on my oath that Joanne will never suffer as my wife I will honour her and her feelings, She will be treated with the utmost care and respect.

Well that's very commendable replied Joanne's Mother, and what of finances Father stated how are you to support her, Her dowry went with the last disastrous marriage, as I remember correctly said Joanne's mother You chose Him, our poor darling Daughter had to suffer a terrible life with that awful family, the demise of that marriage was not our Daughters fault.

It was just a pity it didn't end sooner, then her mother began to sob then maybe we would have been able to enjoy our grandson, meet him in the flesh not bury that poor baby, Joanne moved to comfort her mother, as she sobbed, she carried on, when his poor mother was so ill, delirious with grief, let her choose who She wants to be with, cried her Brothers, at least it will be her choice and not forced on her.

Nevertheless Father said are you looking to have an income through Joanne's estate to support you both, Sir replied Joseph I am a very wealthy Man I can support Her we will not be asking for one penny out of your estate, I own all the merchant Ships in Jerusalem port, I may have been a quiet bereft Man before meeting your beautiful Daughter.

Today I am the happiest man in the world, your darling Daughter has lifted me from the depth of despair, I can't wait to spend eternity together, She is my soul mate, I only wish I could have met her earlier in our lives, I want to make her happy and content, and I ask again Sir, may I marry your daughter, will you give us your blessing. Father smiled, of course you may, welcome to our Family Joseph.

The couple decided that they couldn't wait to be together they enjoyed a simple ceremony at the local temple binding them legally together as man and wife, Joseph joked that they will be married properly when Mary and Jesus give them their blessing, after the Family party, they went together to the family crypt to lay flowers at Her sons grave, Joseph noted that this was the first time he saw her smile as she gave her offering of fresh flowers to her Son. It was as if she was saying goodbye to the unhappy past, leaving it behind her forever.

It was decided to travel back to Mary and Jesus with the whole Family, everyone was excited to meat first-hand the living Gods, they had heard much gossip about them, and it was exciting that they would actually meet them in person.

The going was much harder with a large contingent of Family, it took much longer, Prince was getting a bit frustrated at the slow movement, he wanted to gallop with his princess back to Mary and Jesus as fast as he could, Joseph had to keep holding him back and correcting him, still he danced along tugging at the rains snuffling and snorting his frustration.

Princess gently, softly slow cantered at his side, behind them came the carts holding the Mother Father and two servants in one cart the family of the youngest brother, Wife and three children complete with their two servants, and then the cart which had the older brothers family of which consisted of his wife two servants and eight children.

The Family were in good spirits enjoying the journey even when it rained, Joseph found that their joy and good humour infectious it rubbed off on him, he found himself smiling and humming a tune he heard the children sing, as he rode alongside his beautiful wife, he suddenly realised he was truly happy.

After a few days journey the road became familiar, nearly home, just round that corner and we will be able to see the villa, called Joseph to the Family, Prince and Princess knew it also, they were trying hard to get their heads and go galloping home to Mary and Jesus.

As they got nearer to the villa Joseph became concerned its very quiet, it's not usually so, there are People coming and going all the time, yet it seems to be deserted, He looked over to Joanne somethings very wrong.

He was beginning to feel aprehensive, when Prince decided he could wait no more he set off at a mad gallop with Princess right behind him, it was all joseph and Joanne could do to hang on, hang on for dear life they did, as they drew close to the arched entrance, a great cheer went up hurray they are home congratulations, surprise surprise happy throngs greeted them, the whole place was packed with everyone Joseph knew, and then

IN THE BEGINNING

some more, Jesus and Mary stood before them and the crowed became silent as the rest of the family arrived, they cautiously dismounted moved forward to greet firstly Mary and Jesus.

Mary asked Joseph to introduce them to his new Family, After all the introductions were made, Jesus addressed everyone, Greetings to all our Family Old and new members, we are here to celebrate Joseph and Joanne's marriage, they had no idea we knew, it's a complete surprise to them Did you think we would not celebrate, and find a good excuse to have a splendid feast in your Honour, we are especially blessed to receive Joanne's Family, who are now our Family because our beloved Son Joseph is already legally Married to our lovely Joanne.

As Jesus spoke a group of Women surrounded Joanne dressing her in a beautiful gown, arranging her hair and placing a garland of flowers upon her head, a similar group of men surrounded Joseph dressing Him in fine apparel as a bride groom should be dressed.

We are honoured to bless you both, declared Jesus, and Mary, they addressed them both asking them to always love honour and protect each other and the children they would bring into this world, with a final embrace the blessing was over and with great cheer declared the wedding reception to begin.

It was a wonderful wedding evening even the elderly couple who owned the villa were present.

They made a wedding present of the villa to Joseph and Joanne, with condition that they and Mary and Jesus would be allowed to stay in it for as long as they wished, Joannes Family were amazed at seeing the Governor Pontus Pilot greet the couple as warmly as his own Family.

The guest list was amazing including the highest in the Land Lord Chaffe Chancellor to King Herod and his beautiful wife Simone, everyone was treated as equal in the eyes of Jesus and Mary even the servants were allowed to join in the fun, the wine was plentiful, the food never ended, the dancing music and merriment went on well into the following morning Joseph and Joanne, declared it was the best wedding surprise ever, a wonderful happy day that no one wanted to end.

The following day all rested, on the second day everyone arose early watching the sun rise, they saw Jesus and Mary walking out of the Villas entrance, being greeted by Prince and Princess, who walked by their sides, suddenly there appeared many men, women and Children who had slept in the fields surrounding the villa, some were weeping, Children ran towards them with their Arms outstretched as if they were greeting their Parents.

The Air felt apprehensive as the rest of the guests followed them out to the pastures, Mary looked to the little Children who appeared traumatised, Jesus spoke to the adults as they limped towards Him Tell me what has happened to you, why are you here in such distress.

We are refugees come from the Syrian border we were thrown out of our village ransacked by Elamites, we cannot go back, we seek refuge from Pontus Pilot the governor of Judea, we wish to ask him to send an army of Roman Soldiers to get our lands back.

So that We may return back to our Homes, however I believe our community has been laid bare and nothing is left of our Homes, we small band of refugees is all that is left, Jesus looked at the ragged and worn out faces of the poor people in desperate need.

He was filled with compassion for them He instructed all the guests to help everyone they found in need, bring them into the middle quad of the Villa where Mary and He would be able to administer healing, He looked over at Mary engrossed in helping the young ones with Miriam as always at her side, She looked up and caught his look, She immediately told the Children to follow her, Joanne's Mother ran towards Mary to help with the Children.

Joanne's Father enquired from one of the Men survivors where this happened, because He was concerned about His Home and People left there, all of a sudden a blood curdling scream was heard a young Girl threw herself at Miriam slashing and stabbing Her with such forceful screaming that it was hard to hear.

Jesus ran towards the commotion catching the Girl in his arms and ripping her away from their precious Miriam, Mary had been thrown backwards by the attack, and Poor precious Miriam lay dead before them, Her blood was everywhere and it was difficult to see the wounds, Mary screamed NO, JESUS HELP US,

Mark came dashing up He saw the fountain of blood and screamed NO DEAR GOD NO, Quickly Jesus took command as Mary and Mark were in shock He held Miriam in his Arms, to heal her but She had bled out fast, it was all He could do to stop the terrible bleeding, He had never encountered this before, he called Mary quickly I need you, they both placed their hand on Miriam and held her body between them, everyone bore witness to the blinding light that enveloped them after a few moments the light receded and Jesus and Mary looked down on to their beloved Miriam, who appeared to be waking after a long sleep, they breathed a big sigh of relief and kissed her, poor Mark was still holding his hands over his face as tears streamed from between his fingers, Miriam said what's wrong with you, Mark quickly dropped his hands while trying to wipe the tears, Oh Nothing you alright Miriam, Mary said Oh for goodness sake would you both please except that you love each other beyond reason I think you both have been in denial to long, then out of relief they all started laughing.

 The Girl who attacked Miriam was being held down by some of the Men, her face held a most sinister gaze her mouth seemed stuck in a crazy grin, she was completely manic, her face was filthy, and her hair looked like it hadn't been combed for ever.

 Jesus looked around at the refugees who had gathered around them, Who does this Girl belong to, no one came forward, Someone must know this Girl, a Woman holding a Child who was no more than a year old, stepped forward, She followed us here She was a feral Child, no one here owns Her She would come into the town and eat scraps, I have never heard her speak and She would never come near anyone, I don't know her name or anything else about her.

 Jesus knelt down towards the Girl She looked to be around ten or twelve years old, He studied her Face, observed that the manic grin was unnerving, and called to her COME OUT OF HER, The girl started writhing like She was having a fit spittle shot from her mouth, then her body lifted into the air spinning around, She spewed forth her last meal over everyone gathered watching the spectacle, Jesus said again more forceful COME OUT OF HER NOW!! The girl slammed down to the floor but immediately jumped to her haunches and faced Jesus, the same manic grin looked back at him defiant and dangerous looking.

 The Men fell backwards away from the Girl in obvious terror, Mary stood at Jesuses side and said you heard him come out of her now!! a voice came out of the grinning mouth, you cannot command me.do you not know who I am, I hate you, I will kill anyone, or thing, that tries to take this body away from me its mine, she gave it to me with her free will, she no longer lives in it or wants it.

Mary said again come out of her, the body started to shake again, another nasty fit, stop this now, come out of this body Jesus shouted, and what will you give me she said in a little girls voice, there's lots I can give you. I can tell your future, it's not a nice one, she chanted, when you are hoisted up a yew tree, naked for all to see, blood weeping eyes, stabbing sides, he dies, you all crys, ha ha ha.

Jesus lost patience and shouted go to hell, the girl let out yet another blood curdling scream and fell to the floor, She did not stir, People started to whisper has he killed her, is she dead, James gingerly edged forward and poked the Girls body with his foot, still She didn't move, everyone held their breath, Jesus walked forward to the girl, gently turning her over.

The evil grin was missing, a little girls face took its place, Jesus looked for a sign of life, there wasn't one, Mark said if She is dead, it may be a blessing, this body looks emancipated that thing must have held on to her a long time.

Mary moved forward taking the Childs body in her arms, looking at the Childs face, She is in there only just, I can feel her life force, Mary spoke softly to the Child, Come forward little one, no one will hurt you anymore, come forward open your eyes, slowly the Girl opened her eyes, come to me dearest child, Mary kept giving her encouragement until the child was fully awake, Her eyes looked terrified, Mary was filled with sorrow love and compassion for the Child.

Mary stood up still holding on to the child's hand, bringing her to her feet, the poor Girl started to weep, Miriam came forward and said, I will take her and look after Her.

Mark rushed forward No Miriam She nearly killed you, don't have anything to do with this thing pointing at the Girl who wept harder than ever, Mary comforted the child, then said to Miriam are you sure you want this responsibility, Miriam replied am not keeping her forever, just to clean her up bring her enough Love and care until we find a home or She is able to tell us who she is.

Jesus said Thank you Miriam, you are always an incredible example for us all to follow, He addressed the rest of the crowd see how this great woman forgives the Girl who stabbed her to death, and is willing to take care of her, this is the height of an example of forgiveness, and unconditional Love as I could ever tell you, is it any wonder that the living Gods love and depend on our beloved Miriam, She is blessed as a Woman and disciple like no other.

Come with us, all refugees follow us into the villa, you must be very hungry and tired, there is room inside the quad for you, then, when you are ready, elect a spokesperson to be presented to Pontus Pilot I will take you to see him and your message of help will be heard.

Jesus turned and spoke to Mark, take Miriam to her room stay with her and the Child, give her time to change out of her blood soaked clothes, make sure the Child eats well, find other clothes for her, can you do this Mark, Yes Lord of course I will.

Luke counted twenty-five refugees some were critically injured one Man had his Arm nearly ripped off his body, The Children were emotionally and physically injured, some crying and some so traumatised that they could not speak.

Everyone attended the poor people even the twins Star and Moon delivered healing to the Children, they did not need to be asked, they saw the need and they joined in to help, Every bit their Parents Children.

The refugees were stunned at the loving attention and the instant Healing they received, they had heard about the living Gods, never did they think that they would stumble on them and be healed and given respite by them, they were grateful and ready to hear Jesus and Mary speak, about Creation and the seven realms of enlightenment.

After resting Jesus accompanied two Men for an appointment with Pontus Pilot, after hearing their story He deployed two garrisons to secure the area, Pontus asked Jesus if they could stay at the Villa until the region was declared safe to return.

Pontus took Jesus to one side, and said thank you for bringing these people to him, this act of moving over borders for raids, was becoming a big issue with Rome, Jeopardising peace and stability in the area, it could mean actual war to be decaired if these renegades are not captured, Jesus said that they would give the refugees a shelter until they can go back to their homes.

Life returned to normal at the villa all the guests that had attended the wedding went home, which left more room to accommodate the refugees, these people busied themselves making bread tending vegetables taking care of the daily running and upkeep of the villa, they were skilled carpenters, candlemakers, gardeners, seemstresses, one of the women made beautiful crochet lace, out of cotton threads.

Mary Miriam and Solitous enjoyed learning the technique from her, Another Woman made fabulous cheese and butter out of goat and sheep milk, Jesus gave them leave to buy livestock mainly a milking cow for Milk for the children, four Sheep and one Ram, six goats one billy goat and one dozen laying Hens and one Cockrill.

The villa became a cottage industry, everyone working hard to make life better and more comfortable for everyone who lived there, it was a fun place to be, the Children who had been so traumatized were encouraged to play together and attend classes with Star Moon and Pilots Children, afterwards they would swim in the outdoor pool laughing and splashing each other and any unfortunate Adult that walked passed, at night the fire pits would burn and everyone took turns to tell a story or sing or recite poetry.

Days turned into weeks and weeks into months, The refugees felt at home and most of them did not want to go back to their old village, only Joanne's Family wanted to return home, they were advised by Pontus Pilot to wait until the Garrisons returned with news that the offenders had been captured and the area made safe.

They took the advice and waited at the villa and after attending Jesus and Marys preaching to the masses that always turned up, especially on a Sunday, became Disciples themselves, It was a three months before word came that it was safe to return to their homes, manny did not wish to return they had found a more pleasing existence living and working at the Villa, so much so, that the People called their new home a commune of the first Christians, who only wanted to be near Jesus and Mary, they worked hard to give comfort and praise to their distinguish Hosts.

The young Girl that Miriam bravely gave a loving and carefree home to, would not leave her side She would hold on to Miriam's skirts and cry if She went out of her site.

Mary spent time with the girl and concluded that the poor girl had been held back in her normal development, her chronological age at eleven

IN THE BEGINNING

years old, was severely retarded, her behaviour suggested a Child of only about three years old.

Mary and Miriam decided that She should be allowed to grow up as any other Child, with help and love, develop towards her true age, Mary stated to Miriam that three years old, must have been the age She was when the Demon that possessed her took over her body.

She had no recollection of any Parents, or memory of her life, although She could speak, it was like a Baby's voice, very inquisitive, asking what was that for, and why, learning fast, after a couple of weeks Miriam persuaded her to attend the school classes with the other Children.

She was very tentative, Miriam encouraged her, still She was reluctant to leave her side like a little child starting her first day at school, She hung on to Miriam, gradually She started to enjoy learning, let go of Miriam's hand, but after class instead of swimming, She would run to find Miriam, She was always willing to help at any task, specifically She liked to help Miriam, She positively glowed when Miriam praised her and thanked her for being such a good girl.

Thankfully there was no sign of the demon returning to claim her.

Joanne's Family and the refugees were given the news that their region was now safe to return to their village and homes, only a few wanted to return together with Joanne's family.

Those that wanted to stay were very welcome, and those that wanted to go home, left in a much better state than they arrived, they took Jesus and Mary the living Gods, with them in their hearts and minds, all became staunch disciples, Joannes Parents were more than happy to leave her in the company of Joseph Mary and Jesus who they knew would watch over them both.

Joanne's Mother talked with Miriam about the Girls future They reached an understanding that there was much better chance of finding the girls Family if She returned with them, they would be in a position to make enquiries into her past, and maybe return her to her Family.

Miriam explained this to the girl, at first she was reluctant to go wanting to stay with Miriam and Mary, then Jesus took her for a walk, and on returning announced that her name was Poppy, and She was ready to go back with Joanne's Family, nevertheless if Her Family can't be found She would be able to return to Miriam.

That was agreed, when it came time to leave, Poppy hugged Miriam and Mary, tears of departure were shed by everyone, but especially Poppy, who took hold of Joanne's Mothers hand and said under tear strained eyes, are you going to be my Mother now, Yes dear, She replied until we find your own Mother, like Miriam I am to be your foster Mother, I promise to look after you with as much love and attention as if you were my own Child you have nothing to fear.

After they left, a group of Men approached the Villa asking to speak to Jesus, Mark and James with Luke faced the Men, asking why you want to talk to our Lord, before they finished the sentence Jesus approached.

My friends feel they have to stand before you and defend me, yet I have nothing to defend, can I help you. the speaker was called Simon I heriot a Phereses and big important Man of the Temple.

He said are you the Man Jesus, Yes, then I am to serve you with a summons to attend the Sanhedrin council, They wish to ask you about certain discrepancies that have been brought to the councils attention, you are delivering Sermons and healing the sick on the Sabbath, This is against the law.

Jesus threw his head back and laughed, when he finally composed himself he asked, when is this meeting to take place, tomorrow at eleven am in the morning, you are to attend alone without the Woman, Jesuses face suddenly became serious, His eyes flashed with Anger How dare you tell me that the best side of me cannot attend because She is a Woman.

let me say this before you, it would be better for the Sanhedrin if She does attend with me, she will be the only thing standing before me, that will stop me venting my anger at the hypocrites of the Sanhedrin council.

Go back to your council and tell them this, I will be awaiting their reply, surfice to say that if they do not reply I will not attend any meeting without Her.

Jesus promptly turned and left them, James said well you heard the Man, and with that final rebuff they turned and walked back the way they came, Jesus went to find Mary to tell her about the Sanhedrin command, She gently held Jesus in her arms, calm now my Darling, you know how men see women in this world, they are as they have always been ignorant, and unknowing.

Your sermons always tell us that God can do nothing with the simple unknowing, but wait until they gain their spirituality, you know that creation can only create new souls until they reach spiritual perfection, until this time which you say will only begin to happen in over two thousand of the earths years from now.

I know it's hard for us to face in this time, the hypocrisy, narcissistic cruelty and downright wickedness of bearing false witness, We are here to teach our Children consciousness, goodness and Hope, with unconditional love, the same love that we have for our Girls, would you not want this for their Children our Grandchildren and their Children and on and on.

Until they reach the two thousand years of spiritual knowledge and understanding, is that not what we want this world to become, brave to stand against tyranie, become knowing, understanding of another's pain, Loving each other as they love themselves, casting out forever the beast that prays on their fear, and invades their bodies and minds, given the fallen and miserable a loving home, compassion, is that not what we are about, Did our dearest Miriam and Poppy not show us all the way.

Jesus stood contemplating for a moment, Yes, oh great and good right side of me, what would I do without you, He whisked her up in his arms my dearest love, right as always, he kissed her gently.

Sometime later, another delegation arrived to speak to Jesus, Simon the Pharisee appeared more cordial He stated that although the council initially opposed bringing the Women, they have had serious thought and discussion on the matter.

They do not wish to appear unyielding and are willing for Her to be present. Jesus studied them for a moment, alright we will attend, the Men turned and again went back the way they came.

The following morning at breakfast Jesus and Mary told everyone that they would be going to the Temple of Solomon to meet with the Sanhedrin council, the other Men expressed their unease at them going alone, after some debate all the Men decided that they would accompany them.

This now became a large delegation a show of force for their beloved God, they walked together talking cracking jokes in good spirits.

They walked up the steps of the temple, they were met by the Men guarding the council who guided Jesus and Mary into the large court room where all members of the council sat waiting for them, they stopped the others from following them, locking them out of the council room.

Jesus and Mary were beckoned to stand in the middle of the large round room, they stood hand in hand and waited for their unofficial trial to begin, after a lot of shuffling and murmuring Simeon Ihariot started the questioning.

He addressed Jesus; Sir it has been brought to our attention that you have violated the laws of God by working on the sabbath is this true.

Jesus replied You hypocrites, if only you had eyes and ears and minds so that you could see hear and understand, but you are blind and without reason, because you lack the knowledge to see, hear and understand nature.

Therefore you lack insight into the laws of creation, that would enable you to see, hear and understand that Creation does not keep the sabbath holy, so I will enlighten you, Every sabbath day Creation rotates the stars through the heavens regulates the Sun, winds and rains and nourishes all Creatures on earth, it keeps the rivers flowing in their beds and everything goes its normal way on one Sabbath as on another, just as Creation made it.

Someone shouted out, are humans not much more than all the creatures and plants, thus they are the Masters of them when they follow the true Sanhedrin laws!

Jesus replied, Oh you Snakes and vipers, you distorters of the scriptures, who because of your greed for money and power spread false teachings, Had you but one sheep that fell into a pit on the Sabbath day, who among you would not take hold of it and pull it out, how much more is a person worth than a sheep, or your deceitful and false teachings, it is a human law that the Sabbath be kept holy, and that no work be done on that day, but it is a law that escapes logic, since this law is a false teaching, emanating from the Human mind. Not from God.

Truly I say to you, no Sabbath is holy and no laws of creation dictates that no work may be done on the Sabbath, thus the Sabbath is a day like any other day on which the day's work may be done, Humans are creatures with will of their own, thus they alone are masters over the Sabbath, as was previously written in those ancient scriptures and laws that were not adulterated by false profits, distorters of the scriptures and Pharisees.

A man came forward stretching before him a withered hand, shouting at Jesus, is it not a sin and unlawful to heal someone on the Sabbath, Jesus spoke to the Man stretch your hand towards me, and he stretched it out, and it became sound again just like his other hand.

The council leaders and Pharisees were full of shock and left the chamber, they held further council in private about him, and how they could destroy him, since He made known their lies and false teachings in front of, and witnessed by the people, Jesus turned from them, taking Mary by the hand left the temple and the people followed Him including many sick people and the Man with the withered, now healed hand, rejoicing praising Jesus as the true God on Earth, He and Mary healed them all.

They walked hand in hand while their friends walked behind them whispering among themselves, He showed them up said one, they will try to get even, we all know the Sanhedrin's justice is biased, few people will go back on the sabbath, they are beaten and dangerous to Jesus and our beloved Mother, we must be vigilant, the whispering continued until Jesus stopped dead and they all fell into each other.

We can hear you whispering away said Jesus, Judas Iscariot stepped forward it's just that we are concerned for your safety, you have exposed them to be vipers and false teachers, they are Men of money, and power, should we not be afraid, Mary said, no, there is no place for fear, spiritual enlightenment cannot flourish in fear, it will only hold you back, so fear not, ask your God what you want and he will always give you what you need, according to the laws of Creation.

So please tell us how do we ask how do we pray, asked Judas, Mary replied take a candle to represent the light brought into this world by your living god, candles are always conduits in that they can give and receive Angelic messages, so make your prayers and adulations in front of your lit candle, ask always for the giving and receiving of love, meditate on your wants, and your God will always send what you need.

They continued the walk home in contemplation, Then when nearing the Villa Mary shouted Race you, and set off running for home, everyone started running and laughing behind her, no one could catch her, She ran faster than the wind, even Jesus could not match her pace She shot through the arched doorway.

I WON She shouted, Jesus ran up behind her and stated I let you win, HA HA HA the Children heard their arrival and ran towards them they swepped them up and spun them around looking like any happy family. Everyone else arrived puffing and panting still laughing that was fun.

Shouted Mary that's a really good way of getting rid of unhealthy thoughts and anger, better to find a way to relieve tension than give in to it, don't you think? everyone agreed.

Miriam remarked should we set up a running track for the purposed of venting emotions that are volitile, because I have pent up emotions, should I go for a run is that the answer, Mary replied in part yes, but running is only a way to let off steam and allow a person to think with clarity, so they may face their problems and find a suitable conclusion, it's also good for general health and wellbeing, isn't it strange that by physical exertion we have more energy in our bodies and can finish more tasks without tiredness it seems the busier we are, the more we get done.

Miriam what is on your mind pray tell me, Miriam looked ill at ease, oh nothing really, you will think me silly, Mary replied never would I think of such a thing about you, so tell me, Miriam said well it's just that ever since I was looking after Poppy and now She has left, Mark will not speak to me, He avoids me and turns away when I try to speak to him.

I thought we cared for each other, his behaviour is making me feel bad about myself, I can't explain the confusion and hurt I feel, when He will not talk to me.

OH dearest Miriam I felt something was wrong Mary replied, do you want me to talk to him, OH no said Miriam he will think me too needy, I will work it out and go for a good run, Mary gave Miriam a hug and said dearest little Sister I am sure everything will work out for you let's wait and see, now go for a run.

Mary told Jesus about Mark and Miriam, Jesus said I will talk to him, Jesus found Mark in the gardens He had become a very good gardener, growing fruit and vegetables was his passion.

It served everyone at the villa with fresh daily produce, Hello Mark hailed Jesus, Mark looked up and exclaimed OH I wasn't expecting you Lord, well you have been rather quiet as late and I wondered what was on your mind, Mark looked down trying not to engage his lords eyes, He knew if he looked up Jesus would know his deepest and private thoughts so he avoided his gaze, Jesus knew this, and said Mark, why do you not look at me when we talk together.

Mark replied still looking down at his hands I I I He stuttard, its well personal, How do you feel about Miriam remarked Jesus, III don't understand he stammered, what do you mean Lord, Oh you know, and look at me when we are in conversation, Mark immediately looked into Jesuses face, Marks eyes were filled with tears, and Jesus said AHH now I see what ails you, you are angry with Her yet sad, tell me about it.

Mark replied Angry Angry yes I am Angry and very upset, She was murdered stabbed by that Girl, if it wasn't for you and Mary I would have lost her forever, She gave that girl a home and looked after Her, despite knowing how I felt, She did not consider that my heart was broken, the very thought that I would never look at my beautiful Miriam again was terrifying for me, every day She was near that Girl She rejected me, yes I am Angry and many more emotions and feelings I cannot put into words.

Jesus spoke, the Girl has left, why can't you now approach Miriam, and tell her your fears and feelings, because you have not considered how Miriam feels when you reject her, when you avoid her, refuse to speak to her, and act like you don't care, I tell you now, how you are treating her, you deserve to lose her love, but strangely She still loves and cares for you.

Tell you the truth I don't think you deserve her, She is an exceptional Human being, and She has shown me so much, I have learned great lessons by observing Miriam, Her kindness, and willing to do anything to make others comfortable, is exemplary, She is loved by Mary and myself like no other, It pains us to see her so unhappy, and She doesn't know why, because you haven't had the good grace to talk to her honestly, however Mary has spoken to me and of course Miriam has told Mary her feelings and She is Sad and deeply unhappy.

What! Mark exclaimed her hurt feelings are because of me, I thought She had fallen out with me, over that Girl, you mean Poppy, Jesus said, let me tell you Mark, Poppy was scared mentally by the horrors She witnessed, She reacted as any persecuted Animal who is backed into a corner, She was also possessed of a terrible demon, Miriam knew this, and with her love and guidance, She was nursed back to normality, mostly by the loving attention of our Miriam.

If I was you and had wounded my beloved as you have Miriam, I would drop your precious vegetable and run to her immediately, apologise for being such a selfish arrogant idiot. I would be begging her forgiveness, telling her how much I loved her, and could not live without her.

So go now stop this sulking, grow up, and talk to her as a good Man should, but first wash your Hands and maybe comb your hair, Mark replied, you know Lord you are right, but what if She refuses me, OH for goodness sake just go, now, and He did.

As they finished their conversation Pontus pilot arrived He looked serious and troubled I must talk to you in private he said to Jesus, Pontus said to Jesus that he had received a letter from Tiberius Cesar regarding Mary and the Girls, Tiberius states that he heard of their beauty and wisdom, He wishes to give the Women a home with him, and honour them by making them concubines, what better compliment can he give you, to know that your Women will carry future Cesar's.

thereby Jesus turned to Pontus And said with passion and Anger, I would sooner place my wife and children in a cave full of vipers then send them to live with him. It will not happen, Pontus said yes of course you would not send them, but we must be contrite.

I will write back saying thank you for the invitation, but the twin Girls are indisposed with sickness and also that they are too delicate to take the long journey to Rome at this time they are still babies and perhaps you would honour us with the same requests when they are grown.

The Children grew into beautiful lovely girls, so much so that musicians wrote sonnets and poems to them, it also seemed that Mary had started a new fashion craze in the women and girls took to dying their hair red with henna, to emulate Marys shining bountiful locks.

The Children had also inherited their Mothers colour, as they went from their Baby Platinum locks to light auburn, their eyes stayed the most compelling blue.

Solitous and Children spent most days visiting the villa, all the Children spent time having lessons then played in the pool splashing and enjoying themselves, Pilot remarked the palace had become so quiet without them all, nevertheless He was most relieved that the hordes of people had left his gates, and he had time to govern.

Jesus and Mary would meet the people outside of the city at the banks of the river, it became a regular meeting place on Sunday hundreds if not thousands of people would journey to see them and listen to them mesmerized.

Some of the disciples also attended, mostly the Women, Mary had given them the power to heal, they helped Jesus and Mary they would walk amongst the faithful heal the sick cast out the devils and bless the Children.

They chose Sunday as their day because the Sabbath day was Saturday, yet the synagogues and temples were being deserted by their faithful, the heads of these religions were becoming broke and outraged at Jesus.

They refused to believe He was a living God, they quantified their suspicions by spreading gossip, and making up tails behind their backs saying that He was merely a man, who was a good magician, and nothing more, they spread awful lies that Mary was a harlot entertaining Men when Jesus was not with her.

The media wheels were turning and although they reported about Jesus and Marys good works the wind was changing and as the Pharisees Sanhedrin and social elite owned the wheel, they were starting to spread doubt about the legitimate claim of Jesus and Mary being a living God.

The media was turning subtly, the first celebrities were being put under scrutiny, this was the beginning of the lies and blasphemies committed against Jesus and Mary.

It was at a meeting of the people that Juda Ihariot a Son of one of the leading Pharisee Simon Ihariot approached Jesus, He wanted to report a potential wrong doing of Judas Iscariot, He informed Jesus that Judas was secretly collecting gold silver and copper in his money bag so that he could live vainly, he took from the crowds of people who came to hear Jesus speak, He further claimed that Judas had become disloyal to the teachings of Jesus and lived only for his own gratification.

He dropped hints that He wanted Jesus to pay him for the information he held, after delivering the news Jesus thanked him and sent him away without giving him one penny, Juda Iheriot thought of revenge for he was jealous and greedy, he craved the gold silver and copper for himself, it did not work out the way he envisaged.

Jesus talked with Judas Iscariot, taking him in to the desert, for three days and three nights, Jesus taught Judas the concept of right and wrong, whereupon Judas repented and became a believer and trusted disciple, forthwith followed Jesus and Marys teachings, He wrote about the teachings and life of Jesus and Mary, One day Judas came to Jesus, Lord I am afraid that my writings on your teaching have been stolen.

Jesus spoke to Judas, truly truly, I say to you Judas Iscariot, you will have to suffer even greater evils than the mere loss of your writings about my life, I have sadness for you, because for over two thousand years my friend, you will be wrongly accused of betraying me, because Simeon the Pharisee wants it so, His Son Juda ishariot is the real culprit,

Like his Father Simeon Ihariot the Pharisee who seeks my life, It is He who stole the writings from you and brought them to the scribes and Pharisees, so that they could judge me and put me to death, Juda Ihariot received seventy pieces of silver for your writings and he will receive another thirty when he makes it possible to hand me over to the executors.

Truly I say to you, He will certainly succeed and for two times a thousand years you will innocently have to pay the penalty for it, subsequently you will become a martyr, but write down my teachings and my life story another time, for the time will come, in two times a thousand years when your writings will be revealed, until then my teachings will be falsified by unscrupulous Men they will turn my words into evil cults, which will cause much heartbreak and blood to flow, because the People are still not prepared to comprehend my teachings and to recognise the truth.

Not until two times a thousand years, which is only a blink in the eyes of creation, will the truth come out as a result of the deceitfulness of the chief priests, and the ignorance of the people, but my Friend, Judas pay no attention to this, do not feel hurt, for the teachings of the truth demands sacrifices that must be made.

The People are still not very great in their spirit, consciousness and knowledge, thereby they must first take upon themselves much guilt and error before they learn thereby to accumulate knowledge and wisdom, so as to recognise the truth.

Only after two times a thousand years will an unassuming Human being come who will recognise my teaching as truth and disseminate them with great courage, they will also be vilified by the established cult religions, and advocates of the false teachings about me, and be considered a liar.

but you Judas you must pay no attention to the lies, because until then, you will be innocently reviled as my betrayer and thus be condemned again as the result of the deceitfulness of the chief priests.

Who hide behind your back so to vindicate themselves as liars and False profits, they will always point their fingers at others, what they are blind to, is that, as one points a finger accusing another, three point back at them?

Judas listened intently to Jesus and threw himself at Jesuses feet, Lord I care not what they say about me, all I care about is what you see in me, Jesús replied, behold my son Judas Iscariot with who I am well pleased, who was wanting and now blessed as my beloved Son, you shall sit on my right side of me in heaven for all eternity all discrepancies paid in full, life without end.

Over the next ten years life fell into normality, every Sunday Jesus Mary and the disciples delivered their teachings to the People, They healed the sick, gave refuge to the displaced, held the heartbroken and cried with them, the People travelled great distances just to hear them and look upon them, to feel healed simply by their presence.

Life was Good within all the holy lands from Juda to Syria Iran Irrack and Israel to Babylon, crops flourished, trade was plentiful, Children well fed, the Animals and nature experienced abundance, wars vanquished even though Rome was in Charge, It was described by learned men and scholars as a time when Heaven came to live on earth.

Even the Animals flourished seen by their own dear Horses Prince and Princess became parents of four Children, their Foals two mares and two stallions were unique, being born all black until reaching their first birthday when their coats became a pure white, yet still their skin was black, they were also blessed with great intelligence, poise, and their beauty was beyond description.

Ruth and her husband Marcus along with their four children and Horses, came to visit with Mary and Jesus, the Horses were sharing the paddock with Prince and Princess and their four Children, the mares fell in love with the two brothers, they were wonderful stallions.

Many had approached Jesus and Mary to buy them, but they stated that they could never sell them, however Ruth suggested that the two stallions go back home with them to their stud farm, Ruth was in awe and amazement at the intelligence and beauty of the pair, they would be an invaluable asset in giving the Mares incredible foals.

The two Mares would be able to run with their stock, learning the many tricks Ruth taught them, the Mares intelligence was beyond comprehension Ruth marvelled at the responses the Horses gave when Mary was with them, Mary and Jesus asked the Horses if this arrangement suited them, after establishing that it was exceptable, and giving assurances' that the Mares and Stallions would be able to come home if it was their wish, it was agreed.

However, throughout this time there was also a quiet rumbling in the background the Sanhedrin the temples and synagogues were largely deserted.

The Men in seats of power suffered, their coffers became empty, Jealously simmering anger and hate, They complained to Rome bitterly, rejecting Jesus as a fraud and con man, they were openly plotting against the movement of Jesus and Mary, the following became known as the Christians, as Christ the Father and Saviour of Man, walked with them on the earth, the great outside was their temple, compassion, Love Family, forgiveness, looking after Creation was how they lived their lives, and taught others these principals.

The Cesar Tiberius sent more letters to Pontus Pilot He was ordered to put pressure on Jesus to let Mary and the Girls live with him, for their own protection, Pontus spoke to Jesus, the Answer was always the same Jesus stated never as long as I live, I would sooner put them in a snake pit, than give them over to the Devil's advocate.

Pontus playing the diplomat handled the request with politicly precision by telling Tiberius that the Ladies in question were suffering from a terrible illness and could not be expected to travel to Rome at that time, however Jesus was willing to review the situation in time and if the Ladies are recovered, will send a personal message to the Great Cesar, Jesus sends his respect and is honoured that Cesar is willing to give such a generous gift of protection for His females.

However it was several years later when Cesar Tiberius sent the message that surely with all the accounts of miraculous healings that came to his ears performed by Jesus, that he had not seen fit to heal his own Wife and Daughters, Tiberius was losing patience, He was under

IN THE BEGINNING

constant barrage from the sennet, who because of the Sanhedrin Councils constant complaints, were beginning to see Jesus and Mary as a threat to Rome itself.

Pontus was visibly shaken with this last letter, He was at a loss as to what to say to Tiberius, it seemed He was spent as to any other excuse he could use to put to Cesar.

He had used everyone in his excuse book, He expressed his concern to Solitous, she said that She would ask Mary what should be done, Pontus exclaimed that it may be better if She did not spend as much time at the Villa.

Solitouses eyes opened wide at this suggestion and She turned on her husband the first time ever She was prepared to go against his wishes, how could you suggest such a thing, we owe them our lives, our Children, and our happiness.

The Children's lessons are given daily, they can already read write and speak other languages with ease, they are also instructed on cultures and ways people live.

Our Children are being given a brilliant education learning with love, and our dearest Friends and Family are Jesus and Mary, and you have the effrontery to suggest I do not see them daily, well how bloody dare you.

Pontus beat a hasty retreat, not wishing to provoke his Wife any further, nevertheless his feelings of impending doom did not leave him, He would talk to Jesus as soon as possible, after all how could he think that a woman could see the importance of calm relations with Tiberius, who better than Jesus to give him yet another good excuse to send to Tiberius keeping him at bay for yet another year of peace.

Pontus decided that He would walk to the villa that afternoon after completing his papers and tasks as the Governors' as he neared the villa, a great cheer went up, He ran to the gate looking for Solitous, He saw her and shouted over to her, She was part of a large crowd of People who seemed to be giving congratulations to Mary and Jesus.

Solitous ran over to Pilot, Hello Darling She gushed We are celebrating Mary and Jesus are expecting another Baby, isn't it wonderful, Pilot replied oh what wonderful news I must go to them and offer my congratulations, Pilot found Jesus and Mary, and gave them his Best wishes.

Then asked if he could discus something with Jesus they left the party and went into Jesus and Marys private appartments, Jesus spoke first, what is bothering you Pontus, Pilot replied I have had another letter from Cesar Tiberius, asking yet again for the women folk to join the Cesar in Rome where He states they will be well looked after, treated as Queens, He has given me leave to negotiate the terms, Jesus looked at Pontus with dark brooding eyes.

Pontus had never seen Jesus so angry, He was taken back as Jesus said I have told you over the past nine years that will never happen, as long as I live, I am so appalled at the matter of fact way Cesar wishes to take my Familly, use them as he sees fit barter over them as if they are a beast of burden, My Mary, Star and Moon are incredible Women they are always the best side of me, they are free to decide their own lives and to make their own choices.

Pontus Pilot replied, yes of course I agree with you in private, but this is not the way this world works, Women are used as slaves, married for land status and money, they are not free to choose anything.

They cannot own anything including their Children, they are used in many ways, If She dare complain She will be punished by a beating, I know this is not right, its simply the way it is.

Jesus said that is the reason I favour Women over Men, and why most of my closest most loyal disciples are Women, I know they will never betray us, those are the ones I can trust, they are the bearers of the next generation, they will tell their Children and the Children's Children, and so on about Mary and Jesus, the Christian fellowship will not be forgotten in time, but it will still be used by all the Men who will set up cults, to control the masses, our future Children will not be free because of them, and their misuse of our word of peace love and freedom for all.

I suggest that you send another letter back to Cesar saying that Mary is with Child and cannot make a long journey to Rome in her condition, and of course the Girls want to be with their mother at this time.

Pontus sent the letter, He still felt very uncomfortable this feeling of impending doom would not leave him, He was worried for his own position, if Tiberius found out where his allegiance lied He would be put to death by his own soldiers or even by the hands of Cesar himself, he must tread warily.

IN THE BEGINNING

Pontus felt more at ease when news came through via Merchants, that Cesar Tiberius was disappointed but understood the situation, and would expect them to travel to Rome after Marys confinement, and he wished the family congratulations at the Birth of their third Child.

Pontus breathed a sigh of relief at least their position was safe for a few months, He pondered at what he could say after the Birth to keep Tiberius calmed.

Normal life resumed, Mary was well all through her pregnancy, She positively glowed, and was thrilled when Miriam and Mark decided to tell everyone they were in love, and asked Jesus if they could marry, this was arranged quickly, as Jesus said it was a long time in coming and didn't want them to change their minds.

They enjoyed a lovely wedding at the villa, and settled into married life much the same as before, only now they slept together holding and loving each other, they felt their bliss would never end, however dark days where on the arison, everyone who loved Mary and Jesus would find their lives forever changed by events out of their control.

These events started quickly when Tibur Drusus arrived to deliver the news that a garrison of the most blood thirsty soldiers were on their way with orders to detain Jesus, put to death anyone that stood in their way.

There orders were to deliver the women and Girls to Rome, Tibur was beside himself with concern, openly worried that they should hide Jesus and Mary before the Garrison arrived, even Pontus Pilot knows nothing of their coming, Tibur retorted I know because one of the Soldiers Tibor had served with, was a particular horrendous individual, had called on Him and His wife, whilst journeying through Pompei, He had bragged to him, of being picked by Tiberius himself to go on this mission.

Tibur immediately made the journey by sea so he would arrive ahead of the marching Garrison and warn them, help them escape before they arrived, Jesus immediately summoned to him the followers Pontus Pilot Joseph of Amalthea, Philip James Mark john Andrew Simon Peter Luke, Bartholim Jude and Luke.

The women came with them, Jesus thanked them all for responding so quickly and told them of the Garrison on its way to arrest him and take Mary Miriam and his girls to Rome by force.

He told them that they must not oppose threaten or stand against these Solders, for fear that their lives be taken, but they must plan to save his beloved family, hide them until the threat had dissapated, Tibur would you please escort them to Galilee, Simone will be waiting for them and look after them until it will be safe to come back to Jerusalem.

Mary immediately jumped to her feet NO NO I will not leave your side, Jesus replied Yes my darling you must take care of our Children, when this blows over we will be together again, Miriam must go with you, if Mark wishes He should go with you also some of our most trusted friends, Joanne must stay at the villa and keep the people here calm until given instruction.

Tibur came with his uniform because it gave the impression that He was of the highest rank sporting all five medals of valour and status, He would not be challenged by any other guards He also stated that he felt it a good idea for all the men chosen to escort the Women should be dressed as Roman Soldiers and asked Pontus if He could supply them with the relevant uniforms.

Solitous answered for him Of course my husband will do everything he can to help, and I wish to be with Mary, my Mother and Sister can look after the Children, Pontus stopped her No, I forbid you to go, it would be important for my wife to be seen at my side when these soldiers come.

I want to be in a position where I can help Jesus and not worrying about You, Jesus raised his hand before an argument broke out, Pontus is right dear Solitous, you must remain with your Husband, his good name and standing would be called in dispute if you are not at his side, let's not give the gossips any more information that is necessary.

Jesus turned to Luke, my dear brother I am to send you on a mission alone. I want you to take the writings made of our lives into Egypt and hide them, it is hoped that future generations will be worthy of finding them, will you take this mission Luke, Luke looked up into Jesuses eyes, his own eyes were welling with tears, my dearest lord If this is your wish I will do anything you ask.

Gather all the writings you can, load them on a good donkey and be back here in five days, Luke did as he asked however He had to load four donkeys such was the amount of writings,

IN THE BEGINNING

He could only make ten miles out of Jerusalem, the going was too hard for Him, He came onto a series of caves and left the scrolls' and ledgers in them and set off back to Jerusalem.

Arrangement were made in great hast, when everyone was leaving Jesus asked Tibur, Joseph, and Pontus to stay behind, no one knew what Jesus said to them, however when each one came out it was very clear that they had all been weeping, that night Jesus and Mary held on to each other Mary quietly wept.

Early next morning Tibur came for Mary the Girls and Miriam, Tibur had saddled Prince and Princess, Mary and Moon to travel on Princess, Miriam and Star on Prince, a couple of donkeys came along with provisions, after heartfelt goodbyes they set off on their journey to Galilee.

Mary wanted to turn around and run back to Jesus, but She knew he was right She had to safeguard their Children as soon as they were safe with Simone, she would ride back to Jesus immediately, she felt great foreboding.

Nevertheless events would prove otherwise, the going was slow, Miriam was concerned, Mary looked pale and sick although She did not complain She was feeling unwell, the first stage of Labour was upon Her and She was afraid that without Jesus She wouldn't be able to get through the birth, Mirium spoke to Mark to find them shelter for the night.

Tibur did not want to pass through the town of Bethlehem for fear of being recognised, however he had concerns as to Marys confinement, She did not look well, on the outskirt of town was a stable he thought it better to let the ladies rest there, it was warm and dry, the Men would be able to stand fast if they were threatened, however he knew that the Soldiers sent by Rome would by now, be arresting Jesus.

He knew it would not end well, Tibur lifted Mary gently off the Horse and carried her into the stable Prince and Princess followed them without guidance, some of the Men busied themselves looking after the Horses fresh hay was given, Prince ate as much as he could, Princess stood silent with her muzzle gently touching Marys head, She remained head down, no one had the heart to force her away.

Miriam and the twins were busy making a comfortable bed out of straw and blankets they had brought with them, Tibur gently placed Mary on the makeshift bed, it was obvious to everyone that Mary was about to give birth, Her pallor was white, with beads of sweat running down her beautiful face.

Moon and Star began to cry, Miriam as always took charge ordering the girls to find wood to light a fire, whilst She looked to Mary, She was as scared as they were, but giving them tasks to do would keep them occupied and give Miriam time to assess the situation and see how far on Marys confinement was.

It took two days of agonising pain before Mary felt the need to bear down and deliver the child, it was impossible to carry on to Galilee' they waited and looked after Mary, Tibur and the Men felt utterly helpless as there was nothing they could do to help her, the girls were holding Marys hands and still she did not utter one scream 'she looked completely worn out, and very near death as one final agonising push delivered her Son into this world.

Miriam cut the cord bathed the beautiful little Boy and worked as Mary had taught her to retrieve the afterbirth, Miriam saw immediately there was something wrong Mary had not moved or uttered a word her eyes were open and seamed fixed on something above them.

Miriam felt her pulse and She could not find one She realised her beloved Mary was dead, Miriam cried out, a scream that was chilling to everyone, Star and Moon joined her utterly bereft, all the Men came running each falling to the ground with shock and sadness, after what felt like hours, the sobbing became quiet, as each one fell asleep exhausted in grief, the girls and Miriam falling across Marys body. Miriam woke first and went to tend to the Baby, she found a lambs bottle used to feed an orphaned lamb, and asked a cow in the barn if She may take a little milk for the Baby, Mark joined her just as red eyed as she, he took her in his arms and they cried together, She asked Mark to get the milk why she tended the Baby,

He was absolutely beautiful, perfect like his parents, his eyes were the bluest like his Father and He did not cry instead he smiled at everyone that came close to him to hold him he had the same continence as his parents, it was as if he knew everyone around him, Tibur lifted him up and kissed him on his forehead I vow I will look after this child all my days, He walked forward to where Marys lifeless but strangely beautiful body lay, he bent down and kissed her on the forehead goodbye beautiful mother.

IN THE BEGINNING

Tibur then turned to Miriam, we must leave here, it's not safe, the farmer will be here soon and will insist on an explanation, we must bury Mary and leave, Miriam immediately turned towards the men, if you do not wish to stay with us we understand, so take your leave we will wait here until Mary comes back to us.

Tibur exclaimed are you insane, Mary has gone, we must make hast and safety for Moon and Star, and yourself, you will be taken to Rome and God knows what will happen to you Women there, Mark stepped forward and said Tibur, if Miriam says we must wait for holy direction then we must wait, and anyway we can't get anywhere with this tempest, wind rain and lightning all around us, it's very bad outside.

Tibur said I am so sorry I have a wife and my own baby on the way I must get back to Pompei, I do not want to leave you, but if you will not head my warnings then I must go back home to my other family, I will take the baby with me He will be well looked after, Miriam started No you will not take him with you, He has a family here with his Father Mother and sisters.

He will be loved and looked after by his Family, just then a commotion was heard outside looks like the farmer wants his stable back sighed Tibur drawing his sword, A few men virtually fell into the stable from the storm outside bedraggled and wet, they were shepherds.

We were told to come by an Angel who said a king will be born in our stable and we are to pay homage to him, and his Mother, they moved forward looking at the Child and then their eyes met the mother laid out in a makeshift bed motionless.

OH my, its Mary, they fell to their knees in worship, They cried have you not heard, they took Jesus to Golgotha and crucified him, the garrison have ransacked Jerusalem looking for Mary and the Daughters, dont go outside yet, the garrison who took his life will pass right by here very soon, People are running for the hills to get away from them, they don't care who they kill, they are a very bloodthirsty lot, better to wait it out in here, than chance the road today.

Miriam, Moon and Star were in shock, no please they pleaded don't tell us its true, the women held on to each other and wailed and cried then went again to Mary and laid next to her and cried themselves to sleep.

It was on the third day after Mary had given birth, the miracle happened, suddenly Marys body started to tremble then She gulped in an almighty breath and sat up breathing heavily She looked around her, everyone didn't make a sound or move they were in total shock they had started considering her burial and here She was, completely restored.

Star broke the silent spell by shouting Mummy, fast followed by Moon who was so overcome with happiness fainted on the spot, Miriam carried her to Mary, this time there were tears of happiness and joy, Miriam carried the baby Son to her and She held him to her breast.

Everyone was overjoyed at having Mary come back to them, no one wanted to break the happiness by telling her what had happened to their beloved Jesus, they were so preoccupied and overwhelmed with love and thanksgiving to have her back that they just wanted to feel happy for a little while.

for a few hours they didn't bring it up, it was Mary who first broached the subject, She asked aren't you going to ask me, Ask what dearest mother said Moon," where had I been, replied Mary well everyone believed you to be dead replied Miriam, their conversation was cut short by the sound of Men marching, Tibur and James jumped to their feet just as a centurion poked his head inside the stable, he only saw the soldiers sitting resting, he immediately went into Sargent mode.

What are you lot doing, taking it easy whilst we do all the hard work jump to it he shouted, Tibur rose to his feet and walked towards the centurion he shouted, "who are you to order my Men, these are my Men I am the one to shout orders here".

The centurion immediately recognised the uniform as being a high ranking officer, and visible shrank sorry Sir, thought these Men were shirking their duties, Well now you know, be on your way, we have official business here, and have been marching nonstop for days, my men deserved a rest.

Tibur and all the others held their breath, whilst they heard the marching move away everyone breathed a large sigh of relief as they passed by.

Tibur turned towards Mary and the other women, I believe we are at your service Lady Mary tell us all what do you command of us, and it will be done, OH come here Tibur and give me a hug commanded Mary, everyone gather round I have some important news which concerns you all.

I have been to Heaven with my lord Jesus, he is fully recovered from his terrible ordeal it took its toll on him and I had to leave you for a little while as I was needed elsewhere, to be with him and set the laws for your everlasting life and home.

I came back to be with my Children on this earth plane, I am sorry my darlings had to manage without me, I knew I could leave you with my beloved Miriam, Mary placed her hand on Miriam's face, thank you dearest Sister, even though your own heart was breaking I knew you would see to my children before yourself.

I knew you would wait for me to wake up. Miriam cried but I didn't know if you would wake up I simply tried against hope to believe you would, isn't that what true faith is replied Mary, I have so much to tell you it's hard to know where to start, so let's go to the beginning I remember being in such pain that I wanted to die, then I heard Jesus cry out to me saying MARY MARY WHY HAVE YOU FORSAKEN ME.

The next moment I was flying feeling free, to Jesus, I saw him surrounded by many Angels who were weeping in such anguish, and then I was in his arms lifting my dearest home with the Angels.

Then we were in heaven our true home it was so beautiful we stayed, it seemed a lifetime, and then my dearest Jesus said to me Mary do you remember our Children on the earth plane.

I said I think of nothing else except your love, Mary he says, do you wish to return to them, and I say to him Yes, but it will mean leaving you here, you forget Mary, the time here is lucid, very different from the earth plane where time is measured by the Minuit.

if you wish it you can join your earth body at some time after the birth of our Son, you will be able to tell everyone especially our children and our beloved Miriam that I have a plan for them all, and we will be able to walk in that world as a Family.

Before I was taken by the evil, I arranged with Joseph of Amalthea and Pontius Pilot safe passage by sea, we have room for some of our beloved disciples about one hundred who wish to sail with us to a new life, you will see me again soon, kiss my daughters Son and Miriam for me, tell them we will be reunited soon, I have to meet with some of our disciples to make arrangements for our Son to be cared for, as he becomes a Man, if I am to give my only begotten Son unto this world then I am sure to give him the best education I can to survive the evil that so cruelly murdered his Father before he was born into this world.

You must not continue to Galilee you must return to the villa, Joseph and Joanne are waiting for you they know of the arrangements, they will be most happy to see you.

There you have it, am I not back with you, everyone nodded a yes, OH and there is one more thing, at that precise moment they were suddenly joined by two beautiful golden angels.

This is the next thing I was to tell you, we will soon be joined by Angels who are here to heal my earth body as it needs a little care and divine healing, seems it was damaged by the birth of my little Man here giving Jesus jnr a rub with her nose, so he giggled.

Miriam would you take him, Star and Moon go with Aunty Miriam, for a little walk outside, as for you Men about face, if you turn around you will be blinded so don't say I haven't warned you.

the Men went quickly outside turning their backs not one dared to turn around.

The Disciples with Mary hadn't eaten for three days such was their distress, Mary asked Miriam to bring her food bag. Oh yes Miriam laughed we have food enough for everyone, The mood had now shifted there was hope again it felt so good knowing their Mary and Jesus will soon be returned to them, in such hopeless despair and Grief they could not eat, and now happiness had been restored to them everyone was grateful for the food, even more grateful for Marys return.

After eating their fill, they set off back to the Christian Villa, Joanne was waiting for Joseph to return and overcome with emotion when Mary Miriam the Girls and the Baby Jesus came home.

Mary held Joanne as She wept relaying what they had witnessed forced to watch Jesus being scorned and Murdered, Joseph had gone to the tomb to supervise the cleaning and preparation of Jesuses Body for permanent entombment, Joanne held the Baby Jesus.

Mary asked her to look after him whilst She the Girls and Miriam went to the tomb, Joanne replied no you cannot go yet, there are two of the most unpleasant Soldiers guarding the Tomb, Tibur said I will go in front and dismiss them, You must put on birkas so that you will not be recognised.

Some of the garrison sent to destroy you both are still here, we must be very careful, I will go first and you dear ladies will follow later, Tibur was resolute in his instruction, telling some of the Men to accompany him and remember you are still solder's in the service of the Cesar, so please act like them.

CHAPTER 7

When the religious leaders came to the decision to put Jesus to death, they wouldn't even consider that he might be telling the truth, that he was, indeed, their Messiah.

The Jewish high priests and elders of the Sanhedrin accused Jesus of blasphemy arriving at the decision to put him to death.

But first they needed Rome to approve of their death sentence, representatives of the Sanhedrin went directly to Rome taking untrue stories with them, to persuade Cesar Tiberius to commit Jesus to death from Rome, so they could not be accused of contriving Jesuses death," it wasn't us but Rome's doing"

Jesus knew they would be coming to arrest Him, he arranged a supper for some of the Male followers, after ensuring Mary and the Children were hidden and well on the road with Drusus to Galilee and Simones protection,

He told the Male companions that they must look out for, protect the Women disciples above all things, to help them, they would be blessed with the same marvellous attributes as they will be able to heal the sick, preach in many tongues, and know that their place at Jesuses side would be for all time in this world, and the other. Jesus said breaking the bread," this is my body "eat and be full, Lifting a flagon of wine "this is my blood drink and be quenched".

Jesus said He that believed in me shall not die, but have eternal life with me in paradise, all he asked of them was to keep him company until the arrest came, the Men became alive with testosterone swearing to stop this terrible injustice, to fight to the last man in protection of their beloved

IN THE BEGINNING

leader, Jesus smiled a knowing smile, No my Friends you must do nothing but bear witness.

Jesus do nothing let me be taken, some of you will betray me anyway out of fear, some will wait for me to stop them.

They found Jesus with some of the Disciples in the Garden of gethsemane, He appeared to be waiting for them, Simon Is Hariot and his Son Juda Is Hariot pointed Jesus out to the Soldiers.

Although Pilate found him innocent, unable to find or even contrive a reason to condemn Jesus in Public, he thought that there was enough of Jesuses followers to stop this awful persecution of his beloved friend, so he decided that the people should decide on his fate.

However, most of the followers were locked out and the priests had people in the crowd threatening them by knife point, thereby Stirred by the Jewish chief priests, the crowds declared, "Crucify him! "Pontius Pilate washed his hands declaring it was not his wish to crucify a man he knew to be innocent, told the crowd that it was their doing and their conscience, wanted nothing to do with it, and by acting his part had vanquish Rome.

However Pilot had an ace to play, the Jewish feast of the Passover was due, as a custom of showing respect for the Jewish religion it was up to Pilate to vindicate and set free a prisoner, He called to the crowd, should He set free Jesus, who he could find no fault, or Barabbas, who was known as a thief murderer, lier and who had spoken words of uprising against Rome.

To his shock and dismay the crowd called for Barabbas.

Jesus had already commanded him in this matter, to do nothing, to be seen only to be on the side of Rome to act as the Governor of Judea, yet as soon as he walked back into his palace he broke down in uncontrollable sobs, wringing his hands and weeping, Solitous was also so inflicted they tried to comfort each other, their sadness at their role was overbearing, yet he did what Jesus had declared him to do.

Jesus was held in the prison reserved for the ones awaiting death, it was a terrible place dark and fearful, all despair rang through its walls, As Jesus laid trying to sleep, having a brief respite from the cruel taunts and blows, A visitor came to see him, the Devil himself, He asked Jesus, are you not sick and tired of these humans, just say the word that you will leave this world to me and your suffering will be over, have you not learned that I am the one in charge and will always be so, these Humans are not worth your suffering, they will hang you on a cross strip you naked and display your body to show that you are only a Man.

I have dominium over you, in this world and the next, Jesus replied you viper how dare you come to me with your lies and trickery, Get thee behind me Satan, for this is the place you will always be, your number is 666 and mine 777 take your place in the very depth of heaven for soon I will see you there, then watch out, I will meet you with my trusted Angels who will show you as much mercy as you showed to me on this fateful day on earth.

I give this life and Body for them, You will not have dominium over my Children from this day forward they will be able to call on their holy Father and Mother to cast you out, the Angels who love God will work against you to deliver them from evil, I take pleasure in knowing this.

As was common, Jesus was publicly scourged, or beaten, with a leather-tonged whip before his crucifixion, Tiny pieces of iron and bone chips were tied to the ends of each leather thong, causing deep cuts and painful bruises.

He was mocked, struck in the head with a staff and spit on. A prickly crown of thorns was placed on his head and he was stripped naked.

He staggered under the weight of the cross and fell down, Deborah sister of Philip ran under and passed the guards, She was holding a gourd of water and a flannel to wipe the blood and tears from His eyes, All the women started a diversion screaming and holding on to the guards, Deborah quickly placed the flannel over his face and gave him a drink of the water, all the time she chanted, Oh dearest lord what have they done to you, She wept with Him, saying please forgive Me.

I love you so much, I cannot bear to see you so cruelly persecuted, Jesus managed to take a few large gulps of the liquid it tasted a little strange but refreshing,

The guards noticed Deborah grabbed her by the hair and threw her back into the crowd, She was still clutching the cloth and gurd, She sat down in the road and wept allowing the crowds that followed to walk on without Her, Jesus got to his feet but he was Too weak to carry his cross, Simon of Cyrene was forced to carry it for him.

He walked slowly in great physical pain which grew nothing in comparison to the feelings of betrayal, psychological pain depression, fear and longing for Mary,

He alone had allowed them to do this terrible thing to him so that He would know how it felt to be a Human being from the highest tower Magdalen, to the most scourged mocked and persecuted, He walked weeping not for himself but for the People his beloved hundreds He called them, it was to protect them and for his dearest Mary.

Suddenly He felt woozy as if someone was rocking the world, He staggered on and realised the water Deborah had put something in the water, naughty Girl he smiled to himself, yet he was relieved that he didn't feel the awful pain as much, however He felt that everything in the world was moving slowly, then one of the soldiers struck him, then everything was moving fast.

He was in shock, the world around him whirled it seemed to slow down then speed up fast, He felt for the first time a terrible loneliness, He needed Mary He staggered on concentrating on his love for Mary and his children, His mind in another place, untill reaching the execution site He was led to where he would be crucified.

As was the custom, before they nailed him to the cross, a mixture of vinegar, gall was offered. This drink was said to alleviate some of the suffering, but Jesus refused to drink it.

Stake-like nails were driven through his wrists and ankles, fastening him to the cross where he was crucified between two convicted criminals.

The inscription above his head tauntingly read, "The King of the Jews." Jesus hung on the cross for his final agonizing breaths, a period that lasted about six hours. Jesus had already instructed the Angels.

that they had not to interfere whatever they looked on to bear witness, they must not lay blame or seek retaliation they must stand fast and be ready to take him home

During that time, soldiers cast lots for Jesus' clothing, while people passed by shouting insults and scoffing. From the cross, Jesus spoke to the Disciples mostly Women who were assembled to bear witness to this atrocity, Happy is the father that looks upon his children and feels pride in them cried the lord, a little later he cried out in shock and pain again Mary Mary why have you forsaken me.

Then he saw her coming fast towards him flying through the air to him, then She was right in front of him saying My dearest darling what have they done to you, come into my arms and I will deliver you home with the Angels, He stepped out of his bonds and immediately felt lifted by Mary who was surrounded by the most beautiful Angels.

They rose with them into infinity and beyond and such was the ending or beginning of His human life.

However, there was one black Angel that was incensed at his beloved God being treated so badly, he hated human beings and could not understand what his beloved God saw in them, at that point, the dark Angel in his despair hit his fist so hard on the ground it shook underfoot, and darkness covered the land.

A little later, as Jesus gave up his spirit, the dark Angel overcome with sorrow and anger, hit his fists so hard on the ground an earthquake shook the ground, ripping the Temple veil in two from top to bottom, "The earth shook, and the rocks split a great tempestuous storm ravaged the land lightning struck the trees, sending them into burning damnation, the hour of death was abhorrent to nature, and nature itself became unstable for a little while.

It was typical for Roman Soldiers to show mercy by breaking the criminal's legs, thus causing death to come more quickly. But this night only the thieves had their legs broken, for when the soldiers came to Jesus, they found him already dead. Instead, they pierced his side. Before sunset, Jesus was taken down by Nicodemus and Joseph of Amalthea and laid in Joseph's tomb.

Since according to the rules of the Roman Empire, calling oneself king was grounds for treason, the Garrison leader gave orders that the initials INRI be inscribed on Jesus' tomb after the crucifixion. In Latin, INRI stood for Jesus' name and his title of King of the Jews a final mockery of the Human race's saviour.

Thousands of people from all faiths and creeds flocked towards Jerusalem many could not believe that Jesus had been murdered, talking to each other they expressed their Grief and distain at the event, some getting Angry at why and who would do such a thing, conspiracy theories were abound, then some started whispering, if he really was God surely he could have laid waste to his persicutors, after all he would be able to command the Angels to come to his aid instead of dying like a common criminal, maybe he was only a clever Man after all, Maybe the Jews were right.

Gossip and conspiracy theories were everywhere.

Jesus provoked more conscious thought and discussions, but the reality was that He had been taken from the disciples and believers too soon, giving up his life gave into gossip, only deepening his and Hers mystery.

After being laid in Joseph's tomb two of the Soldiers were deployed to stand Guard until further notice at the entrance, the women followers wanted to take over from the Men and wash the body, applying fragrant oils and covering the body in a burial cloth.

The guards had other plans and refused to let the ceremony of dressing the body take place the Women wailed wept and lamented keeping a vigil overnight outside of the tomb, whilst the Soldiers mocked them, even spitting on them if they ventured too close.

The next day was the sabbath no work on this day, so they could not gain entry to the tomb, the second day was Sunday the Soldiers would still not grant them their right to enter the tomb, however the following morning they saw a Roman centurion approaching the Tomb.

As he saluted the Soldiers there appeared a blinding light everyone turned away as they could not stand the light suddenly the two Soldiers guarding the Tomb disappeared in their place stood two Angels, who commanded the large stone placed to seal the tomb to move away, it was at that moment that Mary arrived, walking into the tomb into the blinding light.

Many People witnessed Jesus walking out with Mary hand in hand, a great cheer went up, People ran in all directions shouting HE LIVES, Tibur fell to his knees in homage Jesus looked down to him and said thank you Tibur for keeping the Family safe.

They walked on past the onlookers towards the Villa, Jesus appeared unsteady a testament to the ordeal His body had been subjected to, Mary held on to him and they walked home together surrounded by all the faithful who stood by them in their darkest hours.

Mary Jesus said, how is our Son, You will soon see him for yourself, it was at the moment of my transition our Son was born into this world, Yes darling Mary replied I know we gave our only begotten Son to this World, who will ensure all our Children know your love and compassion for generations to come thus Earth and Heaven will work together to eliminate the Evil ones.

Joseph came dashing towards them My dearest lord he flung himself at Jesus and wept, hugging him like he did not want to let go, when we took you down I would swear you were Dead it's a miracle, those that love you will be elated when they realise you are Alive, all the plans have been put in motion I have three good ships stocked and ready to go as you asked, I suggest we make haste and leave this very day.

And so it came to pass Mary Jesus and Children boarded the first Ship with fifty dedicated followers Adam and His family were the first followed by most of the refugees from the villa, Joanne and Joseph were to stay behind at the villa to continue their work, some people wanted to stay at the villa, which was their free will to do so.

Mary had to tell Prince and Princess they were going away and asked them to help Joseph and Joanne let them ride them, they would be looked after until arrangements could be made for them to join the Family again.

Each ship held fifty disciples Men Women and Children as well as the crew captain and an array of livestock, Jesus stayed with them as they set off from the port at Jerusalem, just as they were casting of from the dock a commotion on the land grasped their attention.

It was Pontus Pilot and his family shouting to Jesus with all his mite, Jesus stopped the departure gesturing for the others to continue on their way, Pilot embraced Jesus, Oh my most precious Friend dearest Lord God, they told us you were risen from the dead.

I so want to come with you, Pilot was weeping but I know it's impossible for now, would you take Solitous the Children and all my family with you, I will join them when I have taken care of my duties as Governer, Jesus said of course we will take them with us if you so wish they are already Family.

I would like you to come as well, Pontus replied Lord I cannot as yet, I must be in position when Tiberius arrives, they could put me to death if it comes to light that I am your friend and follower, I need to make sure my Family are safe, you can protect them better than I, if it goes bad with Tiberius he will be arriving soon, He has taken to come for Mary and the Girls himself.

It is good that you are leaving now, just please take good care of my loved ones he was holding his Children kissing them and instructing them to be good, He kissed his wife and the other family members as they boarded the ship, You will send a messenger to tell me where you are.

Solitous was overjoyed to be with Mary again but so sad that Pontus could not come with them, She wept whilst waving him goodbye, I will join you as soon as it is safe to do so Pontus waved to them, and so they left, sailing on the ocean, the mood was of elation people started to sing laugh and enjoy themselves, slave and master alike felt liberated, happy voices filled the air sailing on a beautiful day with a hopeful future.

Everyone wanted to hold Baby Jesus, so He was passed around while everyone made a fuss of him he rarely cried his little face was always smiling giggling and laughing, when he had enough of this game he gestured to his Mother and She took him in her arms, saying he is ready for his milk.

Days passed the followers were beginning to get fretful and kept asking, are we there yet, where are we going? Jesus addressed them, do not worry we will come upon an island soon where we will depart and live in peace, be patient, sure enough land was sighted, they sailed into the harbour, the island was beautiful and rugged, a natural deep harbour and quaint town Valletta they had arrived in Malta.

They would make this beautiful Island their home for the next forty years, Jesus the Baby became Jesus the Man and Son of God, He enjoyed an idyllic Childhood, they lived in a small Roman house at the very top of the Island, More about this will be published in the Next Book, MARY THE MOTHER, What She did next.

Meanwhile in Galilee the male Disciples talked amongst themselves, debating the recent events in Jerusalem, the more they talked about Jesus and Mary, the more the Men became morose, feeling sad despondent, guilty at having ran away from the terrible events in Jerusalem.

Their thinking was that they deserved to be left behind, they did what most men will do, go fishing and contemplate, It was a beautiful day when they cast off their fishing boat, they tried several attempts at casting the nets, but they were out of luck, they decided to move into the centre of the great lake, they cast their net again and again it was empty, Philip joked even the fish have abandoned us.

Suddenly a great storm blew, tossing the boat around in a tempest of rain wind and enormous waves, The Men were terrified, as they battled to save themselves, Andrew pointed out to sea shouted above the wind,

Look what is that, a bright light seemed to be moving through the storm coming towards them.

The Men remained transfixed as they were terrified, the spectre moved closer, it was a Man walking on the water moving towards them, with each step he made the sea became calmed, Peter shouted out Lord is it you, or some terrible abhorition.

The Men became afraid crying out to God to save them, Jesus moved closer, He called out, Peter, John, Philip, Andrew, James you Men of little faith, do you not see me, who else would walk towards you on the sea.

Peter called out I have faith in you Master, with my faith I come to meet you, Peter stepped off the boat and walked towards Jesus, on top of the water, a few feet from Jesus, his doubt and fear overcame him, He started to sink, Help me Lord, He cried out, Jesus took his arm and walked him back to the fishing boat.

The Tempest calmed, the rain stopped, and the sea became still, Jesus spoke to the Men, where you not aware of my coming, Yes Lord but you look a little different.

Peter said I cannot understand what it is? but you look slightly different, younger than I remember, Jesus laughed Yes my friends, I am Jesus the Son of God, my Father sent me to give light to this world, you are reminded to look at the seventh principle of learning my Father taught you.

When reaching this level, you can bend time. This is the level of God my Father, You Men are taxed by God to accompany me on my travels, I will explain everything presently.

Firstly, you are to take me to Simone, she is fully aware, and waiting for me. {More about Jesus the Son, in the third book, JESUS THE SON, MOON AND STAR

BIBLIOGRAPHY

The Bible New Testament

Pontius Pilate joined his Family two years after they left with Jesus and Mary.

The circumstances surrounding Pontius Pilate's disappearance or death as some assumed are something of a mystery. According to some traditions, the Roman emperor Caligula ordered Pontius Pilate to death by execution or suicide. By other accounts, Pontius Pilate was sent into exile and committed suicide of his own accord.

Some traditions assert that after he committed suicide, his body was thrown into the Tiber River. Still others believe Pontius Pilate's fate involved his conversion to Christianity and subsequent canonization. Pontius Pilate is in fact considered a saint by the Ethiopian Orthodox Church.

Regardless of what truly became of Pontius Pilate, one thing has been made certain—that Pontius Pilate existed. During a 1961 dig in Caesarea a, Italian archaeologist Dr. Antonio Frova uncovered a piece of limestone inscribed with Pontius Pilate's name in Latin, linking Pilate to Emperor Tiberius's reign.

Jesus the living God did walk amongst us, He was amazing and powerful. The religious leaders of His day rejected Him, but vast numbers of people accepted Him. People would chase after Him and gather in His home. He could not escape. In both the gospels of Mark and Luke we read that the people were impressed with Him, therefore the writers of the original Bible and Koran had to recognise and implement the story of the living God, being born of a Virgin, so that it fit with culture and Politics of the Day, becoming the most

incredible catalyst of Controllably invading the Minds of Human beings, by inventing Religion.

And He came down to Capernaum, a city of Galilee, and He was teaching them on the Sabbath; and they were amazed at His teaching, for His message was with authority. (NASB)

Even secular writers were impressed. One major comment comes from a Jewish historian. His name was Flavius Josephus (AD 37-97). He was born into a priestly Jewish family. He was a Pharisee and a historian for the Roman empire. He wrote several famous works: Antiquities of the Jews and the Wars of Rome.

When God walked on this earth as a man, those who observed Him were astonished. They had never seen a man performing the Jews. Here is a major comment from him,

Now, there was about this time Jesus, a wise man, if it be lawful to call him a man. For he was a doer of surprising feats - a teacher of such men as receive the truth with pleasure. He drew over to him both many of the Jews and many of the Gentiles. He was [the] Christ; and when Pilate, at the suggestion of the principal men amongst us, had condemned him to the cross, those that loved him at the first did not forsake him, for he appeared to them alive again the third day, as the divine prophets had foretold these and ten thousand other wonderful things concerning him; and the tribe of Christians, so named from him, are not extinct to this day. (Antiquities of the Jews 18.3.3)

Another major comment comes from multiple authors who quote from documents that Pontius Pilate (1 BC - circa AD 37) had written. Pontius Pilate was the fifth Roman procurator of Judea (AD 26 - 36), under Emperor Tiberius, who lived during the time of Jesus. He sentenced Jesus to death by crucifixion. The quote below refers to missing. Its existence is strongly supported by three ancient authors: Epiphanius (Heresies 50.1), Justin Martyr (First Apology) and Tertullian (Apology).

"At His coming the lame will leap as a deer, and the stammering tongue will clearly speak: the blind will see, and the lepers will be healed; and the dead will rise and walk." And that He did those things, you can learn from the Acts of Pontius Pilate. First Apology 48.

records about Jesus from Cornelius Tacticus (A.D. 55-120), who has been called the greatest historian on ancient Rome; Hadrian, who was an emperor of Rome in A.D. 76-138; Mara Bar-Serapion, who was a Syrian living at least 73 years after Jesus Christ; Phlegon, a historian who lived in the first century; Gaius Plinius Caecilius Secundus (A.D. 61-112), or Pliny the Younger, who was the governor of Bithynia (A.D. 112) and a Roman senator, Gaius Suetonius Tranquilla, who was a Roman historian (A.D. 117-138); Thallus (circa A.D. 52), who wrote a history about the middle east from the time of the Trojan War to his own time; and Trajan, who was emperor of Rome in A.D. 53 - 117. The testimony is loud and clear. Why would secular writers have written what they did? The answer is simple. They recorded what was true. Jesus existed, taught, and healed people. HE AND SHE GAVE THEIR ONLY BEGOTTEN SON TO THIS WORLD.

Susan Alty.